THE ALPHA AND AURORA SERIES

AURORA'S SECRET

DELTA WINTERS

Copyright © 2024 by Delta Winters

All rights reserved.

This book or any portion thereof may not be reproduced in any form or by any electronic or mechanical means, including information storage and retrieval systems, without written permission from the publisher, except for the use of brief quotations in a book review.

All characters appearing in this work are fictitious. Any resemblance to real persons, living or dead, is purely coincidental.

Cover designed by Miblart

PUBLISHED BY

Inkitt

THE ALPHA AND AURORA SERIES

AURORA'S SECRET

Chapter 1

Pack

―――◆―――

RORY

As my eyes flicker open, white shining light fills them and beautiful choir voices fill my ears, hymns of old and new and everything in between.

It's as if I'm lying on nothing, with only the songs of time keeping me afloat.

Only from willing it, I stand, although I feel nothing below my feet but mist and almost inaudible whispers.

Heavenly light covers all sides, blinding me to any fears or evils in the world. Am I even in the world anymore?

What is going on?

I died… I'm sure of it.

Or did I?

Two doors suddenly appear.

To the right, a glowing emerald door appears, thistle branches capturing its frame.

To the left, a golden door, its gilded frame glimmering brightly.

I walk toward the golden door, but when I touch the doorknob it disintegrates into nothing.

"Not yet," an angelic voice whispers to me, "it is not yet time."

I turn to the other door.

This time the doorknob doesn't disappear. Instead, the door swings open with ease.

Suddenly, I am pushed by some invisible force.

As I plummet through a forest canopy, I can't help but think, "How did I even get here?"

ONE HOUR EARLIER

"Alpha Nickolas is holding a pack meeting. He's finally declaring who his mate is," Mama tells me as I walk through the front door from school.

I stop in my tracks at the news.

Alpha Nickolas found his mate?

I can't help but feel jealous. The most advantageous thing about being a wolf is the fact that they can know who they truly belong with… who their soulmate is.

We humans have to go through life, through different relationships, in the hope that we'll be right this time. That this man or woman is who we're meant to be with.

Or, maybe, because we don't have mates, maybe we don't have "the one." Maybe we're destined to look for many types of love.

Still, I adore the mate idea: the feeling of truly belonging with someone, feeling safe in their arms, their wish to make you happy and vice versa.

But alas, I'm human. The chance of a werewolf being mated to a human is rare. The compatibility of soulmates should at least be based on the same species, *right?*

I *do* have a boyfriend at the human school that I go to. His name is Eddie, and while I like him a lot, I could never imagine telling him that I live with werewolves. I mean, I haven't even told my best friend Freya.

How can Eddie and I ever end up together when I have to lie about so many parts of my life?

Mama pulls me out of my spiraling thoughts, frantically tugging on my arm in order for us not to arrive late.

Another thing to know about me is that I'm cursed with clumsiness, so obviously I trip over my feet as we rush out the door.

At pack meetings, Mama and I stay at the sidelines, hoping we are invisible and willing ourselves to shrink into nothingness.

Of course, being human, my scent is wildly different to others, making it impossible for me to stay completely in the shadows.

The previous alpha welcomed me into his pack when my mama brought me home after finding me, abandoned, in the rogue lands.

The new alpha, on the other hand, Alpha Nick, hates me.

In fact, he detests all humans.

"Today is a momentous occasion for me," Alpha Nick begins, his voice echoing throughout the hall. "I have found my mate, right here in our pack."

Wolves can only smell their mate when they turn of age, eighteen.

Alpha Nick has been waiting a few years, so his mate must be just of age, or maybe they've known for a few months if she belongs to this pack.

"Here she is," he declares. A tall, beautiful girl joins Nick on the stage, her glossy hair cascading over her shoulders and hazel eyes glistening in the lights.

Victoria.

A girl, a wolf, who has bullied me every day of my life.

We're the same age and she and her friends were my

tormentors in my childhood. Ever since I started going to a human high school, I see her less. *Thank Goddess…*

But that doesn't change the fact that she will become the Luna, the female leader of this pack, as she is mated to the alpha.

And, like her alpha, she detests humans.

"Now comes time for our tradition," announces the alpha, "when an alpha finds his luna, he grants her one wish. Her deepest, darkest desire."

My mother gasps next to me, a look of panic washes over her face.

We all watch as Victoria whispers into his ear, giggling.

"Can't say I'm surprised," snickers the alpha, before turning to the crowd, "my brilliant luna has requested the immediate expulsion of all humans."

She shoots me a devious smile from across the room, raising her eyebrows knowingly.

For a moment, time pauses. It seems like every single pack member is looking right at me and my mother.

"Here, take this," my mother whispers to me as she shoves a letter into my jacket pocket, "it has all the answers you will need."

I don't have time to ask any questions because the alpha, the beta, and the luna are walking right towards me. Their eyes seeping menace and danger.

The pack stands back, watching as I'm banished from pack territory, driven out across the borders with the alpha, luna, and beta pushing me along.

They didn't even allow me to take anything, and my mama couldn't stop them. Since she's a wolf, getting banished from the pack would actually be painful, the pack ties having to be severed.

She has no choice but to let me go.

I turn my head and catch one last glimpse of her. My Mama, my protector, tears streaming down her face.

"Remember the letter," she mouths to me one last time.

But then I feel Alpha Nick pushing me from behind, and I know that I have to keep going.

Once we're across the borders, we enter rogue territory, and I question why I have to be left out here.

Rogues are notoriously vicious and will kill any unfortunate human that lands in their path.

They remain silent, an amused expression on all three faces as they notice my frightened one.

These three are evil and sadistic.

Suddenly, out of nowhere, I feel a sharp knock to my head, and I tumble to the ground. My vision blurs, the throb in the back of my head mind-numbing.

I cry out as I'm turned onto my back, pinned down by the alpha's large hands on my shoulders.

His full body weight crushes me, and I see the flash of his knife trailing along my jaw. His still-amused face wears a devious smirk.

"What are you doing?" I ask in an almost inaudible whisper.

"Why, little Rory, we're getting rid of you permanently," Nick tells me in a cunning tone. "I can't have your pretty little mouth telling someone about wolves, about the pack.

"Humans can't be banished," he says. "Humans have to die."

With no more warning and no seconds left, the metal digs right into the skin of my neck and slits it open.

I feel the need to cling to my neck, to try to breathe and stop the blood spewing all over my hands.

Before everything goes black, I feel my mother's letter heavy in my pocket, full of all the secrets I would never know, all the questions left unanswered.

It's all over.
They've killed me…
I'm dead.

―※―

Before I can properly get my bearings, I realize I am about to hit the forest ground at full force.

I brace myself for a painful impact, but no such thing comes.

The choirs cease, the almost painful but charming light is now gone, replaced by blackness.

I blink my eyes open and am shocked to find myself back in the woods, back in rogue territory, back where my alpha killed me.

I scramble to my feet to search the surroundings.

The night rolls in as the darkness envelops me like the soft, chilly breeze. Sounds of wildlife echo through the whistling trees.

The rustling of leaves sends shivers down my spine, and I clutch my arms, recoiling at the haunts of this territory.

Just as the next member of any pack, I've heard all the stories about rogues. Lone wolves that refuse to be governed, refuse to bow down and pledge loyalty to any alpha.

They are wolves without discipline, without morals, without the need for companionship.

And I'm in the very heart of their territory, having been seemingly resurrected from the dead.

I'm reminded of how insane that seems.

I freeze, realizing that the warm liquid I'm feeling on the soles of my feet is actually my own blood, the blood from my neck.

It now pools under my feet, staining them crimson with hints of mud and dirt.

How is this possible? How am I here? Am I really here?

Maybe I'm not alive. Maybe I'm a ghost. Or maybe this is the afterlife, and that the door I was pushed through happened to be the gateway to what comes after death.

I touch my neck to find it still tainted with blood, but the wound is fully healed, as if it were never there.

I couldn't have been imagining it all, the blood is the evidence of that.

I dare to take a step and, naturally, I slip.

On my own blood…

I roll onto my back, completely drained of all my energy.

All I know is that I need answers.

Suddenly, I remember the letter in my pocket…

I reach into my jacket and am relieved to feel the paper between my fingers.

This is the last thing I'll ever get from my mama.

I'll never be safe to go back there and she can't leave the pack.

Did she know they were going to kill me?

Unfolding the blood-stained envelope that's tucked into my pocket, I dig at the opening to get to the letter.

I quickly read the letter and gasp in shock.

Right there, on the page, in my mother's neat handwriting, were all the answers I had ever been looking for.

CHAPTER 2

Resurrection

———•◆•———

RORY

Dear Rory,
    I knew I would have to tell you this someday, I just didn't think it would be in a goodbye letter like this.

As you know, I'm not your birth mother. The night I found you, in rogue territory, I was sent out to collect some herbs that could only be found in their territory.

I was wary and scared that night, but the little whimpers of a child took all that fear away.

But I didn't just find you, I found you lying on the ground, dying. I sat with you, holding your little hands, hushing you to sleep, hoping I could make your suffering ease.

You didn't cry, you just…closed your eyes.

And you died.

Or so I thought.

I planned on burying you back in the pack's territory, away from the rogues. You didn't have a good death, but you would rest in peace in a safe place.

I abandoned my mission for herbs and headed back, with you in my arms. I'm not as fast as other wolves, so it would take me a while to run back.

Halfway through my run, I almost had a heart attack.

I started to hear little cries cradled in my arm. I felt your pulse, and this time, you had one. You were alive. I don't know how, but you were.

You died, and then you came back to life.

At first, I thought I must have made a mistake, I must have thought you were dead but you were really alive.

So I brought you back to my home, and I planned to raise you, to look after you, to love you. Your parents had left you in the woods, alone, with nothing.

I wanted no harm to ever come to you, but you were the clumsiest little girl I've ever met. Even for a human, you couldn't walk a couple of meters without falling over.

One day, when you were seven, we were by the river. I was collecting some herbs by there and I didn't notice you were playing in the water.

But you slipped. You hit your head on the rocks, you were lying face down, and you drowned before I could get to you.

You had no pulse, you died.

But I made sure this time. I was crying profusely, but I wasn't going to make the same mistake as I did before.

You were dead. I was sure.

A few hours later, you started coughing up water. You were breathing and alive. This time, there was no mistake.

And I knew that when I had found you, you had died too. But you came back. You're a human, and yet you keep dying and resurrecting.

I knew one day this would happen, that they would kick you out of the pack. I tried my best to make you feel like this was your home, and the people in it were your family.

But the young pups never liked humans, even though their parents brought them up on different teachings.

The moment Nickolas became Alpha, I knew that it was only a matter of time for you.

You can't tell anyone about this gift of yours. I have no idea what else you can do, but people, wolves, they'll exploit it. Don't tell anyone.

I wish I could go with you, to make sure you don't get into trouble, but I'd only slow you down.

When I found you, you weren't mauled by rogues, you were stabbed with a knife, right in the heart.

Someone killed you, maybe your parents, but my point is, the rogues didn't hurt you, even though many would have passed you. And no one came near me with you in my arms.

But you can't trust anyone. And you can't come back to the pack, back to me. You have to run far away from here, where no one knows you. Start fresh.

Please keep safe, Rory.

I love you.

Your mama

She knew. She knew I could die and come back to life.

Why wouldn't she tell me before now? Why give me this information now? Did she know I would die and come back so that's why she explained? Did she know Alpha Nick would kill me?

I have so many questions and she will never answer them because she's right, I can't stay here. They killed me. They slit my throat.

They were ruthless.

And all because I was human.

All those years, I was terrified, powerless against them.

But things are different now.

I can't die.

I don't really know how, but one day I'll get my revenge.

I'll show them…

It's in that exact moment that I hear the crunch of leaves behind me as the low intense sound of growling fills my ears.

Chapter 3

Rogue

RORY

My heart starts racing more than humanly possible, although resurrection is definitely exceeding what's humanly possible.

My eyes widen, and in the faint shimmer of the sunrise, I see the shadow of a rogue wolf.

He approaches, circling me.

I watch him, holding my breath, waiting for the point where he pounces.

What I don't expect is the sound of cracking bones. The transformation of the wolf in front of me causes a little shriek to escape my lips.

His eyes lock with mine as he completely changes into his human, naked form and inches closer to me.

I make sure that my eyes stay with his, not even daring to move any lower, afraid of what I might see.

"Little girls like you shouldn't be out here," he grunts, a menacing smile creeping across his lips.

I slide a little as the wolf approaches, which makes me grab onto the rogue's shoulders. My nails dig into his flesh as I gain my balance—not that I had any to begin with.

"I smell pack wolves all over you. One thing I hate more

than anything is pack wolves. And it appears they hurt you. What happened?"

"T-they…tried to k-kill me," I stammer, the shivers of the chilled morning running through me.

Only in bloodied school clothes, I wrap my arms around myself for warmth, taking my hands away from his hot ones.

"H-hi," I say a little awkwardly. I've been told many terrifying stories about rogues, stories that gave me nightmares for weeks as a young child.

But upon closer look, this man in front of me, this rogue, he doesn't too appear threatening.

However, looks can be deceiving.

A small chuckle escapes him at my response to him, but then his eyes narrow as if he's attempting to figure this human girl out.

"You are used to werewolves," he states, assessing me more. "You shouldn't stay out here."

"I have nowhere else to go."

It's true…I can't go home, I can never go home. They thought they killed me. They think I'm dead.

And I was, I think.

But I can't go back, even if Mama, the only person I truly love, is back there. She'll be safer with me gone.

She'll just be an Omega rather than the Omega mothering the only human in the pack.

"You should go, little girl. I protected you through the night, but now I must leave," the rogue states and my eyes widen at his words.

"You protected me?" I question.

"You were lying out in the open, in rogue territory. Many rogues pass through here, me being one of them. Luckily for you, I was the first. Some don't take too kindly to humans.

"With me protecting you, they backed away or took other routes altogether when they smelled me. But now I'm leaving," he declares and changes back into his wolf state.

"Thank you." His head nods in recognition before he scurries off into the woods, hurtling through the maze of trees and out of my sight.

I can't stay here. Not another night especially. But where can I go?

Maybe I can find my Freya, ask her family to put me up. But taking care of another child is a lot to ask.

Although I am eighteen, would I be too much of a burden?

What about Eddie? He was my friend for a couple of years before he was my boyfriend. But I haven't even met his parents yet, even though they know about me.

I haven't met Freya's parents either. My free time was spent with the pack who betrayed me, who killed me.

And now I don't have anywhere to turn.

As I hear the rush of a stream nearby, I race toward it, overcome with thirst. Having my neck slit has left me incredibly thirsty and my throat incredibly dry.

But, like the klutz that I am, I tumble and eat dirt once again.

I'm cursed. Cursed with clumsiness.

I spit out the gunk in my mouth and scramble over to the water to cleanse it. But catching a glimpse of my reflection halts me, my eyes fixing on the ones staring back at me.

I notice the terrified, insane, worrisome look. The blood smeared all over my face as if it were paint, the dried lines down my jaw making it appear as if I had eaten something raw.

Those lines fuse into a clustered gash of crimson where the slit used to be, and then pouring down and onto my collarbone and clothes.

The rogue must have thought I was a mess. Maybe that's why he protected me, seeing a bloodied helpless girl passed out in the woods.

I don't know how to explain any of this. I don't know how I'm still alive.

I died, I know I did. My soul was taken from my body, to the serene desolate place, but then I was sent back, by that force.

It made me go back. And now I'm here.

Alive.

I have been resurrected. Again.

Why?

Is it a miracle or damnation?

I start walking again, more carefully this time. The crunch of the leaves under my feet make me aware of my surroundings. I don't possess super hearing or super smell. I can't tell if anything is about, if anything might attack.

Sometimes I wish I was born a werewolf, then none of this would have happened. I would have been welcomed into the pack, I would be able to fight my own battles.

But instead I'm a weak little human—who has the power to resurrect apparently.

The whimpering and cries of an animal snap me out of my daze, and I search the area for the source. This animal could appear to pose no threat but actually prove quite dangerous.

As I creep toward the noise, the volume of the cries dies slightly, causing me to hear the thud of my own heart.

But then I catch sight of it: a fawn with bite marks all over. Something must have scared a rogue away for it to leave its dinner still partially intact.

I crouch down to the creature, hoping to ease its suffering with each stroke of my hand.

My hand hovers over the wounds and presses down on them, ceasing the blood from oozing out anymore.

A small whimper is released from the animal but soon enough, the baby beast passes out.

A tear escapes me as I stare down at this animal. Like me, it is alone in rogue territory, a child left to its own devices, running from the terrors of the world.

It deserves to live, it should live. It has done nothing wrong.

Why do the innocent die when evil still thrives, like Alpha Nick and Victoria?

All of a sudden, the fawn awakens, panting as its chest moves up and down rapidly.

I snatch my hands away, only to see the gashes are no longer there, somehow disappeared under my hands.

The blood remains, covering my hands, but like the slit on my neck, this baby's wounds have healed miraculously.

Did I do this? Did I save this animal? How is that possible?

This fawn was dying, and now it stumbles to its feet and gallops off.

Moments before, I had a lot of energy. But suddenly, I'm exhausted, even though it's only the morning.

I drop my head into my hands, my mind heavy from trying to understand all the strange things that have happened to me in the past 24 hours.

And that's when I hear it…

Another growl. Different from the last one. There's no way I'll be so lucky again.

Without thinking, I pick myself up and make a run for it.

I don't look back for fear of it slowing me down too much… that I'll get caught even faster.

But it's a wolf chasing me. I won't get too far, especially if

I keep tripping over every branch or even my own feet every six seconds.

When I feel the creature pounce on me, I'm certain that this is it.

This is where I die. Again.

I should really attempt to stay alive longer. It's only been a day since my last death.

But death doesn't come. Not yet anyway. As I hear the bones crunch, I realize the beast is shifting for some reason.

Replacing the paws that once pinned me down are big hands, turning me over and onto my back.

There's an overwhelming force pulling me toward the creature. A strange feeling of ecstasy washes over me as his body presses into mine.

My eyes flicker open and I see a pair of vibrant blue ones staring back at me. The ones from my dreams.

It's him.

"Mate," he growls in my ear.

Chapter 4

Human

EVERETT

"Alpha, come join us hunting today," Beta Lucius offers as he and Gamma Ace charge into my office like the feral animals they are.

I can't blame them, hunting fuels my virility also. But, as alpha of the strongest and largest pack in the country, I must remain calculating and composed.

When my parents were killed, they handed over the reins of a pack that could be considered a kingdom by size and strength.

And with all this power, the responsibilities also fall to me, to protect the pack, to care for the wolves, and not act like an eager, boisterous pup.

"I would but I have those rogues in the cells to attend to," I reply, attempting to seem uninterested in their activities.

As for many a wolf, hunting and running with my pack is in my nature, in the blood coursing through my veins.

Denying this hunt is like denying my nature, although I have higher duties.

These wolves look to me, trust me to take care of them. I won't let them down.

I've proved my strength to them over the last couple years as alpha, yet I have to continue to do so.

Without my mate, I'm doing all of this alone, making all the decisions.

When I find her, I hope that she'll be as strong as I believe she is, her wolf far superior to anyone else but me, and we'll lead as alpha and luna, side by side, sharing our problems.

"They can wait, Alpha. You've been working all week. You owe it to Chaos to let loose," Ace argues, making a fair point.

"He's right. I might explode if I don't get to hunt," Chaos, my wolf, seethes, completely distraught by the fact that I just run around pack territory in the nights and don't let him run wild.

It's his instinct to be free, to run without restraint, to hunt.

"Fine. But it'll be short. I have to get back to those rogues," I declare, standing up, a little too excitedly so that Ace and Lucius chuckle a little.

We head out.

Once we reach the borders, I shift into my wolf, letting Chaos take control. The others shift into their wolves also, ready for a hunt.

Hunting in rogue territory is always more challenging as we have to hope the rogues don't get to the good catches before we do.

Also, hunting in rogue territory means we can get ambushed at any moment, but rogues aren't often so stupid as to go up against an alpha, beta, and gamma, no matter how many of them there are.

Rustling in the branches causes my ears to prick up and my eyes to narrow in on the target. A fawn. An innocent little fawn wandering in the woods.

I almost don't want to take it down, but a rogue gets to it first, leaping onto the animal with ferocity and digging its teeth into what was meant to be mine.

I let out a beastly growl, which causes the rogue to scatter faster than he has time to look up and see me. I chase after it, with my beta and gamma following swiftly behind me.

I hate rogues with a passion. More than any witch or human.

And this rogue is no match for an alpha. I pounce on him, digging my claws into his fur and skin and causing a whimper to escape him.

But when a scent fills my nose, I immediately let go without question.

Honey and roses. And a mixture of other sweet smells. Everything that I could ever want all at once.

Chaos runs immediately toward it, back the way we came, even with Ace's and Lucius's confusion through the mind-link.

I begin to growl as I see a human girl with her head in her hands, her eyes closed as if she could sleep out here. She carries the scent.

"Mate!" Chaos yells to me. She doesn't open her eyes, but swiftly gets up and sprints away from me, her mate.

Chaos chases after her with nothing else in mind but the fact that she is our mate. I watch her stumble a few times over nothing, as if she doesn't know how to run.

I catch her easily, pinning her to the ground with my paws. The girl's eyes are still squeezed shut, and then I realize she's human.

Maybe she doesn't even know about wolves. She's going to, though, if she doesn't. I shift into my human form, my hands pinning her down.

I sniff her deeply, letting the heavenly scent fill my nostrils.

"Mate," I growl, which causes her eyes to snap open in shock.

"What's going on?" Lucius asks through the mind-link.

"I have found my mate," I state. "Human mate."

How can a human be my luna, though? She's not nearly strong enough. Maybe she's just tired.

But I need a wolf to stand by my side. I need a female who will strengthen me in everyone's eyes, not weaken me.

But this girl, as her eyes connect with mine, I know that I want nothing else in the world but her.

Chaos is leaping around in joy because we've found her, and in lust because he wants all of her. He'd mark her right here and now if she allowed him. I certainly wouldn't though.

Then our little mate proceeds to pass out under me, maybe in shock or in exhaustion.

I lift her up in my arms and race back to where our clothes are, slipping them on in case she wakes up and she's scared.

Lucius and Ace join me, their eyes widening at the sight of my mate.

And I take this time to take her all in.

She's a mess. Blood smeared all over her face, her own blood. Dried blood drips down her jaw and as if someone just painted it all over her neck. It's thick right in the middle, clotted there.

Her body is limp in my arms, so small like she could slip through my hands.

Her mahogany hair is laced with dirt and crumpled leaves and clumps of even more dried blood.

What the fuck did she do to herself? Why is all this blood hers? And where did it all come from? I see no wounds.

I sprint toward the pack hospital, handing her over to a female doctor with others close behind.

They assess her wounds and place her in the room next to Ophelia, my dying aunt. She looks up curiously from her bed as the doctors wheel my unconscious mate by, a thousand questions in her eyes.

I need her safe, and this area of the hospital already has a guard for Ophelia. I sit by my mate, just watching her as the doctors do what they do.

My mate is a human. A young human girl. She can't be any older than eighteen, at most.

She isn't just my mate though. She's the mate to the alpha of the strongest pack in the country—she'll be the luna.

Yet she's human. I smell pack wolves on her, so maybe she was running in fear.

She was in rogue territory, incredibly dangerous for humans.

Did she know that? I can't introduce this whole world to her. I don't have the time and I have a responsibility to the pack to give them a strong luna.

I know what I need to do.

I have to reject her.

"Don't you fucking dare," Chaos hisses as the thought crosses my mind. He reels inside of me as I say it, wanting to fight me and kick me out of control so I can never reject her.

"You are not rejecting our mate."

But I'm the alpha. My duty is to the pack.

What choice do I have?

Chapter 5

Rejection

EVERETT

My wolf lives up to his name; he's the chaos to my composure. I have to think logically, whereas he's thinking with the mate bond.

Yes, I already feel as though I can't live without her. And yes, she's beautiful, even covered in blood. And yes, she means the world to me and I don't even know her.

But she's human, and she's breakable. She can't be my luna.

"Yes, she can!" Chaos screams.

"She's a weak little human. No one in this pack will take her seriously, let alone other packs," I argue.

"We'll make them respect her. We are the alpha. We can do what we want. They all respect us, and we'll demand respect for her."

"We can't tell them what to think. They will openly respect her but talk behind our backs."

"She belongs with us. She's not going anywhere, and they'll say what they want to say. She is our mate. Rejecting her would kill me. I won't allow it," Chaos states stubbornly, and I sigh in frustration.

After a while, my mate is all cleaned up, her beauty even more profound to me.

Her soft porcelain skin makes her look fragile, like she could break at the faintest touch, her tiny figure stirring under the sheets of her hospital bed, a cute pink tint to her cheeks.

She's stunning. And she's mine.

Mine for now, at least.

Lucius and Ace walk in with furrowed, contemplative brows and slight frowns, glancing over at my mate.

"You have a human mate," Lucius remarks, a hint of disgust in his tone, which causes me to instantly growl before I can even think.

He steps back a little, noticing my protectiveness of her.

She may be human, but she's still my mate.

"What did the doctors say?" I ask them.

"It's her blood that was all over her, but they have no idea where it came from. Aside from bruises around her neck and covering parts of her body, she's unharmed. She's just tired," Ace informs me.

How could she have that much blood from no wounds on her body? That doesn't make sense, but it doesn't matter. At least she will be alright.

Not that I can say the same for my aunt in the other room. I remembered her curious stare. She'd find out what was going on eventually.

The girl's eyes flutter open, her breath suddenly becoming heavy as her eyes dart around the room to see where she is.

When her eyes catch mine, they lock in place. Beautiful emerald eyes that glisten with confusion. Confusion and not fear.

Interesting.

"What's your name?" I ask a little coldly.

"Rory," she answers.

RORY

"What's your name?" the man before me asks in a flat tone.

This man called me 'mate.' Or maybe I was dreaming that. I was delirious after my time in rogue territory.

But I feel a pull to him—his eyes are like blue crystals, eyes that have haunted me in my dreams.

How is that possible?

I dreamed of him, his wolf, and now he is here. He's clearly an alpha—his dominant aura filling the entire room and instilling in me a control no stranger could ever have over me.

He's an alpha. Does he hate humans like Nick? Will he try to kill me too?

"Rory," I reply, and his frown grows—those eyes continuing to pierce me as if he could see my soul, as if, as an alpha, he possessed that ability.

Maybe I should play innocent and act like I don't know about werewolves. Maybe then he'll let me go, even though that very idea pains me as it crosses my mind.

I don't want to go. I can't leave him.

But why?

If he is my mate, it's the mate bond I've heard so much about—an indescribable connection pulling mates together, creating the feeling as if they can't live without one another.

"Your name's Rory?" he asks as if confirming that I'm telling the truth.

"Well, Aurora. But people call me Rory," I respond shyly as his unwavering stare continues. "Where am I?"

This question makes him frown even more. I believe he's contemplating his answer. He doesn't know I know about wolves. Or he's not sure.

"You're in a hospital," another man answers for him.

This man gives me a hard disgusted glare—the frustration clear in his expression. If I could guess the cause, I would say it's because I am human.

This man must be his beta; the sheer force of his brutal personality hits me hard.

Another man beside him just holds curiosity with a mix of frustration in his eyes, looking at me as if he didn't know what a human was.

The alpha gives his beta a nod to go ahead.

"Why were you out in the woods?"

It appears as though the questioning has been passed off to the second in command—perhaps because the alpha wants to carry on creepily watching me as if he were a stalker or some private investigator.

How should I answer these questions? Should I lie? Would there be any point?

If the alpha is my mate, he'll keep me around, I think. And lying to him would be unwise from what I know of alpha tempers.

But I can't tell them the name of my old pack, or that I died and came back from the dead. My mama told me to share the existence of my 'gift' with no one.

They could exploit it, and dying is awful.

It feels as though everything is being sucked out of me, and when they slit my throat, I wanted to claw my neck and eyes out just from the sheer pain.

Dying is definitely not on the agenda again.

"I was banished from my pack. They tried to kill me," I answer with a slight frown at the memory.

They didn't try, they did. And they smiled about it.

"Pack? You're not a wolf," the beta states a little harshly.

"My mom was an omega wolf in the pack. She found me in the woods and raised me as her own," I reply, seemingly unfazed by his interrogation, but panicked on the inside.

This beta doesn't seem to like me, and he doesn't even know me.

"When can I leave?" The alpha's head snaps up and he stalks over to the side of my bed, looming over me.

"What did you say?" he demands.

I shrink back into the hospital bed, terrified.

"I-I'm a human," I stutter. "I don't belong with wolves. I almost died because of that." *Did die, actually.*

I glance at the beta who hates me, and I see that he's nodding to himself.

The alpha growls, pure fury in the sound. The beta freezes, as does everyone else in the room.

"Leave us. Now." His words leave no room for argument.

Everyone in the room leaves, and I'm alone with the terrifying, but strangely comforting alpha. It's really confusing. His angry gaze scares me, but I also feel like I belong at his side. Like I'm totally safe.

Sure doesn't feel that way with the way he's glaring at me though.

"Why did they try to kill you?" he demanded.

"They thought I would tell people about wolves if they let me leave."

"Will you?"

"No!" I frown, angry that they would think I would betray my mama like that. "Never."

He stares at me, silently fuming. His fists are clenched at his sides, his knuckles white. I get the sudden urge to reach out and hold his hand, to smooth out his fingers. I blush. Am I crazy?

"Do you *want to leave?*" *he asks, his voice quiet. His voice shakes, and I try to figure out what he wants. He sounds conflicted, like he's having a silent argument with himself. Or with his wolf.*

I think about his question. I imagine myself stumbling around in the dark, afraid and alone in rogue territory. A cold chill of terror rolls through me.

"No," I whisper. "I want to stay." *I want to stay with you. But there's no way I'm saying that out loud.*

"Give me one good reason," he growls. "One good reason why we should keep you. What can you do? How can a human make herself useful to the pack?"

I open my mouth to reply, but no words come out. *What can I do? I'm weak. I'm slow. I can barely walk down the hallway without tripping.*

Tell him about your power, a small voice in my head says. I thought about the dying baby fawn. I can heal things…

But I can't tell him! Mama told me not to. They will take advantage of me. They'll test for themselves and kill me over and over for fun.

But if I don't, I'll be abandoned in the rogue forest again, and I don't think I'll be so lucky to survive again…

"Speak," he demanded. "I won't repeat myself."

I stare into his sapphire eyes, conflicted. Can I tell him? A part of me wants to trust him. I can feel the mate bond between us, but I can't reveal my secret to him just because of that. He's still a stranger. He can reject me.

I bite my lip. Trust him and risk becoming a tortured science experiment, or take my chances in the dark forest and get torn to shreds by rogues…?

I take a deep breath.

"I-I can heal…"

Chapter 6

Interrogation

EVERETT

"Heal?" I ask. I think about all the blood we found on her. Her blood. I watch as my little mate's eyes widen. She averts her gaze and stares down at the bed. "Explain," I continue.

She starts to reply but hesitates. She bites her lip, unsure if she should continue. I can't help but notice how cute she looks when she does that.

I grit my teeth. Focus.

"I-I'm good with herbs and medicines," she stutters. "I helped my mama a lot back at my old pack."

She won't look at me. She's a bad liar. She was going to say something else.

"*She's terrified,*" Chaos scolds me in my mind. "*Can't you see that?*"

"*How dare she lie to me?*" I say to him. I try to focus my fury on the young woman before me, but I can't. Normally lying to the alpha was a serious offense. But could I really punish her? Punish my precious mate…even if she's human?

"*Because she doesn't want to be banished again, you heartless fool!*" Chaos screams. "*Are you seriously going to reject her and throw her to the rogues?*"

I growl, anger white and hot flowing through me at the idea. Rory looks up at me, fear in her eyes. She thinks I'm mad at her.

I take a deep breath and calm myself. "You will stay," I tell her. "You are my mate. I will not allow you to leave."

The fear in her eyes melts, replaced by warm gratitude.

"Th-thank you," she whispers.

My heart swells, and I want nothing more than to take her in my arms. I clench my fists to resist the urge. I will not throw her to the rogues, but that does not mean I'll make her my luna.

"*Stubborn fool,*" Chaos mutters.

I spin around and head for the door before I do something stupid, like hold her and tell her everything will be okay now. I stomp away from the room, away from my mate.

RORY

The alpha's words ring in my ears. I can't believe what I'm hearing.

Just yesterday, Alpha Nickolas banished me from my pack. And now this alpha is allowing me to stay? This alpha that was, impossibly, my mate?

I thought I could never even have a mate, much less an alpha.

I look around the empty hospital room, wondering what I'm supposed to do. I'm feeling much better now, and he didn't tell me I wasn't allowed to look around…

I get up from my bed and peek out into the hallway. I see a guard outside, and he growls menacingly at me.

Oops. Not allowed to look around.

"Be nice," a kind female voice scolds the guard from inside another room. "Come here, child," the voice calls to me. Hesitantly, I walk inside of the other room, throwing side glances at the guard. He doesn't say anything, listening to whoever was inside.

Inside I see a woman. She smiles at me warmly, and I see her eyes fill with wonder when she looks at me.

She's a wolf too, I know she is, but she doesn't appear hostile toward me, a human.

She looks more judgmental, narrowing her eyes as if trying to figure me out.

"Hello," I greet a little awkwardly, but this whole situation is awkward. I'm in a whole new place with a whole new alpha claiming that he's my mate.

And funnily enough, I miss his presence around me already. Even though he's furious at me, I still feel a sense of safety with him by my side.

I push that to the back of my mind as I focus on the woman.

"Hi," she says, sitting up in her bed and continuing to stare. "Don't mind Everett, sweetheart. He's...a very dominant alpha. He cares about his pack a lot."

"Everett," I hum to myself to test it out.

Alpha Everett. Saying his name makes my heart yearn for him, which I can only sigh at. Stupid mate bond. I don't even know him, yet I want him more than anything.

I have a boyfriend though, which, after dying and coming back to life and running from rogues and passing out numerous times and finding that I have an alpha soulmate, I forgot.

"Who are you?"

"My name's Ophelia. I'm Everett's aunt."

"Why are you here?" I ask in curiosity. She doesn't look injured.

"I'm dying. It's a wolf disease. My wolf is dying and so am I."

She's dying? But...she's a wolf. She can't die. She's Everett's aunt too. He'll be devastated, I know he will. I feel that he will.

"I'm all Everett had, but now you're here. You can look after him. I'm happy he found you, even though he'll be skeptical of the match at first."

"Why?"

"You're human. And he's the alpha of the strongest and largest pack in the country." My eyes widen at her words, and acknowledgement crosses my face.

He's the alpha of the Shadow Blood Pack. And if he's alpha and I'm his mate, that means I'll be his luna, if he accepts me, which is why his aunt believes he's skeptical of me.

I am human after all, and weak. He needs a strong mate and luna.

"But don't worry. He'll see sense," she says.

I give her a small smile and walk closer. I attempt to walk a few feet just to her bed, but trip, of course, and end up falling over her legs onto the bed.

I hear her chuckle a little as she makes space for me and pulls me up. "Who tried to kill you?"

I glance at her, surprised. How did she know?

"I heard everything," she says, tapping at her ears. Of course. Werewolves have better senses than humans.

"The alpha and his luna from my last pack," I explain. "They hate humans. Their parents allowed my mama to bring me up in the pack, but their kids took over and soon enough, they kicked me out.

"They took me out into rogue territory and tried to kill me. But rogues scared them off and they thought the rogues would kill me anyway," I lie.

But it's almost the truth. They thought the rogues would eat my body, so there would be no proof of what they did.

And there isn't. My wound is gone. It was like they never even slit my throat with smug smiles.

"That's awful. So it was just you and your mama?" she asks.

"Yes. And my friends at school."

"School?"

"I go to a human high school. The wolves at the pack school would bully me and push me around so my mama put me in a human high school with the permission of the old alpha.

"I like being around humans, I feel like I belong there," I confess to her, and she smiles sadly.

"You won't be able to go back. You have a duty now, as Everett's mate. Did you have a boyfriend?"

"Yes." I grimace a little and she grabs my hand in both of hers.

"He won't like that, but you shouldn't lie to Everett about it either. He can be intense, but he is reasonable. He understands that he can't hurt humans," she says.

"Does he hate humans?" I ask.

"No, he doesn't hate them. He believes in coexistence. He likes that humans don't know about our kind, so we can lead private lives away from them. He's not like those in your old pack.

"Maybe because he's older than your alpha? He's twenty-five, and has already had a good few years as alpha, and he also learned from his father, my brother, before he died."

"I'm sorry," I say.

"Don't be sorry, Rory. Just look after Everett. He's like a son to me. He lost his parents and now he will lose me too. I only have so long. I want to know he's in good hands.

"I can tell you are a sweet girl with a kind heart. He might not know it yet, but you are what he needs."

"I'm not sure that's true. He's an alpha. He needs someone strong. I'm probably the clumsiest human alive. I tripped just walking a few feet from my bed to yours.

"One time I caused a riot in the halls of my school. I

accidentally fell into someone who pushed a girl, whose boyfriend was temperamental and punched the guy I knocked.

"Then all the guys started fighting with each other over in that part of the hall. It was chaos."

She chuckles at my confession but then shakes her head.

"Trust me, you're exactly what he needs."

I shake my head, knowing that can't be true. I am many things, but I am certainly not luna material.

Ophelia's face suddenly crumples up in pain. She closes her eyes and curls down towards her chest, grabbing the bed for support.

"Are you okay?" I ask, panicking. I lean over her, unsure of how to help.

"I'm okay, child," she assures me, her voice strained. "It will pass."

I watch as she takes a deep, rattling breath. I feel frustration building inside of me. This kind lady, one of the only people to show me true kindness in a long time, is suffering. And I'm here sitting beside her, completely useless. There's nothing I can do to help her.

But suddenly, I realize that that's not true. There *is something I can do. I remember the dying baby fawn, how it had been miraculously healed after I laid my hands on it.*

Could I do it again?

Ophelia smiles at me, trying to reassure me even though *she's the one hurting. It's okay if I heal her, right? They won't know it was me. This power is less obvious than me resurrecting. It could just be a surprise recovery…*

I almost told Alpha Everett before, but I chickened out at the last second. But now there was someone who needed my help.

I smile at her, trying to hide how nervous I am. I reach for her hand, an innocent enough gesture. There's no way she'll guess that I'm trying to heal her.

Ophelia takes my hand, her grip so heartbreakingly weak.

I close my eyes and focus, trying to find that strange, draining feeling from before. I feel something begin to build up inside of me, only slightly terrified of what might happen.

Here goes nothing…

Chapter 7

Tour

RORY

I focus on Ophelia's hand in mine. How exactly am I supposed to do this?

When I healed the baby fawn—*if I even healed it—I wasn't trying to. It just sort of...happened. Is this something I can control?*

"Aurora?" Ophelia asked. I opened my eyes to look at her. "Are you okay? You look a little pale, child."

Before I can reply, I'm interrupted by the beta and gamma marching into Ophelia's room.

"It's time to go," the gamma says. "The alpha told us to show you around the pack."

The two of them are staring at me, clearly waiting impatiently for me to get up.

"What are your names?" I question, standing up from Ophelia's bed, stumbling over air as I make my way over to them.

"I'm Ace and the beta is Lucius. I'll tell the alpha that you're still unwell," Ace declares.

"Why?"

"You can barely walk," he replies, steering me back into the bed without touching me.

"I'm not a sheep," I mutter, frowning at his attempt to herd me into bed. "And I'm not unwell. That's how I normally walk."

I flash the wolves a sweet smile as I herd them out toward the door.

Lucius gives me an unwavering glare, paired with his scowl, and Ace seems amused by my actions.

But both reluctantly walk out the door, leading me through the halls, despite their snickers at my slips.

As we make it outside, the sun hits my skin fiercely, knocking me on my behind before I can even blink.

Disregarding my estimations of their expressions, I slouch in my position by the entrance of the hospital.

"Are all humans this...clumsy?" Lucius sneers.

"What is she doing on the floor?" a familiar voice roars, his footsteps on the ground like a beater of a drum as he marches over to me.

I look up to meet his eyes, which are filled with fury and confusion. But it soon quells as he glimpses my shy smile, and he sighs.

"She can't even walk. She's like a toddler," Lucius says, insulting me, but immediately regrets it as Everett's scowl returns, directed toward his Beta. "She's fallen at least ten times from her hospital room to here."

"I can't help it," I mutter, staring at Everett's face.

He's the most gorgeous man I have ever seen, his broad muscled shoulders and chest showing his value of physical strength.

He's double my size, making me feel as if he could squish me between his thumb and forefinger. His shirt clings to his abs, so defined that they bulge through the material.

His dark features are complemented by the sapphire of his eyes. There's so many emotions in them, full of longing and doubt and frustration and serenity.

How can so many conflicting emotions be displayed all at once?

"I'm sorry, Alpha," The need to apologize overwhelms me, as if I needed to apologize just for being myself. But he looks disappointed in me. Disappointed that I'm his mate."

I would be too.

His hand reaches out to mine, and as if they were made to lock with one another, my small one fits with his large one.

The sparks diffuse throughout my body just at the touch of his rough skin on mine. He tugs me toward him and onto my feet.

His expression appears as conflicted as his eyes; he squeezes my hand but attempts to look away from me.

"I have work I must do," he declares, dropping my hand and hurriedly turning back the way he came. And my hand is left with this lost feeling, the vacancy of its other half making it grieve.

"He'll do what's best for the pack," Lucius tells me as he notices the dazed expression on my face, staring after the way the alpha went.

My eyes snap to his, my heart dropping as if I'm missing the biggest part of myself.

He'll never mark me. He'll do what's best for the pack, and he'll eventually reject me.

Lucius and Ace begin to walk ahead, expecting me to follow behind, which I do but in a stumbling manner.

"Will I get to go to school?" I ask innocently, and I hear an instant chuckle from both of them as a reply. And they don't choose to respond with their eloquent words.

"I'm eighteen. I want to finish school," I say.

They slow a little so that they're strolling on either side of me, and I'm presented with their amused faces.

"You could be luna of this pack, and you're talking about school?" Ace questions with the quiver of humor in his voice.

"Yes," I state with certainty and furrowed brows toward both of them. But it receives another laugh and a roll of the eyes from Lucius.

Whilst Ace points out different buildings, such as the school, the library, the bank, among many others, I attempt to listen and simultaneously not fall over again, which I think I'm doing well.

It just takes a bit of concentration.

When we arrive at the pack house, they had clearly mind-linked the wolves to clear out of here, maybe to not see the embarrassment that is the alpha's mate.

I guess he can't introduce me as anyone if he doesn't know what place he's going to give me.

Ace and Lucius lead me to an elegant building that stands a bit apart from the others. This must be where the leaders of the pack stay. We walk into a large foyer space, and they have me sit down in a waiting area.

"Wait for Alpha Everett here," Lucius orders.

"Is this where you live?" I ask.

Ace nods. "Lucius, Alpha Everett, and myself live here. Other pack members go in and out, and we have meetings in the big hall-like room downstairs."

The two of them leave me there, leaving quickly as if they would get infected with some human disease if they spent a minute longer with me.

I sigh, looking around at the space. It is quite nice, with comfortable modern furniture and large windows that let in a lot of natural light.

"This can't be any worse than my last pack, who killed me," I say to myself with a small chuckle.

It's strange, knowing I have this world-changing gift.

They had killed me. They didn't just try. They actually killed me. And now I'm here, alive, having found my mate.

I want to call Freya, or Eddie, to let them know I'm okay. But I never had a phone anyway. And as far as they know, I'm dead now anyway.

It's not like I'll ever see them again.

Everett won't let me finish out my year at school, with my friends. I'll be surrounded by pack wolves for the rest of my life unless he decides otherwise.

If Everett does accept me, he can protect me from Nick and Victoria.

But they did kill me. They slit my throat. And I don't even have a scar for it.

They would be suspicious of that if they saw me. And they *would* see me, if I became the luna of this pack. They think I'm dead.

Maybe it's better to stay dead, to start a life somewhere else, to make Everett reject me so I can leave.

But Everett...I can't do that. He's my mate. I already feel like I need him, and I have no idea who he is and what he is like.

But since he's contemplating whether he should accept me, despite the mate bond, he clearly cares about his pack and the future of it, and I have to respect that. He's an alpha.

He has a huge responsibility, and any decision affecting the pack has to be considered carefully and intelligently.

He can't make decisions on the strength of the bond, even though I know he feels it. And it must take a lot of strength to not fall prey to it instantly, even though I wish he would.

I want to get to know him, and I know he'll be distant with me, keeping me at arm's length.

I look around at the empty room, wondering what's taking

Alpha Everett so long. Lucius told me to wait here, but I could probably look around a bit, right?

I get up, but of course I trip on the legs of the chair and slam into the ground, relishing in the lovely familiar ache it brings.

I'm so used to getting hurt and bruised, I barely feel some injuries. But this one hurts like a bitch. However, to be ignored. I need to go.

Is this against his orders? Technically, Lucius told me to wait, not Alpha Everett himself...

I will just say nothing about being his mate, so as not to anger him. It could make his decision easier, and I'm still not sure what conclusion I want him to come to.

I stroll through the long hallways, while several other pack members throw some glances my way. They are wolves and can smell I'm a human, after all. If only they welcomed humans.

How can I tell people what I'm doing here? Do I tell them I'm just some wolf's mate?

That would only make them curious. Maybe I should tell them the alpha helped me when I was injured in rogue territory. He did, after all.

And perhaps that's all I am to him, an injured little human girl who just needs to rest up before she's sent on her way.

I come across a large mahogany door, with the word 'Private' embossed into it in a delicate golden filigree. My curiosity burns inside me, but I decide it's probably best not to trespass into restricted areas on my first day. I file that room away for later and continue exploring.

Eventually, I find a room at the end of a long hallway, the door slightly ajar. I peek inside and I see a large suitcase sitting on top of a lush bed. I see a piece of paper folded neatly on top of it. It reads '*Aurora.*'

I blink. *For me?*

I step inside, and immediately the scent hits me. It smells *so good*. My fingers run over the silk bed sheets, and I realize too late where I am. *I'm in his room.* That's his scent I smell. This is Alpha Everett's bedroom. So why is there a suitcase with my name on it?

Suddenly, I hear a door to my left open and I turn to see Everett.

"I thought you were told to wait for me," he growls. My jaw just about hits the ground.

He's dripping wet, with only a towel around his waist. My eyes follow as beads of water roll down his distinct jawline, over his perfect body, down his abs…

My face is on fire.

"S-s-sorry," I stutter. "I'll leave right away." I stumble back towards the bedroom door, desperate to escape. But I'm clumsy, and not very fast, even on a good day. Just as I get there, the door slams in front of me. Alpha Everett holds it closed with one arm as he leans over me, trapping me between him and the door. My back is pressed up against the wood, and I can feel the heat radiating off of his body.

His half-naked body.

I look up and I feel like I'm drowning in his sapphire blue eyes. I have to remind myself to breathe.

"Where do you think you're going, little mate?"

Chapter 8

Belonging

RORY

"I was going back out to the foyer," I say, trying to keep my voice from shaking. "To w-wait for you."

"A little late for that, don't you think?"

I continue to stare into his eyes, too embarrassed to look anywhere else. I want to let my gaze trail down his neck, lower and lower… I can't move. Could hardly breathe. It's like his gaze had locked me in place. My heart pounds so loudly in my chest I'm positive he can hear it.

Some drops of water drip down his hair and land on my face. I flinch, and that seems to break the spell. He leans away from me, and with a heavy sigh walks back into the room.

"Well, you're already here. I had one of the females of the pack gather clothes for you. They're inside that suitcase."

I take a breath, easier now that he isn't leaning over me.

"Thank you," I say, too shaken to walk. I'm afraid I'll just fall over. "Where will I be sleeping?"

I see him go into a walk-in closet, tossing the towel around his waist to the bed after he turned the corner. I blush.

"Here."

My face, impossibly, gets even hotter. I try not to think about how a naked Alpha Everett is telling me I'll be staying in his room.

"B-but this is your room," I squeak.

"And you're my mate." He walks out, dressed in a simple jeans and T-shirt combo. "Where else would you sleep?"

I open my mouth to answer, but no words come out.

"I have another meeting," he says simply as he walks past me and out the door. "Get settled in."

I can only stare after him in shock. I'm seriously going to be sleeping here? In his room? In the same bed? I feel all panicky. Nervous. And the worst part? I'm kind of looking forward to it...

I walk outside the room and head outside, needing to clear my head. This mate bond is so intense that it's got me excited about sharing a bed with a practical stranger. A very intimidating stranger that is very good-looking and makes me feel strangely safe, but still. Still a stranger.

I walk down the street and recognize a library. Excitedly I walk inside, eager to find some new reading material. It's quite empty inside, and very quiet. Just how I liked it.

Skimming through the wonderful books on the shelves, both old and new, I slide out a few and flip through them, feeling the pages slip through my fingers.

A cough to the side of me causes me to jump in surprise and drop the book on my foot, not that I needed any more help being clumsy.

I glance over to the librarian, who narrows her eyes at me in a curious way.

"Hi," I greet her with a cheerful smile in hopes of receiving an equally friendly one. Instead it makes her frown, not in anger or disappointment, but confusion.

"Hello, can I help you?" she asks a little warily. "You're human," she states, more to herself than to me.

"Yes. Alpha Everett found me injured when he was hunting

yesterday. I'm very lucky he helped me," I tell her, which grants me a smile from my praise of her alpha.

"Alpha Everett may be young, but he cares a lot for the pack and everyone here respects him. I'm Melissa, the librarian. Are you staying here long?"

Her questions are in no way hostile, conveying to me that she has nothing against humans among wolves.

I admire the stance Everett takes in the feuds between humans and wolves, and I assume he preaches this to his pack, even though Lucius detests me and Ace merely tolerates me.

But that's more to do with the fact that I'm human and I'm the Alpha's mate. They wanted their Alpha to have a strong wolf mate to lead them, not some eighteen-year-old human girl.

But I'm not as weak as they believe me to be, nor as human.

Yes, I may be the clumsiest human in creation, but I can also resurrect myself. That's definitely not something everyone can say.

I need to learn more about it, to know if it was dangerous or not. To know why I have this power.

"Alpha Everett has invited me to stay for a while. My adopted mother was a wolf, so I know about the wolf world, and I don't really have anywhere to go. I'm Rory," I explain truthfully.

She nods in some understanding and then glances down to the book on the floor.

She and I move to pick up the book at the same time, causing our heads to knock into each other and sends me to the floor—just me though.

"Oh, I'm so sorry," she apologizes, also realizing I said I was hurt yesterday and checking to see if I'm still all right.

She helps me up, along with the book, and flashes me a hopeful smile.

"This book is amazing," she gushes.

"I know. It's one of my favorites. This is a really nice edition," I exclaim.

"Actually, the Alpha has a better edition of this in his library along with every other book. He has more books than what's in here. But no one's allowed in there because it's his study."

"Oh," I reply, sounding a little disappointed. I remember the door marked as 'private' in the packhouse. Was that his study?

I love books, classics like Dickens or Hemingway or the Brontë sisters. And Everett has piles of books that no one else can get to.

"There's a limited selection in here, but there's enough."

"I should be going. I was planning to explore today, and since I love books, I thought the library would be my first stop. It was nice meeting you, Melissa," I declare with a bright smile.

She nods in agreement and bids me farewell.

As I wander back out onto the streets, I notice a boy with his elbows resting on his knees and covering his face, as if he were crying.

His curly hair sits messily on his head, flopping all over his hands.

I decide to take a seat next to him, keeping the silence, even though I know the pup smells me.

"I'm Rory," I introduce myself, extending my hand out to him. Reluctantly, he looks up with puffy red eyes and narrows his eyes at my hand.

"I don't speak to humans. Why are you even on our land?" he sneers, making me sigh a little and retract the hand. But I stay put, knowing he is only angry because of something else.

"Your alpha helped me when I was injured," I tell him.

"You shouldn't be here."

"And yet your alpha says otherwise. Why are you upset?" I ask.

"That's none of your business," he snaps defensively, looking away from me.

I know that look. I've had it myself.

"You know, I used to be in another pack. And because I was human, they would bully me, call me names, made sure I knew I didn't belong. And eventually, I let them win, I let them run me out."

His eyes snap back over to me, small growls coming from him.

"I'm not getting bullied."

"I didn't say that, you did." He huffs and rests his chin on his knees with a frown plastered on his face.

"I...I don't know why they pick on me. Just because I'm an orphan."

"They pick on you because pups like that, need someone to torment. I was an easy target because I was different to them, and you are an easy target because you're different."

"I don't want to be different," he furrows his brows at me.

"Why not?" I say. "There's nothing wrong with being different. Who wants to fit in? Fitting in is boring."

"It might be boring, but at least I might belong," he tries again.

"But forcing yourself to fit in, it goes against your own nature. They could only dream of being as interesting as you, and that's why they're picking on you." I don't let it go.

"I wouldn't say not knowing my parents is all that great," he says with a small chuckle.

"No, it's not. I know what it's like to be an orphan. But we are orphans, and we can't change that. It's what makes us interesting. We develop emotions that some people never do in their lifetime.

"They don't experience grief or loneliness or being different.

And they may not be great to feel, but you're much more complex than any of them could be."

"I'm Orion," he says.

I chat with Orion for a while, attempting to raise his spirits and also make a friend. I don't want to feel so alone in this pack.

Victoria made sure I never had any friends in my old pack, turning everyone against me and against humans.

Sometimes you just need someone to talk to, someone who isn't family; you need a friend.

And if I don't have friends here, I might as well just go back to the pack that tried to kill me; it would be like living there.

I decide to head back to the hospital to see Ophelia. The guards by her door stop me, scowls on their faces and their tree trunk-like arms blocking my entrance.

"Let her in," that sweet voice calls out through the door, making the reluctant guards let me pass, still scowling as I send them an 'I told you so' smile, before swanning in with unearned confidence.

"I thought I'd keep you company if you want," I say with a bright smile. Ophelia chuckles and nods as she pats the space next to her on the bed.

In the short time I spent in this hospital, she was my saving grace, giving me hope in this pack and Everett, despite her bias.

"You are easily the sweetest girl I've ever met," she tells me, sighing and grasping my hand in her shaking one. Must be a symptom of her illness or side effects of her treatment.

"What's Everett got you doing today?"

"Nothing. He told me that I was to stay in his room, and then left," I complain with a big huff as if I have the whole weight of the world on my shoulders.

And then I proceed to pout like a three-year-old. In my

defense, the past few days have been unbelievable, especially for a human like me.

"Just give him a chance, Rory. He's not bad, really.

"He's distant now because he's fighting the mate bond, and he believes that the bond will make him blindly make his decisions, whereas he's an alpha and is incredibly responsible.

"He does what's best for the pack."

"Which I respect. But I'm… I just got here. He's put me in a place I don't know, allowing me to have nothing familiar. And he's barely had one full conversation with me."

"He'll come around. I'm sorry, Rory. But please stick it out. I'm a dying woman and I need someone to look after my boy when I'm gone."

I already know Ophelia is a mother figure for Everett, her caring nature so evident to me.

Everett needs her. She can't die. It can't be left up to me to support him. He might even reject me.

"I don't want you to die."

When I don't get a response, I peer over to see her unconscious figure, her hand still intertwined with mine. I remember what I tried to do before Ace and Lucius interrupted me. I was going to try and heal her.

I look around, making sure I won't be interrupted again. But before I can prepare myself, suddenly I feel this horrible sucking sensation in my chest. It feels like my soul is being siphoned out of me, and a terrifying emptiness spreads inside me.

My eyes widen but I can't move, I can't even take my hand away.

I just stare at her with heavy eyes.

My chest begins to tighten. The breath in my lungs escapes me so I can't scream. But I want to.

I really want to.

My hearing turns to only muffled words, like bubbles have jammed my ears. My sight melts away too, the scattering of dots crossing my eyes before darkness.

It feels as if my life force is being taken from me.

And when I can no longer think or hear or see or breathe, my mind fades too.

There it is again.

The blinding white surrounding that stretches for miles with no end, and that same leafy-green door to match the plants wrapping around the frame.

The same glowing mist filling me with emptiness as if it was made of ghosts, lonely lost souls, pleading to leave through the door but being denied.

Then it hits me. Maybe that's what they are. Maybe the mist is souls. Maybe to each of them, I am mist too. I am lost and dead. Because that's what happened. I died. Again.

From…nothing. I did nothing. I wasn't clumsy. No one killed me. I didn't kill myself as believable as that might be.

I just…I was on the hospital bed, with Ophelia, trying to make her feel better.

And now I'm dead. Again.

And this mist at my feet and clawing at the door, these are the dead.

"Aurora," a voice whispers, causing my head to swing around, searching for the source.

"Aurora," another voice chimes in, almost hissing it. Soon enough, others join the calling of my name, for some unknown reason.

Before I can ask what they want, I'm forced through the door, passing through the wood with no problem, no branches brushing me, no thorns pricking me, completely phasing through this door, over the threshold.

I startle awake, finding Everett's and Ophelia's wide eyes looking at me as I catch my breath.

What the hell?

Chapter 9

Confidence

———•❖•———

EVERETT

Finding no sign of Aurora in my room, I mind-link Ace.

I attempt to keep the annoyance down, telling him to locate her, knowing Lucius's apprehension toward her.

"With your aunt," Ace says. I furrow my brows at this news. Why would she leave my room, and the pack house, to go back to the hospital?

"I'm heading over there."

Without even a second thought, my legs spring faster, longing to see my little mate, and curious to know why she disobeyed my orders.

Upon arrival, I push my way past the guards at my aunt's door to be greeted with Ophelia herself hushing me, awake, and looking invigorated from her usually pale skin.

And then I notice my little mate, looking dead to the world, everything about her soft and delicate and perfect.

Her dark brown-red hair is scattered over her face, splayed on all of the sheets too.

I stalk around to her bedside, brushing the locks from her beautiful face and tucking them behind her ear.

Her neck is bared, tempting me to mark her right here and

now, on impulse with no added thought. But I must fight the feeling.

No decision in this whole set-up can be rash, especially not when the pack is at stake. The right luna is paramount for the pack and for me as the leader.

"Why is she here? I told her to wait in our room," I query Ophelia in a hushed tone.

"You expect her to just sit around and do nothing? When she's barely even had a conversation with you, and you just go about your business as if she weren't here?" she responds in an equally quiet yet harsh voice.

"You're supposed to be on my side here. You're mad at me?"

"There aren't any sides, but if there were, who would be on Rory's side? Even for a wolf, uprooting your life, attempted murder at the hands of people you once trusted—she stayed out in rogue territory for an entire night.

"She doesn't have any scratches though. She's a mystery and she's alone. And you don't make it any easier on her. This is your family, your pack.

"You know these people, but is she supposed to just wait for you?" Ophelia lectures.

I know she has a point but Aurora hasn't been here that long. I have a pack to lead, I can't babysit all the time. Most of that time, she spent in the hospital.

And I had to learn how to control myself around her, so I kept my distance. But I can understand that she might feel alone.

Is that what she told my aunt?

Speaking of…she looks incredibly well for a dying woman.

"Are you feeling okay? You look great," I tell her with a small smile.

Ophelia has been like my second mother. The only family I

have left. Sure, I made peace with her dying, but it doesn't mean I hurt any less to know it.

Even with her lectures now, it gives me this warm feeling inside, the feeling of family, of caring.

Rogues killed my parents, and ever since then, Ophelia has been all the family I've needed to get through it. And now she's going too.

"Yes, I'm fine. Don't change the subject," she snaps.

"Aurora can wait. She's human, she practically sleeps all day—"

"Don't pretend like you don't sleep, Everett," she replies in a sassy voice. There are only a few people I allow to call me Everett and who are allowed to speak to me this way.

One, of course, being my aunt, and Lucius and Ace.

"She's literally passed out right now. What's she doing here anyway?"

"She probably got bored of your boring room. She decided to give me some much needed company. She's adorable and very sweet and caring. She'll make an excellent luna."

"In your opinion. You barely know her."

"The Moon Goddess matches soulmates. You are an alpha, the perfect match for you would make a good luna and also better you, as you would her. Rory is your mate."

"I can't make decisions based on some mate bond. She's human, she's clumsy. When I found her, her face was covered in her own blood, as if she slipped in it.

"She's more likely to die from her own stupidity than die by the hand of anyone else, and I can't keep watch over her all the time to make sure she doesn't get hurt.

"As a mate, I could do it, but as an alpha, I don't have the time." I finish hotly.

Ophelia sighs, glancing over at Aurora.

Like waking up from a horrific nightmare, Rory suddenly shoots upright, her breath uneven and shallow, panting as if she had run a marathon in her sleep.

Her eyes stare wildly at me and Ophelia as her hand raises to her chest to calm herself down.

Just at that moment, the doctor wanders in, to make sure Ophelia is comfortable and to take her blood to assess the progression of the illness.

I notice her hand no longer shakes, strangely, maybe because she has gotten a lot of rest. I know nothing about medicine.

When the doctor leaves, I grab Rory's hand, ignoring the tingles and sparks I feel that warm me up inside and set alight all the feelings of lust and longing and protectiveness and possessiveness.

She reluctantly gets to her feet and follows me out, stumbling only a couple of times. I take her into a private room and sit her down with me opposite her.

"I told you to get settled into your bedroom, our bedroom," I say.

"You didn't tell me I couldn't leave," she argues, although then adding, "Alpha," like the polite girl she is.

Anything that comes out of her mouth is like listening to an angel, the tones sweet but attempting to hold authority.

"Did you only go to the hospital?" I say.

"No, I went to the library first," she answers.

I sigh and run my hand down my face. Great. I don't want anyone to know about her yet. Just in case she's not staying.

"*She's fucking staying, you asshole,*" Chaos yells at me, and I just internally roll my eyes at him.

"But I told Melissa, the librarian, that you found me in rogue territory injured and you helped me," she adds, which causes me to promptly frown.

If she knew the ideas swarming around in my head, she would know not to share the mate situation. I must have given her those signals.

Signals that I wasn't sure about us, that I might not want her.

I do want her, badly. But I have to think about the pack.

"Should I not have done that?"

"No, you should have. I just… Tell me something about you."

"Tell you something? There's not much to tell."

"Tell me anything. I know nothing about you."

"I was three when my parents supposedly left me in rogue territory and my wolf mom found me. I…love school and books. Books especially. My favorite color is blue, but not the normal blue, an electric kind of blue."

Weirdly enough, the color of my eyes.

"What about you?" she asks.

Is it strange that I'm already in love with her, or I feel like it at least? This mate bond is incredibly powerful, especially when we're so close.

"I like green," I get out. Funnily enough, the color of her eyes. "Running through the woods, with the trees rustling and the fresh smell of nature.

"Being the alpha, I don't get to do it as much as I would like. My parents were killed by rogues."

Her face pales and I see sympathy, which I absolutely hate. I don't need anyone's pity.

"Don't feel sorry for me," I order.

"You can't tell me what to feel," she declares in a firm tone that surprises both me and her, "Alpha," she adds again. "I'm not feeling sorry for you. I'm relating to you. I'm an orphan too, and knowing what my real parents are like and what they would say haunts my mind every so often.

"And as much as my adopted mother tried, she couldn't tell me who I was, and I always hoped that maybe she could."

She almost sounds wise, this small human who trips over air.

Her words are…intelligent, like she could understand my pain. And I almost admire this sudden courage to speak to me this way, although if it were anyone else, they'd be put in their place.

She might be my luna after all and then she would be able to speak to me this way.

I had assumed she was this shy sweet little girl, especially after the few words I exchanged with her when she had fallen on the floor earlier.

Before I can say anything, the doctor bursts into the room, his eyes widened towards me and his expression shocked.

"Alpha, it's a miracle. Your aunt has a clean bill of health. She's not dying."

Chapter 10

Books

RORY

"What?" Everett questions, almost flying out of his seat toward the doctor. Instead, I just race down the hall to Ophelia's room to see for myself.

Did it actually work? Did I heal her?

Her bright ecstatic face tells me it all. Her sickness must have been really bad. It took my entire life force to heal her. That's why I'd had to die for her to live.

Can I really cure people?

If I can, that's an important gift that could be dangerous. What if someone finds out and takes advantage of it? The power to save people…

"Rory, you heard the amazing news!" she exclaims as I hug her tightly.

"It's not amazing," Everett's voice remarks behind us, and I turn back to question his tone. "It's impossible. It's a miracle."

His expression is one of disbelief and shock. I can understand. He had worked to come to terms with his aunt's passing, and now she's healthy and living.

Aurora's Secret

After spending the day at the hospital, Everett walks with me back to the pack house, the crisp night air hitting my bare arms.

Slipping like the klutz I am, my ankle rolls and I tumble to the graveled ground, Everett's disapproving expression staring down at me.

With the reluctant reaching out of his hand, I grab it and he tugs me close to him to wrap his arm around my waist and steady me.

Silence engulfs us as the streetlights flicker; only guards patrolling and the occasional snatch of conversation can be heard around us.

The thick tension-filled air becomes a little uncomfortable, more so for Everett than me as his breath quickens and his hand lightly rubs my waist.

Perhaps the animosity between us is due to my outburst earlier. Perhaps I should apologize.

Having just died and come back to life has given me a new sense of confidence. However, he is an alpha, and I'm assuming not many people speak to him in the same way I do.

But I let the silence stretch, continuing to just walk. His strong arm around my waist heats my cheeks, his large hands on my body, even over clothes, makes me feel more connected to him.

I know the mate bond in humans is weaker than in wolves, but the attraction I feel toward him is undeniably strong. If he feels it stronger, how can he push it away?

"Are you hurt?" his deep voice asks, glancing over at me before his eyes quickly flicker back to straight forward.

"No," I lie. I'm forcing myself onto my hurt foot to not raise his suspicion, which may have also raised his suspicion as he saw me fall on it.

But I maintain a high pain tolerance level, having hurt myself every which way over the years.

"You're lying," he deadpans, as if he didn't just accuse me of being a liar. His cold tone sends shivers down my spine, uncontrollably making my body press into his for warmth.

He grips my waist tighter, most probably fearing I'd fall without support.

Once we get inside and to his room, he lifts me up with ease and sets me down on the end of the bed.

He dashes into his bathroom, and I hear him rummaging around, opening cupboard doors and slamming them. I almost jump off the bed to ask what's wrong when he comes charging out and right up to me.

Without uttering a word, he grasps my injured foot that's swinging off the bed and drags it up onto his lap.

Removing my shoe gently, he presses an ice pack around my foot as I just watch him curiously. He doesn't say anything, but his face shows his disapproval from a mile away.

"It's fine, really," I tell him. My hand brushes his as I reach for my foot, but he swats my hand away and glares.

"You should really stop lying to me. You hurt your foot. It needs to be iced. Are you disagreeing with me?" he asks in a low tone, as if to say, "Do you dare disagree with me? I'm the alpha."

"No, alpha," I reply submissively, bowing my head slightly so he can't see my eyes anymore and I can't see the disapproval in his.

I know I'm human, and a clumsy human at that, and that's the last thing he wanted in a mate. I understand that he needs to think of the pack, that he has a responsibility, and I respect it.

I just wish he could be happy, and have a better mate.

After bandaging up my foot to give it more support, he shows me a wardrobe decked with female clothes a bit bigger than would fit me.

"These are the clothes that were in the suitcase," he says. "Though now that they're laid out I see that they're too big for you. I'll tell the female to get you some smaller—"

"Don't. I like wearing bigger clothes. It's fine," I tell him with a polite smile, picking out some night clothes.

I can feel his stare at the back of my head, but for some reason, his eyes on me don't make me feel too uncomfortable, as if on me are where his eyes are supposed to be.

"You're lying again," he comments before moving over to the bed. I skip to the bathroom and slip these clothes on, finding them baggy but comfortable.

He's right. I prefer fitted clothes for the day, then slipping a jacket over the top. But it is fine.

As I pop out of the bathroom, I suck in a breath, staring at Everett's bare back, his muscles in his shoulders making me drool.

His sweatpants hang low on his body and as he turns around, he raises a brow at me when he notices me.

Averting my eyes from his chest, which has abs so defined, it floors me as to how anyone gets them, I limp over to my side of the bed and crawl in. Am I going to be seeing him half-naked so often from now on? The thought makes a flash of heat blitz through me.

Nothing is said between us as he crawls under the covers too, but he faces away from me, his back on full display again.

I feel my eyes flutter closed as he shuffles around in the bed.

I shoot up with my hand around my neck, in a cold sweat and my breathing heavy. I miss him, the smell of him lingering in the air, easing my fear from my nightmare a little.

Having my throat slit like it was nothing was bound to give me nightmares sooner or later.

But I also heard those voices. The terrible, tormented voices calling my name in that white, misty plane of existence. Who were they? How did they know my name?

I decide to push those thoughts to the back of my mind, even though I know they'll be plaguing my thoughts later and in my sleep.

I throw on a baggy sweater, which rather looks like a stylistic choice instead of a sizing issue, with some blue jeans and head down the stairs.

As I reach the kitchen, I notice Ace and Lucius milling around, and they both glance over to me at the same time when I enter.

"Why are you up?" Ace asks me.

"Should I not be?" I retort, raising my eyebrows in question.

"It's five in the morning. So… I don't know," he replies nonchalantly and continues to root through the fridge. I fill up a glass of water with Lucius's eyes trained on me.

After finding a snack for my breakfast, I head out of there, not wanting to have their stares on me any longer.

Being the curious yet clumsy girl I am, I carelessly blunder into a door, the smooth wood slamming painfully into my shoulder.

I look up and see the door marked 'Private.' Alpha Everett's study. I remember Melissa, the librarian, telling me how many beautiful books were inside. Rare copies. Limited editions. More books than the library.

I look around guiltily, making sure the hallway is empty. I really shouldn't...

I try the doorknob. It's unlocked. Heart thudding, I peek inside, but I don't see anyone. Just a little look won't hurt...

I gasp. The space is filled with the most beautiful books. I can't help myself but travel in further, ignoring the warning in my mind.

It has a downstairs too, with long-stretching windows by his desk and books spanning the entire walls of the room.

I know it's against the rules to be in here, but my desire for books gets the better of me. I scan the shelves, logging into my brain every interesting book I see.

All of my favorites are dotted around the room, gorgeous copies that look to be untouched. I'm a firm believer that if a book is not creased, it hasn't been loved like it should have.

Books aren't just for decoration. They're to be held, to be read, to be treasured. These books need that. As I'm scanning through the shelves, a few books suddenly catch my eye.

One is about the Moon Goddess, Selene. Another about Greek gods and their myths. And one title written in silver.

The Myths and Truths of Immortality.

I gasp. Maybe I could find some answers about my strange powers here...

But before I can reach for them, a furious voice booms from behind me, causing the books to tremble on their shelves.

"What. Are. You. Doing?"

I hear the fury in Alpha Everett's voice, and I'm too afraid to turn around.

Aw, crap.

Chapter 11

Research

EVERETT

My little mate begins to tremble, half frozen as she was reaching for one of the books. I scan the section of my study she's in. My private study. Myths and Legends.

Hmm…

"Well?" I demand.

I see her take a breath and shyly turn to look at me, her face red with embarrassment at being caught.

"Sorry, Alpha," she says. "I was just so curious. The librarian told me that you had so many more books here than in the library…" Her eyes widen. "But don't get mad at Melissa, please! It was all my idea."

I hear Chaos chuckle in my mind. *"Even when she knows she's in trouble, she's trying to protect others."*

"You know you weren't supposed to come in here," I say.

Her eyes drop to the floor, guilty.

"Yes," she whispers.

I glare at her, deciding what to do. But even when she's breaking the rules, I can't completely focus my anger on her.

"How will I be punished?" she asks. She meets my eyes, clearly afraid but resolute. She isn't making any excuses, accepting responsibility.

Chaos rumbles with approval.

"Get out of here." I sigh. Her eyebrows scrunch up in confusion. "Don't let me catch you in here again."

"Th-that's it?" she asks, disbelieving.

"*Now*," I growl. "Before I change my mind."

"Y-y-yes, Alpha!" she stammers. "Thank you, Alpha!" She hurries past me, her intoxicating scent making me want to grab her and never let go. I see her hesitate, her eyes flickering back to the books on the shelf behind me before she stumbles outside into the hallway.

"You know she's going to sneak back in," Chaos snickers. *"Our little mate is too curious."*

My lips twitch as I try not to smile. She's braver than I give her credit for. I was afraid she'd be too timid. I don't want an obedient puppet as a luna.

"We'll see."

RORY

As fast as I could, tripping along the way, I manage to get out of the packhouse. My heart still hasn't calmed down, and I take some deep breaths of fresh air.

I was positive that Alpha Everett would have banished me after I got caught in his private study. Why is he letting a human like me get away with so much?

Maybe...because he likes me? Maybe the mate bond...

I sigh and shake my head. He's probably just being nice to me because I'm so weak and frail. Still, I wish I'd gotten just a few more minutes in his study. I wanted so badly to read those books...

I walk around the town for a little until I decide to visit Orion to distract myself.

Knocking on the door of the orphanage, I'm greeted by a woman my height with a kind smile, short legs, and flour all over her body. I beam back at her and introduce myself.

"Hi, I'm Nellie," she responds, opening the door wider to allow me inside. "The alpha saved you? He's quite the hero. Everyone in the pack loves him. So are you staying here for a while?"

"Yes, I am. I met Orion yesterday and he mentioned this place, and I thought I would come visit," I tell her and her face brightens up.

"You're the reason Orion came back so happy yesterday? Bless him, he always comes back with puffy eyes. The pups at school can be cruel to outsiders.

"You're welcome to stay a while. I could use the help. The kids are baking in the kitchen rather messily. Would you mind?"

"Of course not. I'm happy to help," I declare and follow her into the kitchen. I'm greeted by six or so kids, all throwing cake ingredients at each other and giggling.

I notice Orion reading in the corner, and just as he glances up and sees me, he hurries over with a wide grin on his face.

"Rory!" he exclaims. "Hi."

"Orion, hey. You seem happier," I say with a smile. "Whatcha making?"

A couple of the other pups catch my scent and look over to me with curious eyes.

Most of them are younger than Orion, who is around nine I'm guessing, but then a scowling girl walks through the backdoor of the kitchen, tugging her headphones from her ears to her neck.

"Why is there a human here?" she asks in a disgusted tone. She must be a teenager, maybe fourteen.

"I'm a guest, courtesy of your alpha," I tell her with confidence. "I'm Rory, it's nice to meet you…"

"Cassidy. And it's not nice to meet you," she snarks with a glare. "Alpha Everett invited you here?"

"I was injured in rogue territory and he—"

"Rogue territory?" Her sudden interest almost startles me but I just nod at her question as I see her curiosity is piqued. "You were out there? How long?"

"A day really. I was exiled from my pack when I came back from school, and I slept overnight in the woods," I reply as I begin to help two kids, Chloe and Wes with their cake.

The others play outside whilst Orion and Cassidy sit at the table just staring at me.

"How did you survive the night? You're human," Orion asks me.

"I was passed out, and I woke up in the morning to find a rogue protecting me from others for some reason. He shifted, and he told me I shouldn't be out here and then left."

"A rogue? My parents were killed by rogues," Cassidy tells me in a sullen tone. "A rogue helped you?"

"Not all rogues are the same," I answered.

"I was always taught that all rogues are vicious and selfish and dangerous, and I go by that because you don't know what they're like," she spat out.

"You have to stay wary. But not all rogues leave their pack by choice."

"Why did your pack run you out?" Cassidy questions.

"Because I'm human, and my pack was intolerant." I help the kids pop the cake in the oven, and they go join the other little kids playing outside.

I join Orion and Cassidy after I make some coffee for myself and get sodas for the two of them.

"Thank you, Rory," Nellie says as she enters the kitchen, plopping down on the seat next to me. "The kids were making quite a mess in here."

"Well, the alpha hasn't really given me anything to do, and I thought I'd help out around here if you'd like."

"Yes," she replies immediately, followed with a sigh. "Thank Goddess you said that. They are a handful!"

"Just don't mention it to Alpha Everett. He always seems distressed or disappointed around me," I tell them.

"Why?" Cassidy queries, narrowing her eyes.

"I'm quite clumsy, which is partly why he's letting me stay, and the fact that I have nowhere else to go.

"I just think that he wants me to spend all my time locked up in the pack house where I can cause no damage," I explain with a light chuckle. "Speaking of which, I should get back there soon."

"Aw, really?" Orion complains with a pout and slumps onto the table.

"I'll come back tomorrow if you like," I tell him with my brightest smile, and it seems to appease him.

I bid my farewells to the other pups and Nellie before heading back to the pack house. On the way back, I can't help but think about all those books in Alpha Everett's study.

I need something. Something to tell me who I am, what I am. I can resurrect from the dead. I died. Twice that I know of now, and twice before that.

I died. And I came back. I need to know why. I need to know the limits of it all.

The clumsiest person alive can bring herself back from the dead, can heal wounds. The irony isn't lost on me. The person who is most likely to die can bring herself back.

But I have to know why. I need answers. And, hopefully, if

I read enough, I'll find some answers. I could really help people, like I helped Ophelia.

I have a gift, but I need to understand it first.

I suddenly find myself standing before the closed door, the words 'Private' staring down at me. I cringe, remembering the alpha's words from earlier. If he catches me again, I'm *definitely going to get banished. But I have to know.*

I sneak inside and grab as many books as I can carry. I bring them back to our room and scatter the books on the bed to begin my research. I'll have to be quick so I can return them before he notices.

I plague my thoughts with old and new texts, myths that were thought impossible, stories of the Greek Gods, the Moon Goddess too.

She created the bond between Everett and me. Yes, he is a wolf, thus would have a mate. But to be mated to a human is very rare, and the Goddess would have a good reason for it.

Those humans would be strong, fearless women with worthy hearts, destined to be powerful leaders.

I am not anything like that. I stumble over my own feet as a toddler would.

It becomes late at night, when I had warily hidden the books away in case of Everett returning, but the clock strikes one and yet he is probably still working, or hunting, or doing something alpha-associated.

So, I carry on reading, studying text after text, reading stories of powerful gods who fought among themselves and over humankind.

Can they make an immortal human is my question. Maybe in return for being so clumsy, nature balanced it with resurrecting. But I can heal others, save them from death even.

"Why am I not surprised?" A heavy sigh startles me out of my studies.

"Well? Do you have anything to say for yourself?" he asks. He doesn't sound as angry as I thought he would. He sounds... resigned? Maybe a little tired.

"Well? Do you have anything to say for yourself?" he asks. He doesn't sound as angry as I thought he would. He sounded... resigned? Maybe a little tired.

Great. He didn't even care enough to get angry anymore. There wasn't even anything I could say. No excuse to save me.

I put on a brave face, trying to hide how terrified I was.

"No, Alpha." I say. "But, can I stay for the night, at least?" I see him frown in confusion. "I don't have to stay in your room," I add quickly. I can sleep out in the hall. I just...I don't want to leave at night." I shiver. "I'll leave at first light, I promise."

"WHAT?" he thunders, his face filled with the fury that was missing before.

I cringe away from him, terrified. I couldn't even stay the night. I'd have to go out and face the rogues alone...at night...

"You AREN'T leaving," he fumes.

That brings me up short, and I look up at him with confused eyes.

"You aren't banishing me?"

"No."

"But I broke the rules. Twice."

His lips twitch. It looks like he's enjoying a private joke. "Yes."

"So...?" I don't finish, confusion plain in my voice.

"My order is final," he says, suddenly angry again. "Don't question it."

I know better than to push him. I'll be counting my lucky

stars that I wasn't getting banished again. I nod and keep my mouth shut, looking down submissively.

He's silent for a while, and then I feel him sit down on the bed beside me.

"Why are you reading about Selene, the Moon Goddess?" he asks in a softer tone.

"I want to know why I am mated to you," I mutter in response.

"Aurora, look at me," he commands, and my eyes immediately snap to his in obedience. "You won't find the answer to that in a book," he tells me a little harshly and slaps the book down on the bedside cabinet.

"No one knows why the Goddess does the things she does. You can't read about what our fates will be. There's no such thing. We make our own futures, and you won't find anything in these books."

He picks up a few of the others and examines their covers with his eyebrows furrowed in what I would call a cute expression.

He slams more books down and inches closer to me, his eyes searching my face as if it were a puzzle.

"Years ago, my father, the previous alpha, taught me a lesson. He would teach me all sorts of lessons to prepare me for becoming the alpha, and one I mastered fairly quickly was whether someone is lying to me.

"You, my little mate, are an awful liar, which I suppose is a good thing. Good liars are practiced liars, bad ones are truth-tellers, most of the time.

"I don't like liars, Aurora. And you are lying to me. What do you want with Greek gods? And what do you want with healing and resurrection books?"

Chapter 12

Stronger

EVERETT

"Answer me, little mate," I demand as I watch her eyes go wide and her body freeze. I know I caught her in a lie, but she seems thoroughly paralyzed by my question.

"I believe in miracles. But I believe there are reasons that miracles happen. Ophelia had an impossibly curable disease. And she was cured. I wanted to know why."

The words are convincing, only if she wasn't the one saying them; she's a terrible liar.

Why is she hiding things from me? I don't know why. With her, my instincts are heightened, like I know what she's feeling and what's going through her mind in the most basic form.

Of course, that's due to the strong mate bond. If we were fully mated, I would know what she's thinking and feeling.

"Very well. Go to sleep, Aurora," I declare, brushing the other books aside and peeling back the sheets so she can get under them.

She slips her legs in and just watches me, following my every movement.

I stand to head back to my office, where I had smelled her scent and became furious over the invasion of privacy, but I'm stopped by her angelic voice.

"Are you not coming to sleep also, Alpha?"

Every time she calls me Alpha, it infuriates me. As much as I value the respect she holds for me, she doesn't feel comfortable around me.

I want her to call me Everett, but I know I'll enjoy it too much, and that will blind my judgment. I have to think like an Alpha, not like a mate.

But I will comply with the hidden request she has made, for me to go to bed, to sleep beside her.

I turn to face her, expecting her emerald eyes to be staring back at me, but I watch her snuggle into the covers and her head rolls to get into a resting position.

A soft almost inaudible sigh falls from her lips that makes my body tingle with excitement.

"Fuck you, Chaos. We need to be rational here," I tell him.

"Bullshit! She's our mate, and I can get excited if I want to be by her. She's adorable and intelligent. I don't even know why you were scolding her," he argues back with a huff.

"She was told specifically not to go in there."

"But she's our mate. She's allowed to be in our space. Don't tell me you weren't excited too when you sniffed her scent in there," Chaos advocates.

I roll my eyes and stalk toward the bed, sliding into the other side and turning over so I can look at her.

My little mate. My curious mate.

I guess I can't just expect her to stay in our room forever. It's understandable that she's bored.

Lucius and Ace even told me she asked about going to school, her human high school, with her human fucking boyfriend.

She didn't tell me about him, but Ophelia did, knowing

that I'd most probably lash out if Aurora told me. I lashed out when Ophelia told me, but she's used to it.

I don't like getting angry at my mate, especially when she hasn't done anything really. Just dated a guy who isn't anything to her now.

When I hear her light whimpers, I automatically stroke her cheek to calm her as if it was a reflex action. And she does calm.

She leans further toward me whilst still in her slumber, sensing my protection of her and wanting to be close to me.

My girl, my clumsy girl, my little mate.

I wake up to a harsh crash on the ground beside me and a quiet "damn" from the other side of the bed—Aurora's side of the bed.

Shit!

I almost hurtle over the bed toward her and a shy smile appears on her face as her eyes connect with mine. A red tint colors her cheeks as she scrambles up and back onto the bed.

"I'm sorry for waking you up, Alpha," she apologizes meekly, trying to decipher my reaction to her casually falling out of bed like it's normal.

Maybe it is normal for her. She's only spent two nights in my bed.

If this is what I have to wake up to every morning—my little mate smashing her body onto the floor—Chaos and I might go crazy and strap her to the bed or start holding her close and tight, never letting her go.

"Are you hurt?" I ask, sitting back on the bed and checking all over her little body.

Please tell me she's not hurt. Although I have a feeling I'll be praying for that a lot.

"I'm fine, Alpha," she replies with a sweet smile. "It's just

Aurora's Secret

my morning routine," she jokes with a giggle. Her giggle is what makes me chuckle, not the fact that this does happen regularly.

But then she gazes at me like I've done something obscene. Then she smiles. A real smile, not the shy or sweet or embarrassed ones she gives me.

She needs training. She needs toughening up and knowing how to defend herself and maybe learn some balance along the way.

She's a fragile little thing, body covered in bruises—old yellow ones and new purple ones.

I want to protect her, but she has to help me out a little. She has to be able to walk without hurting herself at the least.

"Aurora, you're coming to my warrior wolves training."

Her eyes widen and a little unconscious pout works its way onto her lips. I take a second to admire her cute expression, her "I don't want to" face.

But she'd never tell me that, she wouldn't outright disobey me. Because she's a good girl. My good girl. And she respects me.

"Why, Alpha?" she asks shyly.

"Because I want you to train. Are you disobeying me?" I question her, even though I know she'll do as she's told.

As easy as that makes things for me, my Luna can't be so submissive.

I know that her life in her old pack warranted her to keep her head down and follow orders, but to be my Luna, she has to be a leader and stand up for what she believes.

Maybe she can learn that, but sometimes it's just nature whether you have the will or not.

"No, Alpha, of course not. I'll get changed," she declares with a wary smile and skips over to the closet, almost falling over clumsily.

I leave to allow her some privacy and wait for her outside

the door. I hope she doesn't get tangled in her own clothes. But I wouldn't put it past her. Are all humans this graceless?

"This isn't a good idea. What the hell are you doing?!" Chaos yells at me.

"What?"

"She'll get hurt, you know she will."

"She'll be fine. I'll put her into some boxing gloves, and I'll be there, and Ace and Lucius. Even though they don't like her, they know she's my mate. That assures their protection over her."

"I'm telling you, this is a bad fucking idea."

"She needs to get tougher. I can't watch over her all the time."

Just as I am about to imagine more scenarios of her getting hurt, and worrying myself even more, Aurora pops out from the door in some sweatpants too big for her and a baggy hoodie.

Thank God she's small and the clothes are too big. With all my unmated warriors about, my little mate showing skin could result in some violence, by me to anyone who looks at her that way.

"Let's go." I reach out to grab her hand in mine, giving myself a calming feeling and a sense that she's a little safer.

Her little hand interlocks with mine, almost sending me into overdrive by the skin contact. "Walk beside me. I don't want you falling again," I tell her, and she nods.

As we reach my training grounds, my warrior wolves turn our way, narrowing their eyes at the human holding my hand.

Thus, I drop it and allow her to walk in front of me so that I can watch her step. I growl lowly at a few wolves I see checking her out, although they can barely hear me.

I don't want them to know she's my mate yet. She's just a girl I helped in rogue territory and brought back here.

"Alpha, what's Rory doing here?" Ace asks me as both my Gamma and Beta stroll up to me with questioning looks.

"She needs to train, to get stronger," I reply nonchalantly. "Take her and get her some boxing gloves her size," I command Ace, who nods and leads my mate away.

"Training with the warriors? She'll get laughed at by them," Lucius tells me, although hiding his wicked smirk.

He doesn't like my mate because she is human, and she's clumsy and he doesn't think she can be the Luna. I do share his doubts, but she is still my mate, and he will respect her.

"Watch it," I growl to him, which makes the hidden smirk slide right from his face. "She's my mate, although no one else here is to know that.

"She's a human we found in rogue territory and gave a place of refuge. But she is my mate, you shouldn't forget that."

I give off a threatening tone to make him understand, to which he slowly nods.

"Sorry, Alpha. I meant no disrespect. It's just… don't you think Rory training with the others is a little… The girl can't walk without falling, let alone train."

"I know, but I can't constantly watch over her all the time. She needs to get stronger quickly, and training with the warriors from time to time will get her there faster."

Hopefully before she falls or trips or drowns and dies.

I don't think I could ever live with that.

Chapter 13

Warriors

———•◆•———

RORY

When Everett orders me to do something, I find it hard to disagree, as he is my mate and my alpha now.

But I really don't want to train. My gym teacher even told me to sit out most lessons or do something like walk around the field, even though I would still manage to injure myself even doing that.

Now Everett wants me to box.

"We didn't have any kids' gloves, which would be her size, but the female ones are the closest," Ace tells Everett in an amused and mocking tone as he glances at my hands.

Everett huffs in response, his hand clasping around one of the gloves already on my hand and dragging me away with him.

Everyone around us stares intently, some with scowls, others with curious looks, and a few with amused expressions, most probably from seeing their strong powerful alpha next to a small, weak and human girl.

Everett then draws my attention back to him when he removes his shirt and reveals his washboard abs, his built shoulders, and bulging biceps.

My Goddess, he's as hot as a god himself. I purse my lips

to prevent my jaw from dropping and myself from drooling all over him, but he does notice my staring.

I just awkwardly act like I am not dazzled by his looks and my eyes dart everywhere but his body.

I see a slight smirk appear on his face, but it's soon pushed away as he raises his arms, palms facing toward me.

"Throw a punch, Aurora," he orders, urging me with his expression. Bringing the gloves up, I jab his hand with a tiny bit of force, but then I slip in the dirt and into him.

His hands quickly move to my waist, holding me up, but I can tell he's disappointed. I hear faint chuckles and see other wolves giving me strange looks as I try to regain my balance.

"Oops," I mutter in a quiet voice, but I know Everett hears it.

After a few more failed punches, he passes me off to Ace as he has business to attend to as alpha. Ace holds a more amused expression as opposed to Everett's dismayed one.

As I slip again while taking my right glove off, I don't notice Lucius behind me and my right fist thrusts back right into him.

It sends him right to the ground, his body slapping to the earth with a grumbling thud. My eyes widen as I turn to face him, dark red blood streaming from his nose.

Did I really do that? What the hell? So I can only punch by accident? That screams me all over.

"I'm sorry, Beta Lucius. I didn't realize you were behind me. I-I—"

"Rory, it's fine," Lucius replies with a grimace as he pinches his nose and scrambles to his feet.

The other wolves' smirks have been somewhat wiped from their faces, now confused and surprised expressions adorning their faces.

"You can pack a punch only when being clumsy," he mutters bitterly, his eyes narrowing at Ace, who's chuckling at his friend.

"I'm really sorry," I tell him with my best pleading eyes, to which he rolls his own. He's never liked me, so I shouldn't be surprised by his hostility.

While neither Everett's beta nor gamma approve of me, Lucius takes a disgusted and openly judgmental approach toward me, whereas Ace just appears amused and mocking of my weaknesses.

"Well, little human, let's continue," Ace announces, allowing Lucius to leave and get cleaned up.

"I didn't mean to hit him, although I may have enjoyed his stunned expression," I admit with a smirk as Ace grins at me after Lucius goes.

"I know, Rory. He does have a point. That was one powerful accidental punch. You can't do that again?"

"I think I'm cursed. I don't think it's normal to be this clumsy. I did learn to walk as a toddler, I just can't do it," I say and he chuckles at my statement.

"We can take a break if you want. Does your hand hurt? You are a human, and you punched a wolf's nose, hard."

I take a look at my right hand, my knuckles raw with blood, swollen and purple.

"Fuck! That looks serious." It should feel serious, but my pain threshold has always been high, luckily. The fear of hurting Lucius must have distracted me from the pain.

Now it aches, throbs. But not as bad as it looks.

"It's fine," I state nonchalantly and start to prod at my hand, testing the pain of it and whether anything is broken.

Before I can do anything else, my arm is violently dragged back and my body crashes into a stone-hard chest from a force that could have shattered more bones.

From the sparks streaming throughout my body, I know who it is.

"Moon Goddess," a gut-clenching, butterfly-making, spark-creating voice grumbles. I look up at him, expecting to glimpse a disappointed Everett, but instead, he's concerned.

His brows are pinched together, his eyes examining my wrist and the back of my hand and my knuckles. "I caught Lucius with blood pouring out of his nose and he told me what happened."

"It was an accident. I didn't mean to do it. I'm so sorry. I wouldn't—"

"I'm not mad, Aurora," Everett interrupts me. "I'm more concerned about you, and your hand and wrist. I think you broke some bones. Why weren't your gloves on?"

"I was fiddling around with the glove because it wasn't on right. And then I slipped, and Lucius was behind me, and I whacked him. I'm sorry."

For some reason, I always feel as though I should be apologizing to Everett, for everything. I'm only a burden for him. He has to take me in, since I have nowhere else to go and I'm his mate.

Which makes it harder for him to reject me, if that's what he wants, because I have no one else but him. I'm no luna, especially not for a pack as big and as strong as his.

These warrior wolves train every day, three times a day, whilst also hunting and patrolling and keeping everyone safe. No wonder they're looking at me with disapproving expressions.

"Stop apologizing, little mate. I have to get you to the hospital," he declares, leading me in front of him with his hands on my shoulders guiding me away.

"I don't need to go to the hospital. My hand's fine. It barely hur—"

"Don't lie to me, Aurora."

"I'm not lying," I complain, turning around in his hands

with a pout on my face and my brows furrowed. "It just needs to be iced and bandaged. I don't need to go to a hospital for that."

This confidence seems to only appear when I'm hurt or tired. But I generally lose it completely.

Especially when Everett is looking down at me with that threatening and dark glare.

"You won't disobey me on this, Aurora. Not on this," he growls. Which, in the moment, actually fuels my need to argue with him.

"Disobey you? I haven't disobeyed you once since I've gotten here."

"You went into my office," he argues, although taken aback by my attitude.

"You never told me to stay out of it yourself. I didn't directly disobey you. And I obeyed you this morning when you told me that I had to train.

"And it was obvious that I would probably end up in the hospital, but you didn't care," I rant, but my eyes widen hugely as I realize what I've just said.

"I do care," he growls, stepping even closer to me so he towers above me. His eyes darken and his wolf, Chaos, tries to gain control over him. "We care a lot, little mate. More than you know."

"Chaos?"

He tilts my chin up so that my eyes can meet his eyes easier. Dragging his thumb up my chin, he tugs my bottom lip down in an intense moment.

"We both want to protect you, but whilst Everett thinks as an alpha first and foremost, I think as a mate. He wants you to be able to protect yourself. We didn't mean for you to get hurt."

Chaos is different to Everett. More forthcoming. And more openly affected by the mate bond.

Our bond.

"I didn't get hurt. Like I said, I'm fine. There's no need for a hospital."

He assesses my face, looking for something; what something, I'm not certain of.

"You don't like hospitals?"

"When you're as clumsy as me, you tend to not see the need for trips to the hospital. I've had many injuries similar to this one. I don't like the hospital for minor injuries," I explain truthfully.

He lets out a big sigh, staring directly into my eyes.

"Fine." Without another second passing, he effortlessly lifts me into his arms bridal style and hugs me into his body.

"If Everett won't take care of you, I will."

Chapter 14

Mystery

———•—◆—•———

EVERETT

I KNEW I SHOULDN'T HAVE LET HER OUT OF MY SIGHT. BUT all she was doing was falling over. She didn't even fall and hurt herself.

She punched Lucius, giving him a bloody nose and a grumpy mood, and broke a couple of fingers, some bones in her wrist, and bruised it terribly.

How she managed that, I have no idea.

And how I managed to lose control to Chaos and let him look after her like I should have. She wasn't listening to me.

She wasn't obeying me, which took me by surprise to say the least.

I don't usually enjoy any defiance, but she almost made me proud, if it wasn't for the fact that she was seriously hurt and should have obeyed me by going to the hospital.

Now she's reading a book quietly on our bed as I'm surreptitiously watching her from the crack in the door.

She intrigues me.

Of course I feel the connection between us, and the pull of the mate bond which would draw me to her.

But it's not just that. It's her. She's different. Not like most humans. Certainly not as balanced.

But she's also a mystery of sorts. I've tried looking into the pack she came from, but I have no idea how I should approach the subject with her, and I can't just go around asking.

They think she's dead. They think they killed my little mate. They almost did too. She was just incredibly lucky with the rogues that night.

They normally tear humans apart almost as fast as pack wolves, which they detest. However, they didn't harm her. Very lucky.

Yet, she's very clumsy. She didn't complain or cry, or even hiss in pain from her injury. When I first caught sight of her hand, I wanted to rip Lucius's head off for indirectly causing it.

But her eyes were dry. Her cheeks too. Her face was more confused than in agony as she should have been.

She flinched a few times whilst I was bandaging her up, but there was nothing more than slight grimaces.

Since then, which was three or four hours ago, her hand is now turning green, as if it had been several days old.

See! Mystery.

And now I've got the pack on my ass about her.

To quote one of the warrior wolves: "clumsy little useless human."

I would have cut out the wolf's tongue had that not been a dead giveaway that she is my mate.

Why do I want it kept a secret? Because I still don't know if she can stay. But the longer I wait, the more everyone's perception of her solidifies, that she's a clumsy little useless human.

And she's not. Not to me. But it's not about me. It's about the pack. I'm responsible for a great many lives, and making her luna would share that colossal responsibility.

I'm not certain that she can do it.

"It doesn't matter. She's not going anywhere," Chaos states as a finality.

"I'm still mad at you for taking over yesterday. So shut up!"

"Someone had to look after our mate."

"I was. I was trying to get her to the hospital," I countered in annoyance.

"But she was telling you she didn't want to go. She's our mate, you can't just order her about all the time."

"While she's staying in this pack, I'm her alpha, so I can order her about any time I want."

"She doesn't even think you care about her. Our little Aurora probably thinks we're cold and cruel and bossy and couldn't give two shits. That's down to you. It's your fault Aurora doesn't like us."

"She likes us fine."

"Oh really? After you ordered her to train and got her hurt? She hates us."

"Maybe that's for the best," I muttered, more to myself than to him.

"I swear, if Aurora doesn't want to be with us because of you, I'm fighting you for control all the time, and soon enough, I'll permanently be in control, and I'll care for Aurora like we are meant to."

I roll my eyes inwardly at his threats, which he has been making constantly since we found Aurora in the woods.

She doesn't hate us. She doesn't even know us. I've been too... cowardly to have more conversations with her. I don't want to open up to her if she doesn't stay.

But I guess that's in my hands.

Ophelia loves her, claiming she's perfect for me and so sweet. She thinks Aurora will make the best luna.

Lucius, on the other hand, has a very different opinion. Even though he doesn't voice it, knowing my temper when insults are thrown at my mate, he believes she's too weak.

He isn't opposed to humans at all really, and doesn't even refute the idea of a human mate, but for an alpha—his alpha—to have a human mate who would become luna, he doesn't think that title should be entrusted to a human.

He only voices the doubts I already have. She doesn't have the strength or fast healing or heightened senses that wolves have, which are useful in being a luna.

Lunas have to be able to defend themselves in order to show that they can defend the pack and the pack can trust her.

If lunas do get hurt, they have to show no weakness in the face of it, and heal fast so they can get back on their feet.

And they must be able to do pack activities like hunting and running and training. Aurora would very likely die doing any of those.

Ace, although not approving of Aurora, has different views to Lucius. He's amused by her, and at the pairing of the two of us. Ace believes wholeheartedly in mates, having yet to find his.

He's still young so there's still lots of chances to find her. But his faith in the Moon Goddess is unwavering.

And the mate bonds are the Goddess's work, so they must be fated. Which is why the pairing of Aurora and me perplexes him so much. He doesn't know what makes us compatible.

But just staring at her now, listening to the light gasps or sighs as she goes through the adventure of her book, it seems like there's nothing more in this world that I want to do.

A couple of weeks go by, Aurora visiting the library and spending time with Ophelia, and me dealing with pack affairs and trying to figure out what to do with my mate.

The saving a human in rogue territory excuse only lasts for so long. And this pack meeting is turning into an interrogation.

"I know we believe in human coexistence, but that's only

when they stay away from us," a female wolf, Amber, states with a sour scowl at the thought of my mate.

"We're not a charity. If she has nowhere to go, get her help from humans. We help wolves. She isn't one."

"Alpha Everett, Beta Lucius, and I found Rory in rogue territory, covered in blood and exhausted. It is our duty to help anyone and everyone. Our duty as people," Ace tells her.

"Yeah, and now she's rested and well. She doesn't need immediate help anymore. We should just send her back to the humans," Lucas cries.

"She's not one of them. She's human, yes, but she has never lived with the humans. Her own adoptive mother was a wolf. She lived in a pack.

"She's staying here and that's final," I declare, fed up with their comments about my little mate.

I march out of the meeting with my Beta and Gamma on my tail.

"Why don't you tell them the truth or stop wasting Rory's time?" Ace questions, grabbing my arm and pulling me back to face him.

I growl loudly at him, releasing all my pent up anger that was created in that meeting.

The mate bond, the connection between Aurora and me, is incredibly powerful, so that it almost makes it impossible to think straight. But I must think straight, for the pack.

And I honestly don't know that Aurora is right for this pack.

Ace immediately lets go, taking a step away from me and holding his hands up defensively.

"He's right," Lucius pitches in. "I don't like her, you know that, not as our luna. She's sweet and all, but she's a human, and not exactly a strong human either.

"She doesn't deserve to be locked up and trapped here whilst you take your time deciding."

"She's not locked up," I counter.

"She doesn't know anyone here. Wolves around here don't exactly take to humans. She just reads most of the time. She deserves a life even if you don't want her."

She does. I know she does. But if I reject her, she can't be with anyone else, and I can't let that happen.

Maybe it's too late. Maybe I've already fallen for her, deeper than I should have done.

Chapter 15

Hunt

RORY

The murmurs of the alpha and his beta outside the door awaken me, prompting me to listen in on their conversation.

"The patrol caught a group of rogues sniffing around our territory. They chased them further out into rogue territory and lost them, but one of them injured one of our guys. He's at the hospital now."

"Grab your gear then. We're going rogue hunting today," Everett announces in a confident whisper.

"What about Rory?"

"What about her?"

"Is she coming with us?"

"Are you completely insane?" Everett seethes in a harsh tone.

"What? It's a hunt. We hunt in big groups. She would be safe. A luna has to know how to hunt with us."

"You have gone insane. Or you're trying to further prove to me that Aurora wouldn't make a good luna? Either way, she's not coming, ever."

"Then I don't know how you expect her to ever be luna. And if you don't, you need to cut her loose."

Cut me loose? What is that supposed to mean?

He doesn't think I can go on a hunt with them? I mean, I'm destined to get hurt, but I can still go. I heal like the wolves do thanks to my insane gifts, maybe even faster than they do.

I can help other wolves that are injured. I can help. But Everett doesn't think I can. He thinks I'm useless. He thinks that I wouldn't make a good luna.

He's wrong.

"Let's just go. Come on."

I'm going with them. I'm going to be useful, maybe. But I'm going to prove them wrong.

I gear up myself, changing into my sweatpants and a hoodie in case it gets chilly outside. I sneak outside and follow the wolves as they ready themselves to venture into rogue territory.

Tracking them at a very far distance because Everett would be able to smell me, I'm careful of the sounds beneath my feet, the plants brushing against me, even my own breathing.

When going on hunts for rogues, this pack takes big groups into rogue territory, mostly warrior wolves, and I must be careful due to their heightened senses.

Why are wolves so superior?

"Aurora," a quiet voice whispers, making my head snap in every direction to search for the source. It creates an unsettling feeling right to my core.

And it reminds me of something…

"Aurora," a voice whispers, causing my head to swing around, searching for the source.

"Aurora," another voice chimes in, almost hissing it. Soon enough, others join the calling of my name for some unknown reason.

From when I died the last time. Voices calling for me. It wasn't the same voice, but it was the same tone: menacing, eerie, haunting.

"Aurora…"

This time, the voice is closer, as if it were behind me, raising the hairs on the back of my neck.

Who is it? But I can't make a sound. I can't alert the pack that I'm out here.

I hurry faster and further into rogue territory in an attempt to get away from whoever it is. They know my name. They could know more about me.

They can't be human, maybe not even a wolf.

And then I'm lost. Completely lost, well into rogue territory, yet again.

Even though I've been lucky with rogues in the past, they are still dangerous, especially to humans, especially to weak little human girls.

There's a reason all the pack wolves hate rogues. They have no rules, they follow no code, they have no morals. That's what they've told me anyway.

But the rogue I met, he seemed…principled, honorable.

I hear branches crack around me, and the wind making the trees dance wistfully. Someone is there. Someone's watching me.

Light growls echo through the trees, decreasing the distance between us.

A grey wolf hurtles through the trees and pounces on me, pinning me down to the ground and growling in my face.

My eyes widen at him, small whimpers leaving my lips, and my body squirms underneath him.

As recognition crosses his face, he begins to shift, revealing Ace's distraught expression.

He also rapidly removes himself from me in loyalty to his alpha and acknowledgment of his possessiveness, even for me who he's not sure of.

"Rory, what the fuck are you doing out here?" he growls,

his eyes piercing my soul like I'm some evil demon he wants to destroy.

"I was just…exploring," I lie fruitlessly. However, my real reason may sound a little pathetic, especially since Everett and Lucius were right.

Me hunting is completely insane, and I'll never make a good luna for the pack. Everett should just reject me.

And that thought stabs me in the gut, and them saying it only twists the knife deeper.

"Are you stupid? You're in rogue territory, Rory. The place where we found you before, covered in blood, exhausted and frightened. You were exploring, were you?" he hisses, rolling his eyes in irritation.

He stretches out his hand to me and pulls me up to my feet, checking to see if I'm hurt.

"The alpha will be furious, but he'll be even more furious if you're hurt."

"Where is he then?" I ask.

"Well, I heard noises coming over from this way so I went to check it out alone and then—"

Rustling from among the trees breaks his attention away and he defensively pushes me behind him.

When I begin to hear low growls from all directions, and the fact that Ace has become warier, I know these are not pack wolves.

These are rogues.

"We're outnumbered, and with you with me, I can't risk anything happening to you by fighting. I'm going to pick you up now so don't scream or anything," he whispers.

And just at that moment, he slings me over his shoulder as if I were a sack of flour and sprints away, further into rogue territory, though.

I can only stare at his back, not moving in case I do something accidental that causes disastrous consequences.

We soon slow down once he deems it far enough away from the rogues we almost ran into. But he doesn't put me down.

He just walks at a relatively normal pace for a wolf with me dangling off his shoulder.

"Are you going to put me down now?" I ask him innocently and quietly.

I know he's irritated with me, he could have taken on those rogues if I wasn't there.

I know he saw me as a problem before, like Lucius, and this has only reinforced that idea.

"No. You've already caused enough problems. I'm going to mind-link Alpha Everett and he'll deal with you," Ace announces.

"No, please don't. Can't we just go back to the pack?" I ask hopefully. But he slams me down onto my feet and gives me a harsh glare which makes me cower slightly.

"Do you have any idea what could have happened? Everett would go berserk if anything had."

"Everett doesn't care. He doesn't want me as his luna, but the mate bond is keeping him unable to reject me just yet. When he builds up enough strength, he will reject me," I state.

His eyes soften a little as he listens to me.

"And then I'll have no one. What am I supposed to do when he rejects me and kicks me out of the pack? I have no home. I have no family. My old pack tried to kill me. I don't have anything."

I decide to walk away from him in a huff, my eyes watering a little at my realization. They would flood if I was alone, but I have too much pride.

Everett will reject me, and I'll soon be alone. What's

the point in even trying to get Everett's approval, or Ace's or Lucius's? I'll never see them again once I go.

"Rory..." He's at a loss for words because he knows it's the truth.

He believes Everett will do what's best for the pack, and what's best for the pack is rejecting me as the luna and his mate.

It will leave me heartbroken, and I barely even know him. I just feel so connected to him, even as a human.

The mate bond may be weaker for me than for Everett, but it will still tear me apart if he leaves. I guess that's why I've been lusting for his approval, because I need him.

It doesn't help that he was the one who saved me at my weakest point, after I had just been killed by my pack and was out in rogue territory.

"Let's just go back to the—" He's suddenly cut off, and it snaps my attention back to him. I swivel around.

My eyes widen at the sight in front of me. Ace's loud groan rings through my ears as I rush to his side.

"Hunters..."

Chapter 16

Mistake

RORY

"Hunters...," he grumbles as he grimaces in pain. I quickly act as capably as I can, slinging his arm over my shoulders to balance him and helping us get away.

I try to take most of his weight onto me and we scurry away, much further into rogue territory.

I trip many times, but Ace's crushing weight almost grounds me in a way and prevents me from falling. That's handy.

At least I won't have to worry too much about my terminal clumsiness.

Hunters? I've heard of them, and I know they usually hunt rogue wolves. They're the humans who know about werewolves and decide to hunt them down.

But some hunt all wolves, and most only hunt rogues, knowing that it's the rogues that are the most threatening to humans.

Maybe they thought we were rogues, or at least that Ace was and I was a human he was going to hurt.

They shot him. *Oh Goddess, they shot him.*

But he's a wolf. He'll heal. Won't he?

Then why wasn't he healing? It just looks like it's getting worse as he clutches his chest in agony.

That's a serious injury, even though he's a wolf and he can heal fast. *But why isn't he healing fast?*

Okay. Calm down, Rory. Panicking is helping nothing.

It's not like you're helpless here, remember. You can save people, you can cure people, you can raise yourself from the dead.

I bet no one else in the pack can do that. I guess it's something I'm good for.

But Ace can't know. No one can. Mama told me that. Well, she wrote that.

And she's right.

People can take advantage.

It's not that I don't trust Everett or Ace with my secret, and I don't actually, although my brain is willing me to trust Everett due to the force of the mate bond.

But it's that a secret is best kept if only one person knows it. The more people who know it, the further it can spread and then it's not a secret.

And those with malicious intentions would love to know someone with the gift I have and use it.

Back to Ace, if he's hurt and isn't healing, I have to help him, regardless of whether he knows about my gifts or not.

But he's a wolf. He'll heal. Hopefully.

We continue to trek into the woods with Ace leaning on me for support—very weak support, might I add, but support nonetheless.

"Why aren't you healing?" I question in a sudden panic and urge him to just come out with it.

"They're hunters. Their bullets are laced with wolfsbane. Which is poisoning me and also prohibiting me from mind-linking the pack and telling them where we are."

He groans again as even I can feel the agony seeping from him, resonating from his body in waves.

He's being poisoned? And if he can't mind-link the pack, how will we get back?

He needs medical attention, and we have no clue where we are. We're lost.

"This is all my fault. If you hadn't gone off in search for the source of the noise, you would never have been caught in the group of rogues, you wouldn't have backed away from fighting.

"You wouldn't have run whilst carrying me, you wouldn't have gotten shot by hunters. I'm so sorry," I rant, dragging Ace along with all my strength.

For now, Ace is doing pretty well for an injured, possibly dying, man and wolf.

But soon, I might not be able to get him out of these woods, and we might be attacked again, by hunters or rogues.

That's why this is a dangerous place and I never should have come here.

"I wasn't following your noise. You were pretty quiet for a human. I was following the group of rogues. I thought I heard them and decided to branch off. It's my fault that I went alone.

"I thought I could handle it, and I probably would have gotten hurt by at least one of those rogues if I had fought them.

It's lucky I had you as an excuse to go," Ace admits with a humorless chuckle. "But I'm no coward."

"I don't think you are," I say.

He looks over at me with a pained smile but then slows a little, searching my face whilst doing so.

"You want to know why you're still here?"

I furrow my brows at him in confusion. What is he talking about?

"Everett is a strong and dutiful alpha. Ever since his parents died when he was the young age of twenty, the weight of this massive pack was just dumped on him, and he wasn't ready.

"His instincts as an alpha weren't fully honed yet, and yet, the responsibility of alpha fell on him. So he didn't follow what felt right. He weighed every decision, big and small, carefully.

"He knew making a mistake would not only make the pack lose faith in their young alpha, but it would be his responsibility.

"And, even though he's older now, and he has the respect of everyone in the pack tenfold, and his instincts are trustworthy, he still weighs every decision, assessing the pros and cons, and he takes his time.

"He doesn't follow his heart because he thinks that can cloud his judgment. And the weighed decision about you would be rejecting you, no offense Rory.

"Of course, if you were my mate, I wouldn't. But Everett has to think like an alpha. And you're a clumsy human who would be luna."

I bow my head at his words, tears threatening to spill.

Why is he telling me all of this now? I know what Everett thinks of me. He's disappointed to have me as a mate.

He hates me, but the mate bond has kept me in the pack, has kept his interest. But soon enough, he'll reject me.

"Rory, what I'm saying is that Everett makes the hard choices well, he always has. He'll do what's best for the pack. He has always had the strength to reject you, Rory.

"He's always been able to ignore the mate bond, even though it's strong, and reject you. But he hasn't. He hasn't because you're a mystery to him, you excite him, you intrigue him.

"He honestly thinks that you could be a good luna, even though he has doubts. He's scared to get close to you because he doesn't want to fall too deep.

"But because he won't get close, he can't get to know you."

He grimaces in pain at his injury, but continues to walk and explain to me.

"I thought that you two had nothing in common. I'm a firm believer in the mate bond. Selene pairs people together for a reason, and she doesn't make mistakes.

"When I found out you were Everett's mate, I was dumbfounded. But I see glimpses of why now. And it's my fault I haven't seen more.

"I haven't made an effort to get to know you, like Everett and Lucius, and I couldn't see anything before. Only now am I seeing.

"You take on responsibility that doesn't belong to you, blame yourself for problems that aren't your own, and kick yourself for mistakes that you couldn't have prevented. Everett does that too."

"Why are you telling me all this?" I ask.

"I think I'm dying, little Rory," he replies in a sullen voice, slumping down to his knees to catch his breath and rest.

He looks worn out, pale, and I believe death will be knocking on his door very soon. Of course, I've died myself, so I know how it feels.

"Don't say that," I scold, knowing that a positive attitude might get him a little further.

"We're deep into rogue territory. Hopefully I might just get killed by a rogue before this poison takes me painfully. At least with a rogue it might be quick.

"You should go, Rory. I'm slowing you down, and you can't die out here. Everett would never forgive me."

"I don't care what the alpha wants!" I snap, making his eyes lock on mine. "I'm not leaving you. And don't talk like that. You'll be fine. Stop being a baby, get up, and we'll find our way back to the pack."

A faint smile adorns his face, almost as if he is proud.

"Shit, I really should have gotten to know you more, Rory. You're not the 'rollover and take shit' girl I thought you were," he says with a pained chuckle, clutching the wound on his breast as he scrambles to his feet once again.

I grab his arm and place it over my shoulders again, helping him walk, and we travel a little further, hoping to find something or someone.

The truth is, I can help, maybe. I don't know how my gift even works though. Can I cure poisoned wolves? I cured Ophelia, who had a terminal wolf disease.

But what if I can't heal him? What if I fail?

No, think positive.

What have you been telling Ace all this time? You can't give up.

The next time he stumbles, he might not get back up. I'd try and heal him, but our best bet is to get him to the pack doctors. They can cure wolfsbane poisoning.

No, no, no! Not again!

As I hear the low growling through the trees surrounding us, I'm almost not frightened at all, just from the irritation of it all.

Just as we're about to get somewhere, we hit another roadblock. This is ridiculous.

"An injured pack wolf. It must be Christmas."

Chapter 17

Protector

―――――•―◆―•―――――

RORY

"An injured pack wolf. It must be Christmas," a voice announces in an amused tone.

"Stay behind me and be quiet. I'll deal with them," Ace whispers to me as he pushes me behind him once more, gently. I comply, knowing Ace has more experience dealing with rogues.

All of the rogues shift into their human forms, all staring at us like we're their next meal. Wolves don't eat other wolves or humans, but rogues love the attack.

Rogues hate coexistence with humans and love how easily they can take humans down because we're weak.

They especially hate pack wolves for just being in a pack.

They have rejected the idea of a pack, either leaving their pack or exiled from it, and they hate any wolf who belongs to a pack, a community of wolves.

Maybe because they're just lonely? All rogues are different, I think. I've only met one, but he was honorable and actually caring.

"I'm Gamma Ace from the Shadow Blood Pack. You would be wise to leave me and the girl alone if you don't want the largest and strongest pack hunting you," Ace declares with authority, even though they can all see that he's weak and vulnerable from his wound.

A hunter's wound. They know. They're wolves after all.

"We don't care. A gamma? All the better. An injured gamma wrapped up here like a present with only a little human gir—"

He pauses mid-sentence as his attention shifts to me, and then fully to me. He stares for the longest time, as do the other rogues, the same expressions on their faces that I can't understand.

He steps closer toward us, not threateningly but curiously. However, Ace pushes me further behind him as he slumps over from pain. "What's your name, little girl?"

"Don't answer hi—"

"Rory," I reply, interrupting Ace. Ace gives me a sharp glare and a disapproving look, but I think I'm starting to figure some things out.

There's something about me, I don't know what it is, but it's keeping me safe from these rogues.

All of them are giving me strange looks like they know something, or feel something, that I don't. But I somehow think I'll be protected.

"You shouldn't be hanging around pack wolves, little one. Humans shouldn't be around wolves," he tells me, nearing closer to me.

Ace tries to get between us, but his legs give way, making him fall to the floor and clutch his chest.

"We need to get back to our pack. Can you tell us the direction?" I ask him in a confident tone. From the corner of my eye, I see Ace glance over to me with a confused expression.

"Your friend is dying. The Shadow Blood Pack is about two hours' walk, three or four if you're lugging him around. A little girl like you shouldn't be wandering around these parts with an injured, valuable pack wolf."

"I'm not leaving him. Can you please just show us the way?" I say stubbornly and with a profound confidence.

"I don't help pack wolves."

"But you'll help me?" I question hopefully with a shy smile. He stares at me for the longest time before nodding.

"If you want my advice, I'd ditch the wolf. But the Shadow Blood Pack is in that direction," he says, pointing to the right side of me.

"It will take hours, and he'll die by then anyway. If it was just you, little one, I'd show you the way. But I hate pack wolves." He turns to the other rogues surrounding us. "Let's move out."

I, for some insane reason, decide to stop them by asking, "Was it you who injured one of our pack members?" The leader turns to face us once again, a small smirk on his face.

"No, Rory. And I doubt it was any other rogues," he tells me before he runs off.

"What's that supposed to mean?" I mutter, to myself and Ace now as the others have followed behind the lead rogue.

It's strange, they don't usually travel together, just hunt sometimes. Taking on a pack wolf is a hard task, although this time, their target was injured.

"What the hell just happened?" Ace questions me as I help him to his feet again.

"I guess they decided to leave us alone," I say nonchalantly, hoping to sway the conversation away from everything that just transpired.

Of course, even I found it strange. Either rogues hurting humans is a myth or there's something about me. And I fear it's the latter.

Which would mean maybe they can tell I'm special, that I have weird, unexplained gifts.

The more Ace loses strength, the heavier he becomes as I have to carry more of his weight, and the harder it becomes to travel further. But at least we're heading in the right direction.

"You shouldn't have engaged with him. I told you to be quiet," Ace huffs, wincing every so often in pain. "If he had found out you were the alpha's mate, he wouldn't have let us go.

"I still don't know why he let us leave. If Everett found out you were flirting with him—"

"Flirting?" I blurt out at the outrageous accusation.

How dare he? All I did was have a conversation with the guy.

"I was not flirting. How dare you? You know what? I couldn't care less about what Everett thinks or knows. But I'm technically still with Eddie, my high school boyfriend.

"I mean, we never broke up. I never even said goodbye. But I wasn't flirting with anyone. I was just talking to the rogue and hoping he'd let us leave."

"Everett already sorted it out," Ace says with a little chuckle.

"What do you mean?" I ask warily, looking over to him.

"He broke up with Eddie for you, in a text. He was feeling very jealous at the time. He couldn't let some guy walk around thinking he was dating you."

"Everett dumped Eddie, pretending to be me, in a text, most probably the worst way to break up with someone?" I question, absolutely horrified.

"Yes," he confirms proudly.

Eddie is a good guy, and he was a good boyfriend. He put in the effort even when he couldn't get certain efforts back, like walking me home or hanging out after school, or even meeting my mama.

He didn't care, somehow, and still he had cared about me.

And even though I didn't love him, and we probably wouldn't have lasted forever, I cared about him too.

Dumping someone in a text is cruel. Really cruel. And he didn't deserve that.

"How?"

"He found out his number, texted him like Everett was you, and dumped him. Then he destroyed the phone in case he got a reply.

"Anyway, if you weren't flirting with that rogue, what was with all the eyelash fluttering?"

"What eyelash fluttering?"

"The thing where you flutter your eyelashes. You were doing it whilst you put on the whole innocent sweet girl act.

"Which I can't believe worked because rogues don't think that's adorable, they just think of it as weak."

"I was not putting on some act or flirting! I was just trying to talk to him. And clearly it worked, so I don't know why you're criticizing me anyway," I state with a pout and a scowl.

"Maybe it's not an act. You're just adorable. Is this you trying to be mad? I think you're keeping me alive with your… whole deal.

"Everett's right, you are a mystery," he says with a pained chuckle before sliding to the floor once more and suppressing a loud cry with a grimace.

I try to help him up, but he can no longer carry on. I think this may be as far as we can get unless I can actually save him. I'll just have to try.

I kneel down beside him, opening up his shirt to assess his wound.

There's a big black hole on his chest with black poisoned veins spreading out across his body, taking over more and more of his skin.

"This looks awful," I mutter. A strained laugh comes from Ace, making him cough straight after at the pressure on his wound.

"Thanks, Rory. I love the positivity. I know Everett's your mate, but I am very attractive actually," he comments with an anguished smile.

"So once I'm dead, tell Everett I died protecting you; it will paint me as a hero rather than a guy who got shot by a hunter he didn't see coming."

"You were protecting me," I tell him.

"Then you protected me, somehow. I still don't understand what happened back there. That guy must have liked you and let you go. But I'm surprised he let me go."

"You're dying, and you're still dwelling on that?" I say, shaking my head.

He narrows his eyes at me all of a sudden, like he's figured something out. "You know why he let you leave. That's why you're trying to change the subject."

"No, I'm trying to change the subject because you're dying and I don't know what to do."

"Changing the subject again. Being curious about you will take my mind off the fact that I'm dying. So, tell me Rory, as I am dying, why did the rogues let us go?"

"I don't know," I answer, and honestly, I don't know.

I just know that these rogues like me, or something like that.

They know something or feel something, and it has kept me safe out here in rogue territory, even as a baby, when I was left in rogue territory.

My mama said I had no marks or scratches on me. The rogues didn't hurt me at all, a vulnerable little baby.

I notice Ace's eyes begin to quiver, as if deciding whether to open and close.

"Stay awake, Ace," I tell him, shaking him a little.

"Rory, that's really not helping…" His voice trails off as he loses consciousness. It's now or never. I have to at least try and help him.

I place my hand on top of his wound and my other hand on top of that, pressing down with slight pressure. I close my eyes and push, hoping something will happen.

But it doesn't.

CHAPTER 18

Knowledge

———— • ❖ • ————

RORY

After many long seconds with nothing happening, I begin to panic.

Goddess, he can't die. I can't let him die.

I have the power to save people and now I can't even save Ace. I don't know how to control my gifts, but I had hoped it would just work.

After many minutes with nothing happening, uncontrollable tears begin to fall, rushing down my face. I squeeze my eyes tight to brush away the tears as my hands are covered in his blood.

I know I don't know Ace all too well, but he was nice to me, I guess, in a way. But he's also Everett's gamma, a key member of his pack, and a good friend.

Everett would be devastated, and I would be responsible. Ace was protecting me, because of my stupidity.

He cares about me, even though it's mostly because I'm Everett's mate and his alpha would rip his head off if I got hurt and he could have prevented it.

But Ace is hurt, and I'm supposed to cure him, save him.

Why can't I? When I saved Ophelia, I didn't even realize I was doing it. It just…happened.

I open my eyes to see the area of the black veins decreasing, shrinking back into their originating hole. And then the hole closes up as if nothing happened.

My heart begins to thud like a racehorse's hooves in its final sprint. I try to search for breath, but I find none, and it's almost like I don't know how to breathe anymore.

So I just claw at my neck and my chest and my body, hoping I'll find some, somewhere.

I want to scream, and gouge out my own eyes, and rip my skin off my body from the feeling that envelops me.

My senses melt away, my vision clouding and my hearing muffled like I'm no longer living in the world.

And then my eyes close, overwhelming me with sudden darkness and plaguing my entire consciousness, whisking my life force away from my body once again.

There it is again, for the third time that I can remember. The blinding white surroundings that appear infinite and impossible, yet so real.

The branches around that green door twist constantly, tightening around its frame. And the lost souls wrap around my feet again in the form of the mist; their sullen loneliness, the vacant mist.

It's not so much what it looks like, but what the mist feels like. It feels like a person trapped, alone, desperate for a savior.

If I'm here, that means I am a savior. I died. Not from any wound or illness, but from the feeling I got when I was at the hospital with Ophelia, when I cured her.

I died. Does that mean Ace will live?

"Aurora," a voice whispers like before, but more prominent than the last time, more haunting, closer to me, like at the back of my neck.

"Aurora," another one calls out, nearing me. Maybe it's the

mist. Maybe they're voices from the mist. They must know I can leave by now and want to find a way to go with me. I don't know.

"Aurora." This time, the voice that calls my name is haunting or muffled or whispered. It's loud and clear and almost heavenly like.

And then a figure appears, a woman, cloaked in a stark black dress that wafts behind her, floating like there is a breeze here. But there isn't.

Her skin contrasts completely with the dress, as white as snow, quite literally, perhaps as white as her background.

Her hair is ebony, matching her dress.

Her face is the personification of sadness, although she wears a delicate smile.

"Who are you?" I ask, my voice strangely echoing as if I am in a large hall. But the sound travels for miles, dying out somewhere along the way of infinity.

"My name is Achlys. I'm the one who is sent to push you back through the door. We haven't met before, but with you here so frequently, I decided that I would introduce myself. And warn you."

"Warn me?"

"You're in danger. You always have been. But she's closer now. She can get you here. She can get you in rogue territory. They're unprotected places, and they are not safe for you."

"She? Who do you mean?"

"Her name is—" she abruptly stops when she snaps her head to the side, her bones clearly defined in her neck and collarbone as if she hasn't eaten in years.

"You have to go. Try not to come back here, Aurora. It's not safe for you. It will never be safe for you."

Before I can ask her any more questions, I'm forced through

the door of life once more, leaving this strange place with a little more gained knowledge but not enough.

What I do know is someone is after me, a woman. And I know Achlys. I'll research her, and maybe I'll find some information telling me what's going on.

I needed something to go on, something to look for. I was getting nowhere with finding out why I am the way I am.

And I did notice the way she said, *I am the one who is sent to push you back through the door.*

Who sent her? Is there someone else I should be wary of? Why is my life so complicated?

I had my old pack wanting rid of me, and now some other woman wants me dead too.

A woman I'm guessing even more powerful than Alpha Nick and Luna Victoria as she can get to wherever I go when I die.

I'm whacked awake, back into my body, and I shoot up from the ground. Dirt paints the back of my body, sticking like glue and molding to me.

I look beside me and see a now-conscious Ace building a fire and a comfortable space to lie down next to some trees for shelter.

I notice that it's now pitch-black night in comparison to the relative afternoon it was when I *died*.

"Ace?"

"You're awake," he exclaims, rushing to my side. His eyes are wide and questioning, searching my body and face, checking my health.

"Yes, I'm awake. Why is that surprising?" I ask him.

"I must have fallen asleep at some point and dreamed that I was shot by a hunter, and we met some rogues and it was crazy.

"Then I wake up, and you're passed out next to me. I couldn't even find your pulse," he explains with frantic eyes.

He thinks it was a dream? Um...I guess that's a good thing, right?

He doesn't have a wound, and it was certain that he was dying. Yet now he's alive, and has no wound.

Maybe it's for the best that he thinks it was all a dream. In his position, it would be the most logical explanation actually.

"Yeah, um...you were carrying me through rogue territory, clearly, and we were talking, and you suggested going back to the pack.

"But it was already late and we were tired and you fell asleep. And then I must have fallen asleep."

"We were lucky no rogues found us. But my chest was covered in blood and my hands and your hands. Do you know what happened there, because it doesn't make sense?"

"Yes!" I abruptly say, causing him to jump a little. I have to make up some story that he's not too weirdly forgotten.

"I got hurt on a branch, and I didn't want to tell you because I caused too many problems already.

"And when you were carrying me, I got blood on you and my hands and then when you put me down, you noticed me bleeding but just rolled your eyes and called me clumsy."

"Why don't I remember that then?" he questions, narrowing his eyes. "And if you're hurt, Alpha Everett would kill me. Let me take a look if there's this much blood."

Goddess, I am so bad at lying. Everett was right. Which might be a good thing.

But in my case, being in the situations I've gotten myself into, and my gifts, I need to be good at lying. I need to get better, somehow.

Maybe I need a teacher. Maybe I can find a book about lying.

But for now, I have to make him stop questioning it all.

"You already did. I'm just an excessive bleeder. It adds to my clumsy persona. So, there's no need to worry," I try to say coolly.

He scoffs then repeats, "Excessive bleeder," like it's the weirdest thing ever.

It happens. But I bleed as much as the next human.

Although I did bleed a lot when I got my throat slit. So much that I slipped in my own blood and face planted into it.

Looking back on it, that was incredibly embarrassing.

"It's weird. The dream I had felt so real."

"Did it? That's interesting. So, can you mind-link the pack or something so we can go home?"

"It's already done. Everett was freaking out, so he's coming himself, and I didn't want to move you in case something was wrong. I thought you didn't want me mind-linking him.

"And since when did you start calling the pack home? I thought you hated it there and you think Everett doesn't care, even though he's running out here to get you."

I just want him. I just want Everett. He just feels safe, he feels like home.

He'll protect me from everything, from whoever this woman is who wants to get me. Achlys wouldn't warn me for no reason. This woman is an immediate threat.

And I just want Everett to make me feel safe.

After seeing and feeling all those lonely, lost, trapped dead souls, it takes an effect on me. And I just need him. I need Everett.

"That's because I'm his responsibility, and you told me because he became alpha at such a young age that he takes his responsibilities incredibly seriously, and I'm his mate, so he thinks I'm his responsibility."

Ace nods before staring at me like I have something on my face. Shit, did I slip in his blood or something?

"Are you okay?"

"Yes, I am," he answers slowly and uncertainly, but I accept it anyway.

"Aurora," the voice of the alpha calls out behind me.

Chapter 19

Need

EVERETT

"Everett, calm the fuck down," Lucius yells above the racket of me trashing my office. Why the fuck would she leave? Why would she just run off? And no one saw her?

"Where would she even go? It's been hours now and still no sign of her. I had to return from the hunt when I found out she was missing.

"I have a wolf regularly making sure she's eating and sleeping and checking up on her. But I don't know too much of what she does.

"Maybe she's been planning this, planning to leave me. She can't leave me!"

"Everett, oh Goddess, we'll find her it's—"

A voice through the mind-link cuts off my attention on Lucius.

"Alpha, can you hear me?'

"Ace? Where are you? We couldn't find you during the hunt and then Aurora went missing so I had to come back."

"Rory's with me, and she's fine. She isn't hurt, she's just asleep. I don't really want to move her, just in case she's not okay, so you should come to get her."

Thank the Goddess she's safe. She's with Ace. But that means she's out in rogue territory.

What could she be doing out there? Why would she be so stupid and reckless?

She was lucky enough the first time with the rogues, why would she try her luck again?

What would possess her?

I just hear Chaos screaming at me, telling me it's my fault, which I already fucking know. She could have been hurt, she still can be.

"I'm coming. I'm sending a group out with me to scour the territory. Do you know whereabouts you are?"

"About one and a half hours out. We'll be waiting. I'll keep her safe."

My little Aurora. I thought I had lost her. I thought she had run away from me. Maybe she had. Maybe that was her attempt, but she ended up in rogue territory.

Luckily, Ace found her before anything bad could happen to her.

"You weren't there to protect her," Chaos lectures.

"I can't always be there."

"You should be!"

I immediately gather a small team and head out, my beta by my side. I track Aurora's scent whilst he tracks Ace's. They can't be too far from us.

But I can't feel her, Aurora.

Normally I can just feel her presence, her life, her spirit. Even though we aren't mated yet.

I say yet like it's a sure thing. Even if I decide I want her to stay and be with me, she may decide that she wants nothing to do with me, maybe she already has.

I don't want her to hate me, even though I haven't done anything that would make her particularly like me.

I keep her from everything she knows, force my lifestyle and pack upon her, and give her doubts about whether she can stay or not.

Where would she even go if I did reject her?

She has no home anymore. I'm her home, sort of. But I still need to think of the pack, and I'm not sure Aurora could ever make a strong luna, the strong luna this pack needs.

I continue to trace her faint scent. Ace said she wasn't hurt, thank the Goddess. But she could have been, easily.

And not even from rogues. She hurts herself regularly.

I have slept next to her for over two weeks now, and most mornings, I wake up to her falling off the edge of the bed, no matter how many times I try to place her in the middle of the king size bed.

She just rolls right off and slams onto the floor. Luckily she has both a high tolerance for pain and is used to this morning ritual, plus the fact that I have carpet in my bedroom, our bedroom.

As I catch her stronger scent, I sprint toward it, Chaos leaping at seeing our mate again.

The fright of finding she was missing wrecked us, very badly. My office now displays that same sentiment, books strewn all over the place.

And all because we wanted her. We needed her. Our little mate.

"Aurora," I call out to her as I spot her petite form and Ace's relatively larger one. He nods to me in acknowledgment and Aurora whips her head around to face me.

I can't read her expression. Why can't I read her expression? Does she hate me? Did she really run away?

Of course she would hate me. I gave her every reason to

run away, to not get too comfortable in the pack because I could possibly reject her.

And that's still an option. I have to think about the pack, not just become overwhelmed by the mate bond and give in.

But my little Aurora ran away from me. She'll run again. She'll run now.

But what happens next shakes me to my core. Something I'll never forget.

Something that can possibly make me lose all my senses completely, then and there. All my principles melting away and the logical brain fading into the background.

She hugs me. She leaps over to me and squeezes me as tightly as her little human body can.

She just…hugs me.

And it confuses me more than I ever have been in my life. Her petite body fits into mine, and I never want to let her go. I just hold her. And it feels right.

It's not just the mate bond. This is real. We're real. This moment together, it's real. I need her, and she, strangely enough, needs me right now.

"Why did you run away?" I ask, not trying to sound too pathetic and heartbroken in front of her.

She looks up to me, breaking her body away a little so she can see me, and furrows her brows.

"Run away? I didn't run away," she tells me, almost melting my heart.

She didn't run away? Then what the hell is she doing out here? She could have gotten seriously hurt. And that idea makes my gut boil and the heat rise throughout my body.

"Why were you out here, Aurora?"

"I heard you and Lucius talking this morning," she admits,

her eyes flickering to my chest so she doesn't have to look me in the eyes anymore.

"I just… I heard you talking and I know you're disappointed to have me as a mate, and I'm not a wolf and I can't hunt. But I… In the moment, I just wanted to prove something.

"So I followed you out here. But I heard something and I got lost. I'm sorry, don't be mad," she explains quickly. She's clearly panicked I would be angry with her, and I am.

But more relieved than anything.

So I embrace her snugly into my body, inhaling her sweet scent. It both relaxes and excites me.

"Thank the Goddess we found our little mate again. If Aurora was hurt, I'd slaughter whoever did that to her," Chaos declares.

But she's not, thankfully.

I pull her back to look at her, just to make sure she's not hurt.

But when I see her tired eyes, the small pout she subconsciously does when she wants to sleep, and her little hidden yawn, I pick her up bridal style, much to her content, and trudge back to the pack with Ace beside me.

She almost instantly falls into a deep slumber, exhausted from her trip into rogue territory. I just stare at her beautiful face, wondering what I would do if she wasn't here.

Could I even reject her if that was my decision on what's best for the pack? Maybe I could before, but she's not what I thought. There's more to her, much more.

As stupid and dangerous as it was, she wanted to follow us and prove that she could be strong, that she could be a luna, to prove Lucius and me wrong.

She shouldn't have heard us talking. It was my mistake. I don't want her to think that she's not good enough.

But maybe she isn't cut out for being a luna.

"There's more to her than I originally thought," Ace states through the silence, which catches my attention.

"What do you mean?"

"I don't know…yet. She's a mystery. But I wouldn't be so fast to dismiss her. She's stronger than I thought she was.

"Maybe not in body, although she does have a high pain tolerance, but she has a strong will. And sense of loyalty."

"Why would you say that?"

"She can easily leave, she's proved that. She's staying for you."

"Because she has nowhere else to go. That doesn't prove her loyalty."

"Maybe not. But when we were out here in rogue territory, I told her to go, to run, because we were around rogues. But she stayed and she looked like she wanted to fight.

"It may not have been the wisest choice, but she didn't want me hurt," he tells me.

Why does it feel like there are lies woven into this truth?

But whatever happened to change Ace's attitude toward Rory, it must really show that she is special, that maybe she could make a good luna.

Chapter 20

Suspicious

———◆———

ACE

There's two things I'm certain of after my trip shared with Rory in rogue territory: one, Rory can't lie for shit, and two, there's more to her than any of us know.

I woke up to the little girl passed out next to me, blood painted all over my hands, and her hands and my chest, like my dream was real.

But I had no wound. And I would be dead if it was. So it must have been a dream.

I checked to make sure Rory was okay, her health paramount before mind-linking Everett. But I couldn't feel a pulse, maybe because my hand was strangely trembling like crazy.

I told Everett to come and find us, and soon Rory woke up, spinning some lies. The girl really needs to know how to lie if she wants to do it that frequently.

She slipped up when she told me I had told her Everett took responsibility very seriously. I told her that in my supposed dream, after I was shot by a hunter.

So, either the dream was real and I did get shot with a wolfsbane bullet.

Or the dream wasn't real, her lies are the truth, and for some reason, she explained away that she got hurt, which I have no memory of.

I had blood covering my hands and shirt in the exact same place where I dreamed I was shot.

Honestly, both options sound as bizarre as each other, but I don't think it was a dream. But how do I have no wound? Why am I not dead?

And I seriously bonded with Rory then if it was all real. And I learnt a lot more about her. She knows what happened then.

That's why she was lying to me. She knows what happened or knows something happened.

Why would she lie unless she had something to do with it? I need to know. I need to know why I'm still alive.

She did something.

Maybe she's a witch. They can cure wolfsbane poisoning as well as heal wounds…I think.

That could be the explanation. I have to watch her, every movement that she makes, everyone she talks to, and everything she reads.

She's strangely into books, perhaps they're spell books.

Shit, this is insane.

There's no way that clumsy little human is a witch. If she was she could cast a spell that gives her balance. She really needs that.

I sit, with Rory on my mind throughout the whole meeting, as I'm guessing she's on Everett's too.

As the pack clears out, only Everett, Lucius and me are left with the other two discussing the rogues in the dungeons, trapped behind bars.

Because Everett cut the hunt short to look for Rory, they never found the rogues who injured Freddie in the attack.

If it wasn't a dream, maybe we found that group, even though Rory asked them whilst flirting, and he said no.

Actually, his answer was cryptic, as if rogues hadn't attacked at all. Like something else is.

But I don't trust rogues; they're all manipulative liars, out for themselves.

"Maybe he's in love with Rory," Lucius's voice says, snapping me out of my daze as Everett slams the table and growls. Lucius only smirks and raises his eyebrows at me questioningly.

"What the fuck is wrong with you? Ever since you returned from rogue territory with Rory a few days ago, you've been out of it," Lucius snaps.

Because I should be dead. And I'm not. And I think that's because of the little girl sleeping a few doors down from me, in my alpha's room.

What if she has evil intentions? What if she's all an act, just to trick Everett and destroy the pack? But then why would she save me?

She saved my life. She saved me, I think.

If she wanted to destroy the pack, a good way of doing so is taking down the titled wolves.

She could prey on the mourning of the alpha. Then become luna. And then destroy the pack.

But she gets nothing out of saving me. There was no reason to do what she did. She just…saved me.

Maybe.

That's if she is a witch, or whatever she is.

"He's right. Why are you so unfocused?" Everett questions, narrowing his eyes at me.

"It's because he's dreaming about your little mate," Lucius jokes, creating another huge growl from Everett.

But Lucius remains unfazed in his amused mood.

"Stop aggravating him," I scold Lucius. "I'm just tired."

I am tired.

I've been up for nights thinking about my almost death. I felt myself slipping. I felt myself draining. But now I'm just… fine.

Completely and utterly fine.

The pack doctor checked me over when I got back, and I am perfectly healthy, as is Rory.

Strangely enough, the very clumsy girl is in perfect health. That's just peculiar in itself.

"I bet he's thinking about her now," Lucius mocks, pushing me a little and snapping me out of my daze yet again.

"Can you stop?" I question, irritated and frustrated at everything.

I'm the only one suspicious of this girl for a very simple reason: she acts like an innocent, weak human.

There's no way Everett would ever think she had bad intentions here because she's…lovable, or she acts that way.

I knew no human could be that clumsy.

It would make sense that it's all fake. That she's all fake. Everyone with functioning legs can walk.

And she acts all sweet and obedient and she reads all the time, disguising the subterfuge. And when Everett came to get us, she ran and hugged him.

She knows just how to play him, wrapping him around her finger, my alpha.

⁂

The next couple of weeks, I watch her like a hawk, tracking her every movement. But all I find is more sweetness.

I'm filled with sugar. I might just become fat from watching her.

She actually sneaks away to help out at the orphanage, and

takes—steals—books from Everett's office to let the kids borrow there.

And listening to her conversations with them, I'm not sure whether any of it is fake anymore.

I'm just perplexed. Stuck in the middle between believing the, frankly, unbelievable: that she's genuinely this…adorable.

Or she's a total fraud and possibly a spy.

The rest of her days, she's at the library conversing with other wolves about certain books, or she's reading and studying in Everett's room.

But what was even more surprising was seeing her sneak out into a space of open field that's quite the blind spot in the pack.

When I first followed her there, I had thought she was plotting something, because of the minimal security, and she was aware of that.

But she began to take out boxing gloves from her bag, and weights and weapons too that I'm guessing she stole. And she started to train. Actually train.

She ran around the field, tripping over herself several times. Even with no one about, she's still clumsy.

And she punched a tree many times, whilst almost punching her own face on the draw back, then stumbling, tripping back on a long thick branch, but proceeded to head butt the tree as she fell to her ass.

She excused all her injuries as just being clumsy, which is easy as I hear a soft thump most mornings, even from my room, coming from Everett's room.

By what Everett calls his morning alarm, Rory just falls out the bed. That can't be on purpose.

This time, watching her out in the field, I decide enough is enough. I'll confront her on why she's out here, training.

Does she want to build up her strength to take on the pack,

to take down the alpha? What does she know? Why is she really here? What really happened in rogue territory?

"Rory!" I call out, startling her. Her big green eyes widen at me in utter shock, and she drops her boxing gloves to the ground.

Frozen but not balanced, she sort of topples in a statue-like way to the side and smashes her side into the earth.

Oh Moon Goddess, if this girl is faking, she's an amazing actress. And if she's not, she's incredibly cursed.

I pick her up off the ground and set her down, not on her feet, but sitting on the grassy field. I crouch beside her, checking to see if she's hurt.

Of course she's a little scratched.

"What are you doing out here, Rory? The second time I've found you somewhere you're not supposed to be."

I stare at her, acting all tough as if I'm angry that she's out here. I'm more curious.

"I-I'm sorry. I-I just… I just… um…"

"Rory," I say, hopeful to get an answer out of her some time soon.

"I… Alpha Everett's always disappointed in me, and I just want a little balance, just so I don't get his disappointed face all the time. It's not pleasant," she explains with a pouty expression, as if picturing her mate's face.

She's either a great liar or a completely terrible one.

I think she's telling the truth. I can tell when she's lying. And if she is telling the truth, then Everett's got some making up to do with her if he wants her.

And he does want her. I know he wants her. He used to have the strength to reject her, but after that embrace in rogue territory, things have changed.

He's really falling for her.

And if she's not acting, and she's not malicious, and she is really this sweet, she could make a good luna.

"Can you not tell Everett I was out here?"

"If you tell me what pack you come from."

A way I can know for sure is if I check her story out. "I know you won't tell Everett, but I won't tell Everett about this if you tell me."

"Or about which pack I am from?" she asks. I look at her expectantly, and she sighs. "The Red Moon Pack."

Red Moon? A respectable-sized pack with some powerful warrior wolves.

"What's the alpha's name?" I prod.

"You're testing me? You don't believe me?" she questions, which makes me narrow my eyes at her.

She huffs before replying, "Alpha Nick. And his luna is Victoria. Are you happy now?" she sasses, which almost makes me chuckle.

This little girl is very cute when she's sassy.

But she's Everett's girl. And if he wants her to stay his girl, he better start trying for her.

Chapter 21

Progress

RORY

I don't wake up the usual way. Just to a log restricting my airways. I try to wriggle out of it, but I'm trapped shut against the wall and the log wrapped around me.

Where the hell am I?

I open one eye cautiously to find myself in Everett's room, in his bed, with his arm cutting off my circulation instead of a log.

Although the two are very comparable.

"Alpha?" I call out, my voice strained and almost inaudible. But he must have heard it as he grumbles and tightens his hold. The opposite effect.

"Alpha, you're killing me here," I say, sounding like a strangled cat.

"Aurora, I'm stopping you from falling off the bed," he mumbles in my ear, his breath fanning the back of my neck, almost making me forget that I'm suffocating to death.

What would it matter? I would come back to life anyway.

But Achlys did say that rogue territory and that limbo place are unprotected grounds, so whoever "she" is can get me there.

"But I can't breathe," I squeak, which suddenly makes him loosen his grip and turn me around to face him.

His eyes connect to mine as I breathe heavily, panting and attempting to slow down.

I give him a shy smile to tell him I'm okay, and his hand subconsciously strokes my cheek. But he snatches it away once he realizes his action.

We've had more conversations over the past two weeks, ever since I got back from rogue territory and hugged him.

But we've never been this close before.

"I'm sorry, Aurora," he whispers softly, sighing and staring at me like he's never seen me before.

"It's okay, Alpha," I reply.

"Call me Everett, little one," he says, his hand resting back on my waist and tugging me to him again. "I don't like waking up to you getting hurt. Is this okay?"

I want to, quite pathetically, tell him he can do anything and it would be okay. But his hand on my waist certainly is, so I just nod with a gentle smile.

"Just try not to suffocate me next time," I tell him with a small giggle. "Everett," I add.

I study his morning face, his eyes half open but still luminous with electric blue. His bare chest is definitely drool-worthy for a sight this early in the morning.

His pink lips just look so kissable, like they're begging for me to put my lips on them.

"Can you say my name again?" he asks, and I furrow my brows at him.

Why would he—

Well, I do love it when he calls me Aurora. Or anything really. Like "little mate" or "little one."

"Everett," I say, his name rolling off my tongue. He is my soulmate after all.

His smile widens against all of his self-control, and I smile back at him.

Before, I couldn't imagine staying in a pack like this, with this incredibly attractive Alpha next to me and the strangest and most dangerous gifts.

Or they could turn out to be curses. Whoever "she" is.

Everett will protect me, won't he?

Later on in the day, after spending a few hours with Cassidy and Orion at the orphanage, I stumble into a few warriors, quite literally, and fall back onto the ground, my butt hitting the concrete sidewalk.

"Watch where you're going, human," one of them snickers, raising a brow at me as he looks down at me as if he is far superior to me.

I know the warrior wolves don't like me very much at all, frankly. They don't know that I'm Everett's mate. No one besides the three titled wolves and Ophelia do.

But these wolves are more vicious to me than everyone else, much like the wolves from my old pack, the ones who killed me.

"Sorry," I mutter, shuffling back before standing up to create distance between us. I bow my head and walk around them, quicker than my normal pace.

I hear their chuckles and snide remarks as I run off, but I just try to ignore it. It's nothing I'm not used to.

In fact, it was a lot worse in my old pack because the Alpha set the example to hate on the human to the entire pack, whereas Everett is all about coexistence.

He's not bothered that he has a human mate, he's bothered

that I would become his Luna. Lunas should be strong and preferably a wolf.

There hasn't been a human Luna in... well, I haven't heard of one. But I know there has been a couple at some point in time.

But honestly, I don't know what I am. I don't even know if I'm human.

"Hey, human!" one of them calls out from behind me, and I grimace before turning around.

I can't just run off because that's impolite, and they'll hate me even more, but I wish I got further, out of sight. I look to them expectantly whilst inching back conspicuously.

"Why are you still here? The Alpha and Gamma always seem to be around you, or they keep you locked away in the pack house. Why are they letting you stay?"

I shrug innocently and nervously before averting my eyes to the ground.

"What's your name again?" another of them asks, but not in a vicious tone like the rest of them, but a curious one.

"Rory," I reply.

"Is there a problem?" a familiar voice asks out of nowhere. Gamma Ace strolls up beside me, scowling at the four warriors in front of us in a scolding way.

"No, Gamma. Just talking to our token human of the pack," the one who spoke first responds, a little tenser.

Whilst Everett holds complete power in the pack, and what he says goes, Ace and Lucius also hold that kind of power, just not as excessive as the Alpha.

"Well, stop," Ace states with authority, stepping slightly in front of me to show I'm protected by him.

After my talk with Ace the other day, when he found me on the field training, he seemed suspicious.

Maybe because my lying skills are utterly nonexistent and

he wasn't fooled by my story about what happened out in rogue territory.

But he seems closer to me now, as if he is watching out for me, keeping me safe. And I strangely feel as though I can trust him, not like I'd tell him more than I need to.

It would only create more problems, problems I don't need. Especially when I've been hearing a voice in my sleep.

Of course, I believe it's my subconscious fearing that voice I heard in rogue territory.

There was something about that voice. Something that unsettled me wholeheartedly.

It almost felt familiar, but maybe that's me overthinking it.

The real problem is the fact that I'm losing sleep over it and more frequently falling out of the bed, which is why Everett feels the need to strap me down with his arm now.

"Yes, Gamma Ace. We'll be going," the wolf answers reluctantly before marching off with his little posse.

Once they're far enough away, Ace turns to me with a stern look and rests his hand on my shoulder.

"You shouldn't be talking to them," he states like it's an order. "This pack is quite accepting of the idea of coexistence, but a human living in the pack without reason is not an idea they favor."

"I can tell," I mumble with a slight pout at the fact that this feels like a father telling off his child for the child's naivety.

"Well, stay away then."

"It wasn't my fault," I whine, stomping my foot out of instinct. "Why are you here anyway?"

"You don't like my company?" he teases, taking my hand and dragging me along with him.

"I don't know. It depends," I say, sighing.

"Depends on what?" he asks curiously, looking down beside him.

"What your company is like? I don't like talking to grumpy wolves," I tell him with a bright smile. He rolls his eyes, but is quick to catch me when I stumble.

"Grumpy, huh? When am I grumpy, little Rory?" he teases with a smirk.

"You're always telling me off every time you see me. 'You shouldn't be out here,'" I mimic in a deep, grumpy voice, which he chuckles at.

"'You shouldn't be talking to those wolves,' 'why are you in this field.'"

"I don't sound like that. Plus, you shouldn't have been there," he says with a shrug. "I looked into that pack of yours."

My head snaps to look into his eyes, trying to figure out what he means by that. He can't tell them I'm alive. They'll really question that.

I mean, if Everett makes me his Luna, they'll eventually know, but I don't have the Luna protection yet, and Everett isn't committed to me, which means I don't have his protection.

"What does that mean?"

"Nothing, really. I just wanted to see your reaction. You're so scared because…"

"Because they tried to kill me," I state like it's obvious. They tried and succeeded. They actually killed me.

He narrows his eyes at me for a second before nodding.

He walks with me back to the pack house like a bodyguard, and I take a book from Everett's office. I've concluded that Everett doesn't care anymore that I go into his office.

He knows, he can smell my scent in there.

But after he confronted me the first time and saw that I just wanted to read his books, I think that's his way of granting me permission, just ignoring the fact I've been in there.

I decide to sit outside, a few blocks down from the pack house, on a bench next to this old concrete building.

It was said to be the old pack house, but they say it's used for something else now. I'm not all too bothered about it. It's just peaceful out here, alone with my thoughts.

When a hand clamps over my mouth, I know whoever it is would be a lot stronger than me.

Maybe it's this "she" Achlys was talking about. But Achlys said I was only in danger in that limbo place and rogue territory because they're unprotected places.

Even though limbo is dangerous from what she told me, she's the only one who has and can give me answers so far.

Maybe I should go back there. Purposefully kill myself. Then again, saying that thought clearly like that sounds ludicrous.

But back to the fact that someone is dragging me away against my will.

I still struggle fruitlessly, just to say that I did. Maybe I don't have to kill myself.

The worst thing whoever this is can do is kill me, and it seems that I can't die.

So, bring it on.

Chapter 22

Dungeon

———•❖•———

RORY

Flailing around, presumably looking like a complete idiot—but because I'm small I can get away with it—I knock into an unwavering body, built just like a wolf.

So this isn't the work of "she." Maybe I should name her. Evil lady.

Maybe that's too presumptuous. I don't know anything about her. "She" will work, I guess.

Back to why there's some wolf kidnapping me and dragging me along with him to wherever we're going.

I hear a few different grunts from different people, telling me there are more than two wolves in on this.

Is this a "hate the human" thing again? The last time something like this happened was when I died.

And my life got a whole lot more confusing.

I was thrust into a world of mystery and intrigue and the unknown.

I didn't know anyone anymore and I had to leave my mama behind, especially for her own safety.

I don't know who I am, or what I am.

I'm suddenly thrown into a dark, dingy place, down a flight of stairs, and into a cage, with steel bars enclosing me into it.

I look back out through the bars to identify my captors, but it is too dark to make them out clearly. We're still inside the pack, thus they must be pack members.

There are a number of people who aren't enamored with the idea of a human living in their pack. But not many would do something this daring.

They know I'm staying here with the Alpha's blessing, and doing something like this would be going against his orders.

But perhaps they believe the consequences wouldn't be too dire, considering I'm just a guest here.

Yet they don't know I'm Everett's mate, and entrapping me is a dangerous move. Who knows what Everett will do?

Faint chuckles can be heard from several captors as the distance grows between them and me.

They're leaving me here, in this cell.

Why?

A loud clang of a door that I heard open when we came in tells me they've just left, with no explanation or reasoning.

"It's not every day we get to see a little human girl in here," a menacing voice comes from behind me that almost makes me shriek.

I snap my head around, my body following, and back up right to the bars. My eyes widen, attempting to see in this dimly lit dungeon.

"Who are you?" I ask, my voice shaking. I bite back the whimper threatening to escape my lips and calm myself down.

I haven't quite taken in the fact that I technically have nothing to be afraid of. Whoever this person is, he can't kill me.

I'm stronger than him, because I can resurrect and he can't. If I die, I'll come back. If he dies, he'll stay dead.

That gives me unlimited chances at successfully coming away from this situation. It's inevitable I'll stay alive.

"Well, little girl," he begins, stepping closer to me and more into the light that shines through the petite window from outside the cell.

I can now see his face clearly, and I realize he's a rogue; he holds that aura. He bows to no one, radiates independence and power.

He has that look about him too, his countenance seemingly dangerous, dark features with that rough hint, drained by the lack of sunlight in here.

I assume he's been here for a while. And as I look around the cell closer, I notice other faces in the dark: rogues.

This is the dungeon.

This is where they keep their rogue prisoners. In here. And I was put in here.

Because whoever it was thought I'd be eaten? Because I'm a weak little human girl and easily preyed on?

Rogues seem to like me usually.

"I'm trapped in here, and so are you. Let's be friends. I'm Eden."

He extends his hand to me with a devilish smirk, and for some reason, it makes me eye his movements.

He doesn't appear very trustworthy, but I guess that's why he's in here. Although Everett locks up every rogue that trespasses on his lands, he sees it as a crime in itself.

"Over there, that's Ian," he declares, pointing behind him to a skinny guy with a contrasting dark aura.

"He's Red," he says, pointing to the one at the far back of the cell.

"And I don't know the names of the two over there," he tells me, gesturing over to a dark corner where the two men just glare at me, not maliciously but curiously.

"What's your name?" Red asks, moving over to us.

"Rory," I announce with confidence, trying to appear unafraid of these wolves.

Strangely enough, even with the nameless ones in the corner staring me down, I don't feel too threatened by any of them.

"Why are you in here?" Ian interrogates, narrowing his eyes at me. "You're a human. They must want to kill you, little girl."

"Why would you say that? How would putting me in here kill me?" I question, although already knowing the answer.

But that's the point. They should be trying to hurt me, and he's proving that they do hurt human girls.

So why not me? Not that I don't like living and hate the feeling of dying, my life force sucked out of me.

But why don't these rogues hurt me? Why don't any rogues hurt me? I need answers.

"We're rogues, Rory. Rogues kill weak defenseless little girls like you. Especially ones who consort with pack wolves.

"We hate pack wolves. We hate this pack. They have locked us down here," Red explains.

"Then why are you not killing me?" I ask.

"Because…" He pauses, staring at me like he has no explanation for it, like he doesn't know what to tell me.

Maybe they don't even know why they can't, why they just find themselves protecting me, but they do.

Perhaps it's because they're rogues, and rogue territory is unprotected grounds. This "she" can get me there.

Maybe these rogues are like my protectors when I'm there, from "she." Or perhaps that's a reach. Everything is at the moment.

I have no answers, and without them, I can't understand what's going on, or what danger I'm in.

But what I do know is Achlys is an otherworldly being, and even she is afraid of "she." I could see it on her face.

And just before I left limbo—or should I say, she pushed me out of there—I think she saw her. I think "she" was there. Whoever "she" is, she's powerful.

I just need to know how much. I just need answers. And Achlys has them, I'm sure among very few.

Maybe my parents have them, my birth parents. Maybe they can tell me who I am.

I settle in after a while, giving up hope that I can just wait it out and ignore them. They have no answers for me.

They just…feel like they should protect me, at least that's what Eden tells me.

"How long have you all been in here?" I ask.

"Those two were recent," Red answers, pointing to the nameless ones in the corner who sit silently, just watching my every movement.

"I've been down here for a few weeks with Eden, Ian's been here over a month."

"For what?"

"I accidentally crossed over the border," Ian states bitterly. "I didn't even mean to. Yet I get stuck down here. I hate pack wolves. They can't decide what to do with me though.

"That's why I've been here for so long. Plus, I may have been part of a group that attacked one of their guys a while back. But I didn't do anything," he says defensively.

"Why are you here? Why are you in this pack's territory? You clearly know about wolves."

"I was adopted by a wolf, but my pack ran me out and tried to kill me. The Alpha here found me hurt out in rogue territory and helped me. He told me I could stay here indefinitely.

"I don't think he knows I'm in here, but other wolves in the pack don't like that a human is staying here," I explain honestly.

"Warrior wolves," Red comments, staring at me. "That's

who brought you in here, if you were wondering. They're the same wolves who brought me in."

Of course, the warrior wolves. They were scorned earlier by Ace and this is their revenge.

"So you like the pack wolves here?" Ian asks. "The ones that imprisoned me?"

"Yes," I admit. "Something you want to say about it?" I question daringly.

I want to test the boundaries. Can I really say anything and they won't hurt me? So far, I'm unharmed and they've remained civil, even friendly.

"No," he utters with a raised brow. "You're mated to one of them, right? You definitely are. Which one?"

I narrow my eyes at him and stay quiet, not really wanting to share that information.

But they won't hurt me, right?

They could use me for blackmail if they knew, but they won't, because they can't. They feel the need to protect me.

"The Alpha, right? Am I right, little girl? You're the Alpha's mate. But those wolves don't know that, do they? When he finds you're in here, he'll flip his lid."

I watch him, and all the others, trying to see what they would do with this information Ian has deduced. But they all just seem curious.

"Alpha Everett of the Shadow Blood pack and his little human mate who clearly is more than she seems because I can't even use this information to get me out of here.

"I don't want to hurt you, I can't hurt you. I don't think any of us can. Yet, you're the Alpha's mate. That sucks. You suck."

"Thanks," I reply sarcastically, and he chuckles, along with Red and Eden. Ian definitely has warmed up to me, probably because he has a few more answers, which I would love too.

I really need those answers, because I'm going insane right now.

How to get them? Go back to limbo. But is that too dangerous? And is there a limit to how many lives I get?

So many questions and so few answers.

Chapter 23

Protect

———◆———

EVERETT

She's fucking missing. Again. I will fucking tear the heads off of those patrol guards if she's left the territory.

"Stop pacing, Alpha. The guards haven't seen any sign of her. No one has left today. She's probably still in the pack," Lucius tells me, attempting to calm me down.

But all he's doing is fueling my rage. She can't leave. Not again. I was distressed enough the first time.

I can't fucking take her being gone again.

Bursting through the door is Ace, an unreadable expression on his face until he drags in with him a few of my wilder warrior wolves and scowls at them.

"These four have something to tell you," Ace declares, glaring at all of them without a hint of mercy in his eyes.

"We… We may have put the human down in the dungeons, with the rogues," Tyler mutters, rolling his eyes.

Immediately, at his words, I storm out, sprinting over to the old pack house that's been reformed into secret dungeons that only the warriors and titled wolves know about, and head into the cells.

Following behind me is Lucius and Ace, dragging the four treacherous wolves with him.

These rogues will eat her alive.

What if she's already dead? Fuck!

This is my fault. She's in my pack.

Those wolves would never have done anything like this if they knew she is my mate. But I just had to keep it a secret, because I still hadn't made my decision.

And it could have gotten her killed. I could have killed my mate. It would be my fault.

But when I see her beautiful green eyes beaming out, her petite body surrounded by rogues, I sigh a little but rip the cage door open once I take the lock off.

She's there. Unharmed. Alive. Without a scratch on her.

Still beautiful.

And the rogues group around her, as if protecting her, protecting her from me. I'm her fucking mate and why are these rogues protecting her?

Not that I want her hurt. But I don't understand.

"Everett?" her shy voice calls out, making my heart skip a beat just at the sound of my name leaving her lips.

"Aurora, come here," I order, extending my hand to get her away from these brutes. No one will hurt her.

I know that Ace and Lucius and the warrior wolves are behind me, just outside the cell. But I don't care about anything else anymore. I just need her to be safe.

I need my little mate to be safe.

She takes my hand; her soft little hand fits perfectly with mine. The smile that graces her lips informs me that she's fine, that she's not hurt, that she's not angry with me.

But there are four wolves I'm furious with. Utterly and undoubtedly furious with. I instantly tug her to me and embrace her, not caring who's watching.

I bet these rogues wouldn't have been too kind to her if they knew she was my mate.

But she's safe now. She's safe. She's with me. No one will hurt her.

She accepts the embrace and squeezes me tighter, burying her head in my chest. I need her, all of her. She completes me, and it's not just the mate bond.

It's real between us.

This deep need for each other.

I take in her scent, breathing as much of her in as I can and attempting to calm myself down.

I guess I can't be too angry with those wolves. They didn't know she was my mate, and they should thank the goddess she is unharmed.

But even if she wasn't my mate, this isn't allowed, and they disobeyed me. They need to be punished.

Of course, if she had been hurt, I would have ripped all four of them apart.

She has been in here for hours. Hours!

That shouldn't have happened. And I let it happen.

I should pay more attention to her and what she's doing. I need her to be safe.

I wonder why those rogues didn't hurt her.

But at least she's not hurt.

I drag her out with me and up the stairs of the basement, leading her outside so she can get some clean air.

She's been breathing in that toxic rogue air. The others follow us out, but I'm busy checking her body to see that she's all healthy.

Still clumsy as her ankle rolls, just whilst standing still.

"You're okay, are you? You're fine? You're not hurt?" I question. She shakes her head and smiles at me.

"I'm fine, Everett. No one hurt me," she tells me, even

though it's not true. Those warrior wolves intended for her to be hurt, my mate, my little mate.

I turn back to them, pull Aurora to my side protectively. I scowl directly at the wolves, piercing my eyes right into their souls, making them quake.

They can feel it. They can feel their Alpha's rage, and it's made them understand. Aurora is my mate.

And they've just tried to hurt, possibly kill their Alpha's mate.

"You are fucking lucky I don't rip your heads from your shoulders. What you four did was against the rules, and particularly to my mate.

"If you had known she was my mate or if she had been hurt, you wouldn't be standing here. You would be dead. But I'm going to show you four mercy, and only because she's okay.

"You'll be locked in the cells for as long as I see fit. But first, you'll apologize to Aurora."

They swallow their pride and clearly give their apologies to my little mate. Lucius and Ace lead them away to our official cells, and I'm left with Aurora at my side.

I carry her—although she protests politely at the start—back to the pack house and to our room.

I still don't understand how she's not hurt, but thank the goddess she wasn't.

"I don't want you unprotected anymore," I tell her, probably looking crazy as shit to her with my eyes all wide and a distressed expression plastered all over my face.

"I'm not even hurt," she mutters, pouting slightly in a way that could make me completely melt if I wasn't so enraged inside.

"You could have been," I yell, startling her.

I grab her face in my hands, cupping her cheeks, making sure she's here in front of me, for real.

I don't know what I would do if I lost her. I can't lose her. I need her now. She's my little mate. She's mine. I'm not letting her go. I'm never letting her go.

She'll make a good Luna, a great one. And even if she struggles, I'll help her. We'll help each other. I'll protect her, no matter what.

"I'm sorry, little one. I was…you're in my pack. You're my mate. I'm supposed to protect you and you're supposed to be safe here.

"And you weren't. You could be dead, and it would have been on my territory. I'm meant to protect you. How could I let that happen?"

I shake her head lightly in frustration, wanting to hold onto more of her. I can't believe something like this happened.

"Everett, nothing happened," she says slowly and softly, placing her hands on top of mine and holding my hands to her face. "I'm fine. I'm completely fine."

I'm about to deny that when a knock comes on the door with Lucius's voice calling me to my office.

Due to my sudden need to protect my mate, I bring Aurora along with me, making sure she stays in my sights at all times.

Hopefully this feeling will pass, or I'll find it very hard to do work with Aurora in my office, distracting me with her beautiful entrancing movements.

Anything she does, even her falls captivate me. But her tripping just makes me concerned. Really concerned.

I hate watching her hurt herself, and when she wakes up to her body slamming the carpeted ground, I hate myself for not protecting her more.

Thus, now I'm trapping her to the bed with my body, although a little intimate at this stage in our relationship. Sharing a bed is too, I guess.

But it just feels so perfect that I've never really thought of anything else.

"Does she need to be in here?" Lucius asks skeptically, giving a side-glance to my little mate. This small action makes me growl instinctively.

I've fallen deeper into our mate connection, but I need to hold back potentially.

Although right now, I want nothing else but Aurora.

"Fine. We put the wolves in the cells, but they decided to run their mouths before we got them down there. Practically everyone will know that you and Rory are mates."

"So what?" I question defensively. I know I was the one to keep it a secret, but right now, I don't want anyone doubting us, especially not my Beta.

"If you're okay with that, I guess everything is fine then," Lucius concludes. Ace strolls in, a smirk on his face a little more obvious than usual as his gaze lands on Rory.

It's strange. I've noticed he's been more distant recently, especially after being out in rogue territory with Aurora.

Lucius likes to joke that he has a crush on my little mate, but that may be true.

He has been more attentive to her, looking at her excessively when she's around, and he doesn't have the same expression as he did before toward her.

Ace was curious about her but skeptical. Now he's just curious, and quite mesmerized.

Whatever it is, it better fucking stop. She's my mate.

"Rory's part of our meetings now? How are you, little one, after surviving hours with those rogues?" he asks a little too—caring toward Aurora, even though his tone is disguised in a joking way.

I narrow my eyes at him, but Aurora just smiles politely.

"Actually, I just wanted to say, if I can, that being in those dungeons for many hours, the conditions down there aren't great," Aurora says, which turns all our attention toward her.

Is she really talking about the conditions down there?

"I mean, Red and Ian and Eden look like they've seen no sun, and there are no guards. And they barely get any food. And Ian's been in there for ages and he didn't really do anything."

"Are you defending rogues? Rogues are lying scum," Lucius scolds her, but I can only narrow my eyes at her curiously.

Is she being serious? She knows their names. She spoke with them. She listened to their stories. They told her their stories.

They were...friendly with her.

Why?

Chapter 24

Jealousy

RORY

"How could you not tell us that you're the Alpha's mate?" Cassidy exclaims while all the other kids huddle around me.

It's been difficult to get away for the past week, as Everett has kept me under lock and key.

He barely let me out of his sight, and the times he did, I was showering or doing my business.

It's quite unnerving how attentive he has been, not saying anything but just watching me. And he holds me to him every night, like we're cuddling.

His excuse is to stop me from falling out of bed. But he looks so content when he's holding me, nuzzling his nose into my hair, my body pressed up against his.

Or maybe I just feel content.

He looked absolutely terrified when he found me in those dungeons, and he didn't sleep that night either. He just watched me.

And for some reason, I didn't mind being watched.

He panicked. He was so worried I had been hurt, and furious with the warrior wolves who have been in his pack since birth and who he had grown up with.

But he doesn't want me. He just feels a responsibility to me because of the mate bond, and he was governed by the power of the mate bond when he thought I was in danger.

"The Alpha wanted it a secret for a while, until I acclimatized here," I tell her.

She narrows her eyes at me and Orion looks confused.

"Why don't you lot go play hide-and-seek? We'll come find you."

The kids run off, but Cassidy and Orion just look to me expectantly. They're much older than the others, and therefore a lot more curious about pack gossip.

"You are acclimated here. What's the real reason? He doesn't think you should be Luna? Is he going to reject you?" she questions avidly, making me gulp at her interrogation.

I don't know yet. He doesn't think I'll make a good Luna, who would?

"You don't have to answer that, Rory," Nellie says, giving a sharp glare to Cassidy in a scolding way.

"Well, I don't know. Really."

After playing with the kids for as long as I think Everett wouldn't notice me gone, Ace walks around with me, sent as a bodyguard by Everett apparently, although for some reason, I believe that to be a lie.

I get several stares, and everyone at least looks my way, more than the usual. Gossip like "the Alpha's found his mate and she's human" travels in this pack like wildfire.

"Ignore them, Rory," he tells me with a consoling smile. Sighing, I accidentally trip on a paving slab and almost smash headfirst onto the concrete.

But Ace grasps my arm to steady me a little. But my knees still scrape the rough ground, scratching them up pretty badly.

"Shit, you okay?"

"Yeah, I'm fine," I reply with a small wince as I brush the tiny stones off my knees.

"You're bleeding and you ripped your jeans," he comments like I didn't already know that. "Rory—"

"I'm fine, Ace. You sound like Everett," I complain, pouting at the memories of Everett freaking out over every little scratch and bruise.

"Everett will kill me if something happens to you," he states firmly, bending down to my knee level and assessing the damage.

"What's going on?" the booming voice of the Alpha questions behind Ace, and I look up to meet his sapphire eyes. They glisten with jealousy and suspicion as he eyes the two of us together.

Ace has been hanging around me more often, but it's nothing to do with anything like what Everett's thinking.

Ace is suspicious of me himself after what happened out in rogue territory.

And he wants to know more about me, a lot more, to figure out what really happened.

I didn't think he would fully believe my lies, but I had hoped he would believe some version that everything was a dream.

But I don't think I'm quite that lucky.

Ace snaps back up to standing straight, though, facing away from me and coughing a little nervously.

"Alpha, Rory had a little fall," he says, gesturing toward my knees. Everett's eyes darken as he eyes my knees and grows angry at my clumsiness.

He storms toward me, wolves stopping to stare but quickly averting their gaze as they catch sight of their furious Alpha.

"Where were you, little one?" he hisses lowly and dangerously, one hand grabbing my face and the other snaking to my back.

"Alpha, she—" Ace starts, but Everett cuts him off.

"She can speak for herself."

His tone frightens me whilst his touch sends sparks throughout my body, increasing the dangerous and tense atmosphere.

"I was just taking a walk," I mutter, gulping at the look in his eyes.

He hates me. He really hates me. I must be a big burden to him, practically begging for his help by being covered in blood and terrified and exhausted.

And from the moment he saw me, he knew I was just another one of his responsibilities that he didn't ask for, or he wasn't ready for.

"With him? You were taking a walk with my Gamma, huh? Cause you like him more than me?" he questions in a deep and aggressive voice.

He pulls me with him toward the pack house, attaching me to his side with Ace following behind.

Every wolf averts their eyes, having probably seen their Alpha in a mood like this and having seen the consequences of staring.

Once we get inside, he sits me on the counter in the kitchen.

"We were just walking, Alpha," Ace states, pulling Everett away from me and facing him. "Rory was bored, and on a walk, and I saw her and went to talk to her."

"Leave us," Everett growls in response in that commanding Alpha tone.

Ace does as he's told, his loyalty to his Alpha above all. But now it's just me and the big bad Alpha, who's in a particularly unpredictable mood.

He moves back over to me, standing in between my legs and placing his hands on my waist to hold me still, and perhaps even to stop me from my cursed clumsy ways hurting me from up here.

My feet are nowhere close to the ground; the curse of short legs.

I'm very vulnerable right now, at Everett's mercy. But I know he won't hurt me. He can't. It's not in his nature. It's something I admire about him.

Of course he can hurt people—he's an Alpha after all—but he has his principles that he follows strictly. And I respect that.

It also means that he would never hurt me, no matter how agitated he got. But that's only hurt me physically.

There are still many ways he can hurt me. One being: he can reject me.

And that might just break me.

"I'm sorry," I mumble, my eyes flickering down. But his hand grips my chin and tilts it up so that I'm forced to look into his eyes.

"For what, little one? Have you done something you should be sorry about?"

I shake my head frantically, showing that nothing happened between Ace and me. I know that's what he's thinking.

But I couldn't even if I wanted to. I have feelings for Everett. Beyond the initial mate bond.

"Yeah? So why are you sorry? Tell me."

"For making you angry. I didn't mean to," I whimper, my lower lip trembling uncontrollably.

His thumb comes up to it, pulling it down lightly and back up again. His eyes soften almost instantly as he just stares at me.

"You're my mate, Aurora. Mine. You're not Ace's," he states, like I don't know that.

"I know, Everett. You're my mate. I was just talking to Ace.

I want to have friends here," I explain. He takes his hand away from my face and back onto my waist.

"You were bored? What about all those books you take from my office?" he asks.

"I've read most of them now. I'm trying to keep up my education and learn new things, but I don't have much to do now," I tell him honestly.

"I'm the Alpha, I can't entertain you all the time. I'm busy," he says.

"I know, Everett. And I'm not asking you to entertain me. I just don't like to be accused. I was just walking around."

"I can't keep you safe when I don't know where you are," he states, inching closer to me.

"I'll be safe here. What those wolves did, it won't happen again. I'm safe. Plus, Ace is looking out for me."

He growls at the mention of his name but I touch his face, soothing him.

"He kept me safe out in rogue territory, and he wants to be friends with me. He knows you're my mate. Plus, I thought you didn't even want me as a mate."

"Of course I do. You know that," he grits out, clutching my waist tightly. "I want you."

"Maybe. But you won't keep me. You don't think I'll be a good Luna for this pack. And that's okay. You've given me somewhere to stay and… I'm grateful," I say, a tear slipping from my eye.

"But I…"

"Aurora, don't ever say that to me. You don't need to be grateful and you don't ever fucking say that I won't keep you. I want you, little one."

I look down, avoiding his eyes. He doesn't want me.

I'm just another responsibility.

Chapter 25

Insensitive

EVERETT

But she probably wants nothing to do with me.

I let this happen. I hurt her. I hurt her every day.

I don't even think about how she might feel about all of this.

She was run out of her home, and all I could contemplate was whether she should stay here.

I didn't care about her feelings, I cared about protecting mine, and protecting the pack.

But what about her? My mate? My responsibility? I've been less than considerate.

I let her go back to our room, upset and feeling that way due to me and my insensitivity.

Why the fuck did I get so mad at her? I know she would never do anything. She's too loyal. And she feels our connection too.

But Ace, he's an unmated wolf, and he seems enamored with Aurora.

My mate.

When I saw them together, him bent down in front of her, apparently to check her wounds, I thought he was... I don't know, flirting with her, in some strange way.

I still don't know what's going on with him. Sure, she's too innocent and too much of a bad liar to be lying, but if he likes her, he's sure as hell not going to tell me.

I make my way out of the pack house, needing to let off some steam. I would go for a run, but I have a pack meeting later tonight.

The topic will likely stick like glue on Aurora and me and her becoming Luna. And I'd hear bombarding comments on how I should reject her because she's a human.

She's not just a human to me.

And just as I expected, the comments are out, and the growls are released, and that pretty much shuts them all up.

And whilst Lucius gives me a disappointed glare, Ace remains quiet, either knowing anything he has to say would set me off, or I'm defending Aurora's honor and he's not going to stop me.

Which enrages me even more.

He's changed since the time he and Aurora spent out in rogue territory. It just seems like he has a deep interest in her, and he's unmated.

It's most likely a sexual interest. But she's my little mate. He can't have her. She doesn't even like him.

But I can't have one of my closest allies liking my mate.

Once they all clear out, Lucius, Ace, and I are left alone. And the tension is thick after what happened earlier.

I was working, having finished moving Ophelia back into her house with Aurora, and I have to keep up affairs in the pack.

The wolf council were hounding me about attending the annual conference. Those things are just an assault on humans though, and especially now, I'm not in favor of them.

I had been keeping my little mate close to me, ever since what happened with those warrior wolves.

But I take my eye off her for a few hours and then I can't find her. And then I see her walking along with Ace. My deductions, as rash as they were, were justified.

"So...what's up with you two?" Lucius asks, breaking through the thick air of passive-aggressive silence.

"Why are you hanging around my mate?" I question Ace harshly, cutting right to the chase.

"Because I like her. Not like that, but as a person. She's sweet and she's lonely.

"You don't spend nearly enough time with her, and you don't allow her to do anything but read," he rants, throwing his arms up in the air and resting back in his seat.

"You can growl at me all you want, Everett, but that girl thinks she's not good enough and that's your fault. And then you think you can just get mad earlier.

"If I was fooling around with her, it would have nothing to do with you because you don't act like her mate."

I scoff, agitated now, mainly because I know he's right.

"I'm your fucking Alpha," I yell, standing up and raising my voice. He stands up with me, as does Lucius, attempting to referee here.

"So I don't get to tell you my opinion. You've never run this pack like a dictatorship, your relationship is the same thing.

"You act like you have all the control and you can do whatever you want. What about Rory? Don't you think it's sad that she's okay with being here."

"Sad?" I question.

"Yeah, fucking sad. She's okay because she was run out of her pack, away from her mom and her family and her life and then you come in and you give her a place to sleep and a home.

"And then the threat of kicking her out is making her just deal with all of this shit you're giving her."

"She's lucky. She's mated to a good wolf who might just reject her so she can have a normal life," Lucius says, and that makes me even more furious.

"Both of you shut the fuck up. She's fine. She's just bored. I'll give her more things to do in the pack."

"She's not bored," Ace states like he knows everything about her. "You know what, come with me, she'll probably be where I think she is."

He marches out like he's on a mission, and I just follow, wondering what the fuck he is doing.

"Where are we going?"

"If it were Tuesday or Wednesday or Friday night, she would be out in the field, training."

"Training?" Lucius questions before I can.

"Yeah. She doesn't like how disappointed you always are in her. So she trains, alone, because she's embarrassed and she wants to get more balance so you're not always so disappointed."

"I'm not," I argue.

"It doesn't matter whether you are or you aren't. She feels like you are."

"Look, where the fuck are we going?" I almost yell out of frustration.

"We're here." I stop and look around, just seeing some buildings in the pack and nothing else.

One of them is the florist, a few houses, and the orphanage.

What the fuck are we doing here?

"So…"

"Just listen." I tune into my surroundings, trying to listen to whatever he wants me to hear.

And that's when I hear her voice. My mate's voice.

What the hell is she doing out here?

Lucius listens in too, and I think I hear a boy next to her, a young boy from the sound of his voice.

"Why are you crying?" Aurora asks.

"Some kids from school came by after you left earlier and they were horrible to me. They were playing soccer outside, and I wanted to play but they made fun of me."

"So you're crying?" There's a short pause. "What do you think they want your reaction to be?"

"So you're saying what? Rise above it? That's lame."

"You know I used to be bullied. I mean, it's quite easy to bully the clumsy small human girl. And my mama told me to just ignore them. What they want is a rise out of you. You know what happened then?"

"They stopped?"

She scoffs.

"No. They carried on until they tried to kill me. So, I wouldn't say that it worked at all. My mama didn't understand how these bullies worked. They didn't want a rise. It was the exact opposite.

"They wanted someone to torment. And because I did nothing about it, they continued to torment me.

"Even though I wouldn't have been able to successfully win a fight against them, choosing to fight, even if you lose, makes the bullying less fun for them.

"If they have to fight against resistance, they fight an easier target. Why do you think they pick on the vulnerable and the weak? I wish I had stood up to them."

"Why didn't you then? Sounds like you have it all figured out."

"Because I'm vulnerable and weak," she replies with a chuckle. "And I just thought that it would eventually stop. I didn't know it would end with them trying to kill me. But then I end up here.

"And it's sort of the same thing. They think I'm weak here, and that's why those warrior wolves don't like me. And I guess I'm doing the same thing as I did before: just taking it.

"Sometimes it's hard to be strong because being strong is harder, especially when there's a high chance you can lose. But you know what makes it easier to be strong?"

"What? What does?"

"Having people who'll fight with you. They outnumbered you, right? Next time they're bothering you, come get me. We'll stand up to them together," she tells him, her voice sweet and strong and hopeful.

"I don't like your mate. But I was curious. There's more to her than you know, and you can't judge her based on this image you have of her, a clumsy small human girl."

"What do I do?" I ask Ace, suddenly now realizing what I've been missing.

She's not just sweet and kind and innocent and clumsy. She's strong too.

Maybe not physically, but mentally and emotionally. And I've treated her like shit.

She deserves so much more than what I give her.

"I have an idea. But it's only a start."

CHAPTER 26

Surprise

RORY

"Morning," Lucius greets me unusually as I enter the kitchen. Ace smirks over to me normally, but today, he's grinning as if he's been successful with something.

"Morning," I reply with a shy, uneasy smile.

But I grab some cereal from the counter and pour it into a bowl, watching the two out of the corner of my eye.

"Where's Everett? I didn't see him last night. Is he okay?"

"I thought you were upset with him," Ace says, giving me a confused look as I turn to sit on the bar stools to eat my breakfast.

"Well, I was. But I slept on it," I answer, running my fingers through my hair to get the knots out.

Everett not coming to bed had painful consequences as I got my old alarm clock back.

And I like feeling him next to me in bed, his chest against my chest, his arms draped over me, his hands caressing my back subconsciously.

I love the way he makes me feel inside, the sparks that shoot within me and make me melt for him.

"That's good to hear," Everett declares as he comes up

behind me and takes the cereal box from the side of me, making sure to touch my waist discreetly before pulling away.

He turns to the side, leaning back on the bar to look at me. He appears to be in a better mood than yesterday, almost... relaxed.

Almost.

He seems to be excited about something.

Why have everyone's moods drastically changed?

"Get ready. We're going out this morning," he declares, which makes me furrow my brows in confusion.

We're going somewhere? Where? Why?

"Where?"

"Just go get ready, Aurora. You'll like it, I promise," he says, tipping my chin up to look at him and using his commanding Alpha voice.

He's so handsome it's a crime. He has the body of Adonis with the domineering charm of the perfect Alpha.

I jump off my stool after giving Everett an unsure look, before skipping upstairs.

Where are we going? What should I wear? What is happening?

Everyone is acting so strangely. Everett didn't come to bed, so I thought he was mad for my defiance, but this morning, it's like it never happened.

But if it didn't happen, then he didn't listen to what I had to say.

I have feelings for him, but if he can't listen to me, and can't understand me, how are we ever going to work?

Now we're just going somewhere on his orders.

I'm grateful for everything he's given me. But I don't know if I can stay here anymore. Otherwise, I might fall deeper for Everett, and he doesn't even like me back.

I throw on some blue jeans and a white oversized sweater with the black and white trainers Everett bought me that have probably the most support you can have in a shoe.

He even put extra padding in the soles and tips so that I don't hurt myself stubbing my toe.

They're high tops so my ankles roll less easily, and they cushion upon any fall. They don't even have laces, just Velcro straps, like an uncoordinated child would need.

But, rightly so, as I skid down the stairs, missing at least five steps, but thankfully fall into the arms of my mate.

"Clumsy as always," he grumbles, lifting me fully up in his arms, bridal style, and carrying me out to his car, which I have never been in.

Where the hell are we going? And this is an awesome stylish car. I've only seen cars like this on TV; even Alpha Nick didn't own a car like this one.

"How do you own a car like this?" I ask once he straps me in the passenger seat, slings a backpack on the back seat, and slides into the driver's side.

"My parents left me their business. I have people running it, humans, whilst I am running the pack. The business is thriving, it makes a lot of money," he explains.

"What type of business?"

"Telecommunication. I've never really been too interested in the company, so I pay other people to run it, and it focuses my time on pack and wolf affairs."

"But every now and then I get called in to sort out some problems so I had to learn all about the business."

"That's interesting. I didn't know that."

"I know," he replies, glancing over to me whilst driving, and then turning back to the road.

"So, where are we going?"

"You'll see, little one," he answers shortly.

I look at his mysterious ways and wonder what he has planned. Maybe this is a date, or something like that.

Maybe he had pressure from the pack at the pack meeting to date me or dump me. But he doesn't understand me yet, perhaps it's an Alpha thing.

Because he carries the responsibility of so many lives that he thinks he knows what's best for everyone and he thinks he understands everyone.

As I begin to recognize the gates he's pulling into, my head snaps in his direction, my mouth gaping, unable to form words.

When the car stops, he doesn't even say anything. He just gets out, travelling around to my side of the car and popping my door open.

I decide to get out and stand in front of him pathetically, still at a loss for words. I just stare into his eyes that glisten with amusement for once.

"Why are we here?" I mutter, trying to figure out what this means.

He steps closer to me with a widening smirk adorning his beautiful face. People begin to stare at us, but I just ignore them, only focusing on Everett.

"You're going back to school," he declares. "I know you've been keeping up with your school work and getting ahead. And I know you liked going to your human school and your friends.

"I know I took you from everything familiar, but I want to give you this. That's if you want to go. I called the school yesterday, told them you'd be joining again.

"Because you were only gone for a couple of months, you have the same classes and schedules, and you can ask your friends for work you've missed and check whether you know all of it."

I reach out to hug him, my petite body falling into his and being engulfed in his scent.

But my head, instead of moving onto his shoulder, moves forward right to his, and his lips are right there, begging for my touch.

And I want him so much.

I slam my lips on his, which takes him by surprise. The sparks that light don't even compare to the single touch. They light my entire body, my core going up in flames.

I've never felt so connected to anyone in my entire life, our lips locked and moving against each other in sync.

But what if this is just to get me out of the way?

I'll be at school most of the time, and then sleeping, too, cuts out a lot of the hours in a week.

I pull back, bombarded with doubts. But not a second later, he draws me right back in. His hand supports the back of my head, his other hand moving up and down my back in frantic movements.

But his lips, they move slowly and deeply and sensually, and I love it. He takes complete control, dominating me in this kiss.

He wants this. He wants me. I can feel it.

He dragged me back in to kiss me again. Because he wanted me. He wants me. And he understands me.

He listened to me. He heard what I was trying to say, and he did something to show me what he wanted.

He put me back in school, with Freya and Skye. I love learning and books and work, and he knows that. And he put me back in school because he heard what I wanted.

By the time we finish, it's because we've run out of breath between us, and that's a long time for a wolf, an Alpha wolf.

I didn't even realize I had been lifted up during the kiss and held by Everett until he puts me back down on the ground, restoring me back to my tiny height, especially in comparison to him.

"Rory!" a female voice exclaims from a distance behind me. I turn to see my best friend, Freya.

I've missed her. I only have Ophelia and Cassidy in the pack, and neither of them are my age.

The female wolves from the high school in the pack just sneer at me like immature human-haters. Plus, their Alpha is hot and they hoped to be his mate.

I beam at her, my grin wide and bright, and she returns it.

"Aurora," Everett says, and I turn back to him with the same beaming smile. He matches it, a real smile, a smile I've never seen before.

The backpack in his hands is passed toward me but he doesn't let me take it. He insists on putting it on me like I'm his little first grader on the first day of school.

But it's sweet and protective, and for some reason, I love all of it.

"I don't like that I won't have an eye on you, but you've been to human high school for over three years without dying, so I'm taking a leap of faith. Just...be careful."

He chuckles a little, but his last sentence is an order. He hates seeing me hurt.

"Ace will pick you up, okay? You come right out once you've finished."

I nod excitedly and it makes him chuckle again, a sound I never want to stop hearing. It's like the perfect song.

As he gets in his car, I turn back to Freya to see a bigger group this time. A few footballers, along with Oliver and Bethany. Skye. And Eddie.

Oh no, Eddie.

Chapter 27

School

RORY

"Where have you been?" Freya asks me, wide-eyed and curious. Before I can answer, Bethany cuts in.

"Better question, who is that hottie?"

Oliver nudges his girlfriend, showing his pissed-off expression, but she just shrugs and brings her attention back to me.

"That's Everett. He's my…boyfriend." If I can call us that. I guess that's the closest word to describe a mate.

Although, he's my soulmate, the one that completes me. Yet we're not even quite boyfriend and girlfriend either.

We haven't been on a date, but he monitors everything I do. We haven't had sex, but I sleep next to him in bed every night.

We haven't worked each other out fully and we're living together. It's a complicated situation—for now, to my friends, best described as boyfriend and girlfriend. Particularly because I just kissed him.

I glance over at Eddie and notice him fidgeting, with a distraught expression on his face. I don't quite know what that text said, but I had thought it was the right thing to do, tell him it's over.

Perhaps I shouldn't have done it by text, but if I couldn't have resurrected, I'd be dead and unable to dump anyone. I thought I'd never see him again, so I could at least give him some closure.

Now, it's awkward. Especially with introducing Everett as my boyfriend a couple of months after the text. I wonder if he's moved on. I hope he has, but from his expression, I get the feeling he's still hung up on me.

"That was a cool car. He looks older than college," Oliver comments, narrowing his eyes at me as the other football guys exchange smirks and glances.

"He is. He owns a business that pays for the car," I state curtly. After what I told Orion yesterday, I've decided to actually grow a pair and not take shit from Oliver or any of the other footballers.

Sure, they formerly bullied me and Freya in an obvious way, but over the past couple years, it has felt more passive, more cunning, subtler.

They try and get us to attend their parties and answer inappropriate questions so they can laugh about it.

Their tactics, I think, changed because Bethany is friends with us, and bullying us outright would mean no dating Bethany. And she is one of the prettiest girls in school, plus she's a cheerleader.

Everyone is just following the high school stereotypes—with me, formerly the nerdy clumsy girl, who's now a sort of anomaly.

Do they have a stereotype based on a clumsy bookworm human girl who's mated to an Alpha and can resurrect? I'm thinking not.

I gesture for Freya and Skye to walk in beside me as the others follow behind, talking with some other students, athletes and popular people, and those in between.

"Seriously, where were you? And who is that Everett guy?" Freya questions, genuinely concerned.

"We moved…near where Everett lives…and…it's far away but Everett offered to drive me because he knows I have friends here so I get to go here again," I explain and lie, terribly, again.

I really should start learning. I need a teacher, an actual live being rather than a book. Freya's much like me, she has never had to lie before. She doesn't even believe in lying.

She's absorbed the teachings of hypocritical parents who say "lying is bad" or "there's no need to lie. If you lie, it will only make the truth worse when it comes out."

But the truth is, I'm up to my eyeballs in lies at this point, and there's no way to tell the truth at any point without sounding completely ludicrous or something much worse happening.

Someone could force me to cure a bad person or somehow use my gifts as a weapon. It's safer for everyone if it all stays secret.

"Right," she replies sarcastically, clearly not believing a word I said, but she's taking it for now, seeing as I've only been back two seconds.

We reach our lockers, and I decide to look through the bag Everett gave me. To my surprise, he's bought completely new textbooks for my courses, new stationery, and a notepad.

And he even packed a reading book in there, with a note sticking out the top: *I hope you like this book. It's my favorite.*

The title is *Promise Kept*.

It looks like it's been read over fifty times by the state of the spine, bent back in several places. And, as I flick through, there are notes in pencil on the pages, underlining parts he thinks are important or powerful.

He's like me. I put notes in my books, although I've refrained from doing so in Everett's books. So he wouldn't know that. So that is really something he does.

I believe that when a book is in a state much like this one, it has been loved. Books are meant to be read, not left untouched on some dusty bookshelf.

But I admit, I underestimated Everett. I had thought he didn't understand the way I view books, that he thought it was just a strange obsession. But he's showing me again that he is my soulmate.

Twice in one day. Plus the kiss. The perfect kiss. The earth-shattering kiss we shared passionately.

"*Promise Kept*? I haven't read that book," Freya comments, peering over my shoulder to see. I glance over and smile before I stuff everything back into my bag. "Everett give it to you? The note's cute."

"Yeah, I didn't know he could like a book this much," I say, dazed in my state of euphoria.

I have been since the kiss. I still remember his lips against mine, attacking me, devouring me. His taste of mint and the way he grabbed every part of me, wanting more.

We begin to walk to class together, my feet secure in my shoes, keeping me from tripping. Thank the goddess Everett bought me these trainers, or else I'd be back to causing unintentional havoc in the halls.

"Eddie looked pretty heartbroken back there," Skye tells me with a wincing expression. "I mean, you broke up with him by text.

"That has got to sting. And you completely drop off the face of the earth. Then you come back a couple of months later with a boyfriend. A rich older boyfriend."

"He's not that rich and not that much older. And I know it

must be hard on him. I didn't know I was coming back to school until we arrived here this morning."

My morning classes fly by, although I'm unable to concentrate with everything on my mind.

Everett. Eddie. School. Achlys and "she." The fact that I can heal people and bring myself back to life. But at least I've already covered the content of my classes today.

"Hey, Rory, you okay?" Freya asks as I appear to have zoned out during the conversation at lunch.

Sitting at our table are Skye, Bethany, and Oliver, with a couple of other jocks who follow Oliver around. Bethany just wants to find out more about my boyfriend.

Eddie doesn't sit with us though, like he used to, I suppose because he feels awkward too. He eats lunch a few tables over, constantly glancing in my direction.

"Yeah, I'm fine," I mutter with a small smile. But that doesn't reassure her.

"I thought, with the new boyfriend, you wouldn't be so goody-goody anymore," Oliver comments, chuckling with his jock friends. "A guy like that, you definitely are as nerdy as I thought you were."

"Are you…a virgin?" Bethany questions, and my brows pinch together at the very personal question.

They think just because I have an older "boyfriend" that we've slept with each other. I've slept next to him, not with him.

"Of course she is," one of the jocks, Matt, says with a smirk in my direction. "What are those dumb shoes you're wearing?"

"Everett bought them for me, to stop me from falling so much," I reply.

Freya smiles, looking underneath the table at my footwear. "That's adorable," she comments. "He Rory-proofed shoes for you."

"Yeah, it is," I mumble, hiding my wide smile.

I wanted some sign that he cared about me more than just a burden or responsibility. And this is it. All of it. The shoes, school, the book. He's even made up with Ace, as he told me Ace would be picking me up today.

"How did you get him? It's quite a step up from weak high school senior to rich muscled businessman," Oliver states, glancing over his shoulder at Eddie.

"Hey," Bethany exclaims, scolding her boyfriend. "Eddie's not weak. But he does have a point, Rory. How did you meet him? Is he the reason you've been away?"

"No, I just met him around where we live." True.

Rogue territory is around where the old pack was. It separates Red Moon's territory from Shadow Blood's, along with many other packs on either side. "I know his aunt, too, so we got to talking." True.

"He's really hot, Rory. You've got a catch there."

Chapter 28

Lighter

———•❖•———

RORY

"Who is that?" Freya questions as we exit the school doors.

Bethany and Oliver are already huddled by their cars with their friends. I follow Freya's sight line to see a grinning Ace, arms folded, leaning against his car like he's trying to be cool.

"That's Ace. He's Everett's friend," I tell her. "And my friend," I add because that's what he is.

"Rory!" he calls out, giving me a stern look.

"Get in the car so we can go. Everett's gonna kill me if I don't get you back exactly half an hour after school ends. We're already late, probably because of your clumsy lazy ass," he shouts across the lot.

I narrow my eyes at him and stick my tongue out. He chuckles in response as I walk over to him.

"Friends of yours?" he asks, gesturing behind me to where all my friends are staring. "They're probably thinking, 'Who's the amazingly hot guy?'"

"No, they were thinking that this morning. Now they're thinking, 'Where's the hot guy from this morning?'"

He makes a face at me and I make one back.

"Alright, get in," he says with a sigh and a smile.

I do as he says, sliding into the passenger side as he starts the car, then waving goodbye to Freya as we pull out onto the road.

"Do you all have cars?"

"Yeah, wolf meetings with other packs require cars to get around, even though we stay within the pack most of the time," he explains. "Did you have a good day? Everett sure was happy when he got back."

"It was a good day. I like school," I answer, ignoring his last comment because it's none of his business—like how my life isn't any of Oliver's business either.

I avoided a painful and dreaded talk with Eddie, but we'll have to have one at some point. I hurt him, even though that had never been my intention, and even worse than just dumping him by text, I'm with another guy.

After what feels like a long drive, we arrive back at the pack, parking outside the pack house.

"Everett's in his office," Lucius informs us. "He wants to see Rory."

I give him a quick smile before heading up the stairs and over to his office. I knock before entering, although he's never minded me being in here much.

I'm met with a wide smile as I walk over to him.

"How was school, little one?" he asks after I take a seat in an armchair beside his desk and curl up on it.

"It was great. Thank you. I mean it. For everything. And for the book—I just started reading it."

He chuckles at my excitement. "Did you hurt anything?"

"I was injury-free all day—well, aside from this morning, my alarm," I state proudly, and it receives another chuckle.

What has changed?

I like this version of Everett, the one who doesn't always look disappointed or concerned about me, the one who doesn't look like he carries the weight of the world on his shoulders, the one who actually laughs and smiles.

He still has that responsibility and behaves in the manner of a powerful Alpha, but he's lighter.

"Are you okay?"

"Why wouldn't I be?" he questions in confusion.

Why is he confused? I'm confused. "Well, I don't know. Yesterday, you weren't very happy with me and—"

"Aurora, I'm sorry about yesterday. I just… I want your forgiveness."

"Forgiveness? For what?" I ask.

"For just…everything. I just want you to forgive me." He gets out of his chair and kneels in front of me.

I don't understand. He grabs my face with both his hands, his eyes begging for forgiveness for who knows what.

"Okay. Then, I forgive you."

He smiles, moving in and pressing his lips against mine. And it feels like both the first time and like we've been kissing our whole lives.

When he pulls back, I'm left in a trance, dazed and lost in the euphoric world he's put me into.

"Read in here while I do work?"

I nod, unpacking the book he gave me from my bag and beginning to read.

"How's that Eddie kid?"

"I don't know. He doesn't seem very happy with me," I tell him, peering over my book to see his concerned and jealous expression returned. "What did you actually put in the text?"

"We're over. Sorry," he states rather proudly, and I resist the urge to roll my eyes in front of the big bad Alpha.

"At least there was a short apology in there," I remark sarcastically.

"So you haven't forgiven me?" he asks with an amused look.

"You did put me back in school, so I'm not sure whether they cancel out."

"It was better than not telling him it was over at all," he replies with an easy smirk.

"It's your fault you were dating him instead of waiting for me. You only dated him for a month. He can't act like he was in love with you. 'We're over' is appropriate."

"So we're together?" I ask honestly.

"Yes," he states firmly, his eyes flickering to mine before returning to his laptop screen and the papers on his desk.

"We haven't been together very long, and you wouldn't like it if I sent you a breakup text like we meant nothing."

"But I'm your mate and he doesn't mean nothing," he says nonchalantly. "It's getting late. Why don't we get some food? Come on, little one."

He stands up from his seat and moves over to me. I'm about to get up when he lifts me out of the seat and into his arms.

"I can walk," I whine, kicking a little.

"You'll kick me in the face if you keep that up," he grumbles, shifting my weight in his arms to keep my feet down.

I pout up at him, which just makes him chuckle. I feel like a child in his arms, from the size to the way he looks down at me.

But, weirdly enough, I like the way he takes care of me, how he Rory-proofs everything now: the way I sleep, eat, get changed, walk, descend the stairs.

He even put a stack of pillows at the bottom in case I fall, even though he caught me this morning.

We reach the kitchen to find it empty, so he just sets me on the counter whilst he cooks something. Everett doesn't let me near sharp knives or anything hot.

So that's the stove out of the question, the microwave and

oven, the toaster and the kettle. I just sit here, my legs dangling over the edge, watching Everett cook.

"What did you do yesterday, whilst I was at the pack meeting, little one?" Everett suddenly asks, breaking the comfortable silence between us.

"I was reading," I reply.

"That all?"

"Is this an interrogation?" I question him, furrowing my brows in confusion.

He moves closer to me and in between my legs, his hands resting on my waist.

"It's just a question, Aurora. Tell me the truth," he commands lowly.

"Why are you asking me?"

"The more you deflect, the more I know you did something."

"So you're mad at me?"

"For what? Why would I be mad at you?" he questions.

"Because you think I've done something. Is this about Ace again? Because you sent him to pick me up, so I thought you understood that nothing was happening."

"No, it's not about Ace, and I'm not going to be mad if you don't lie. Just don't lie to me, Aurora."

I pout at him a little, not knowing why he's questioning me all of a sudden.

"Fine. I was at the orphanage. I help out there sometimes and the kids there are great," I tell him. "Are you happy now?"

"Yes, I am," he states proudly before going back to cooking at the stove. "I just wanted you to tell me the truth, little one."

"How do you know that's the truth?"

"Well, you're a bad liar, and I already knew. I saw you there yesterday."

"I thought you were at the pack meeting. And if you saw me there, why are you asking?"

"Because I don't know why you didn't tell me."

"I didn't know if you would allow me. And, you're always disappointed in me," I say.

He leaves the food again and charges over to me, resuming his position in between my legs and gripping my chin.

"This is why. I'm not disappointed in you, little one. I'm concerned. Whenever you fall, it hurts me more than it hurts you.

"I want to be able to protect you, and I'm scared that I can't. But if you're sneaking out and not telling me everything, how can I protect you?"

"You were barely speaking to me before."

"I know. I know, Aurora, and that's why I wanted your forgiveness for everything. But I just… I want to do better.

"I'm not angry that you kept things from me. You had every right to. But you don't have to anymore. I'll protect you. Okay?"

I place my lips on his in understanding, and he responds by taking control, gripping my waist and tugging me against his body.

His hands run up and down my thighs over the material, just feeling me. My hands move up and down his thick arms and all over his back.

"Fucking hell, you have a room!" Lucius exclaims, which makes me pull away from Everett, but he maintains his position, looking back over his shoulder.

Ace appears in my sight too with his knowing smirk. "What are you cooking?"

Chapter 29

Talk

———•◆•———

RORY

"AURORA!" Everett calls out as I reach Freya and Skye outside of school. I look back at him curiously. "Lucius is picking you up today. Ace is going out today, so…"

I hurry back over to him, tumbling into his arms at the end and pouting at him.

"Lucius doesn't like me. He picked me up on Wednesday and it was dead silent the whole way home."

"He doesn't not like you, little one. You'll be fine."

"Can't Ophelia pick me up? Or I can learn how to drive."

He laughs wildly at my suggestion, his deep chuckles incredibly attractive.

"I know you're eighteen, but there is no way I'm letting you ever drive a car—ever. Ever," he reiterates firmly, in case I didn't hear it the first time.

I lower my eyes and then my head, but he proceeds to lift my chin and pecks my lips. "I'm sorry, little mate. It's just… Do you think that's a good idea?"

"I guess not," I say shamefully. "But I can't cook anything, or work any machinery, or do anything. I'm useless."

When he actually grips my chin, my eyes snap back to his and he looks furious.

"You're not useless, Aurora. Don't ever say that. I like cooking or getting takeout. You eat cereal, so I don't have to make you breakfast. And you eat sandwiches for lunch.

"You don't ask me for anything, and I want to do the things I do for you. Fuck, I want to do more. Go to school, and Lucius will pick you up, okay? I don't want to make you late."

He strokes my cheek and kisses my lips, telling me what I need to know.

I stroll back over to Freya and Skye as Everett pulls out of the parking lot, giving one final look.

"What was that all about?" Skye asks, peering off in the direction of Everett's car. "Why was he being all serious and grabbing your jaw?"

She's only seen him for a few minutes every day this week, but she's warned me about him multiple times. She thinks he's using me, trying to get into my pants.

But she doesn't know what I know. And if I tell her I think we're soulmates, she'll lecture me even more. She's usually bubbly and sweet, but can be very protective when she thinks I could be in trouble.

"He's just being… He's sending one of his friends to pick me up—one who doesn't like me very much," I tell her, walking inside so that we can change the subject.

"He calls you Aurora," Freya comments.

"That's my name," I reply in confusion.

"I know. It's just, I've never heard anyone use it. Everyone calls you Rory. You introduce yourself as Rory."

"Yeah, well, I did to Everett. But he likes calling me Aurora. And I like it when he calls me it."

"Hey, Rory," someone calls out as we stand by our lockers, taking our textbooks out.

I peer back over my shoulder to see Oliver and his jock

friends standing there, staring at me. Skye and Freya get called away by a teacher, leaving me standing alone against the jock squad.

"Hey, Oliver. You okay?" I ask.

"Absolutely. But you see, Jax, over there," he begins, casually glancing over his shoulder to a guy I've never seen before who has girls hanging off him.

He's wearing a leather jacket—your stereotypical bad boy. His eyes suddenly meet mine and a smirk grows on his lips.

"You haven't met him. He joined a couple of weeks after you left. He's throwing a party tomorrow and he doesn't really know you, so he asked me to invite you."

"Why?"

"Because he likes you."

I glance over Oliver's shoulder again, and Jax is now fully checking me out, his eyes roaming my body like it's his to stare at. Did no one tell him I have a "boyfriend"?

"Well, like every other party, I can't go," I reply sassily, brushing past all of them.

But Oliver catches up to me and walks alongside me.

"He's my mate and he likes you. I thought you like attention now with the cycle of guys that show up to take you home," he snarks.

I stop in my tracks, very offended, and ready to stand my ground. I've been standing up against Orion's bullies, but I need to stand up against my own.

"I'm dating Everett, the guy who takes me to school every morning. Those other guys are his friends. You can tell your 'mate' that I'm taken," I tell him before swanning off, leaving him stunned into silence.

Settling at my lunch table with Skye and Freya, listening to them complain about Mr. Sykes's math homework, I spot Eddie watching me again. And this time, I build up the courage to go talk to him, to clear the air.

I pull him aside, bearing in mind everything Everett has said to me. I guess a text was better than nothing, especially since now that I've met Everett, there will never be a chance with anyone else for me.

Even if Everett did reject me, which he's told me won't happen, I wouldn't get over it, and I wouldn't find anyone else that I'd have the same connection with. He's my soulmate after all.

"Rory, hey, I...," he starts but soon trails off, scratching the back of his head awkwardly.

"Eddie, I'm sorry. I don't really know what else to say, but I think we just need to clear the air. I know you deserved more than a text, and I'm so sorry for that. Really sorry.

"And...I know I was just gone. We moved. There were some bullies in my neighborhood. And I thought I was never coming back to school here. Not that it was okay to dump you like that."

"'We're over. Sorry.' That's what it said. It didn't even sound like you," he complains, taking out his phone and showing me it.

So Everett really did dump my boyfriend in three words. Not that I expected him to be sensitive.

He's my mate and he's an Alpha. He must have despised the idea I had a boyfriend and wanted to make sure there was no one out there thinking I was still their girl.

"This wasn't you. I know that."

"How would you know that?"

"Because I know you, Rory," he states.

No, he really doesn't. No one does, and I can't tell anyone. I wish I could though. Talk it out. But I'm not sure where that would get me. Still needing answers.

The only way to get answers is to die and put myself in

danger. Who knows, maybe this "she" can actually kill me, and then, in the process of getting answers, I die for real.

"Who wrote it?"

I'll have to tell him a version of the truth.

"Everett, my boyfriend, wrote it."

"Are you fucking serious? Your boyfriend broke up with me for you."

"I don't own a phone. I don't even know your number. I told him about you, and we started dating and he tracked you down, found your number.

"I didn't even know he texted you until well after he did it. I'm sorry. I thought it would be better for you to know we're over than to say nothing. I still don't own a phone or know your number. I'm—"

"Sorry, yeah I know," he finishes, disappointed at my words.

Did he think this would go differently?

"I care about you, Rory. We were friends before we were dating, so I do know you, and I care. That guy who drops you at school every day, he doesn't."

"You don't know him."

"He broke us up. He sent me a breakup text pretending to be you. If that's not messed up as shit, I don't know what is."

"It's more that he's the jealous type. And very protective," I tell him.

"Guys like that are dangerous and controlling. Rory, you shouldn't be with him."

"You can't tell me what to do, Eddie. I just... I wanted to clear the air."

"No, you were going to lie to me about the text, and who knows what else you were lying about. I don't want to see you hurt," he says.

"He's not hurting me. He's nowhere close to that. If

anything, he attempts to prevent me from getting hurt at all, which is hard considering I'm very clumsy."

I chuckle a little and move to leave, but his hand touches my arm, stopping me.

"Rory, you clearly like this guy better than me. What does he have that I don't? I mean, what didn't work between us?" he questions. "Please tell me honestly."

He's right. Even though we were dating for a month, we knew each other as friends for a couple of years. I know him. And he…well, he doesn't really know me.

Being a human living a wolf life and a bad liar, I just avoid the subject of my life, weaving my way around it. I can't tell him about my life. I can't tell anyone.

"I don't know what to tell you."

"The truth. Why are you with him and not me? We've been friends for years, and I thought we had a connection."

"I… He understands me and he takes care of me. He can be a little overprotective, but he's very serious about responsibility, and he protects anything he cares about."

"So do I."

"I'm sorry, Eddie."

When the lunch bell rings, I thank the goddess. Saved by the bell.

CHAPTER 30

Heat

RORY

"Hey," someone snaps me out of the entrancing book world of Alex in *Promise Kept*. I've been reading this book all week, and I can see why Everett values it so much.

I look up and turn my head to the seat next to me, finding Jax smirking at me like he can flirt with any girl and have them begging him for a date.

Unfortunately, this is a regular class for me, which I haven't noticed him in for the whole week. And if he's going to be pestering me, I might just have to change class. Not that I want to get run out of English Literature.

"Hey," I return politely before turning back to my book. But I can feel him staring, leaned back in his chair with a smug expression. "Is there something I can help you with?"

"Friendly conversation. I don't bite, babe," he flirts, inching closer to me.

Everett would slaughter this guy if he saw how close he is to me right now. I inch away, leaning toward the window and shuffling my chair quite obviously to show him I'm uninterested.

"I'm not your babe," I deadpan, not looking up from my book. "So I'd appreciate it if you didn't call me that."

"Oh, so you're sassy, are you? I like hard-to-get girls."

"I have a boyfriend," I state curtly.

"I don't see him."

"You'll see his fist in your face pretty soon if you don't stop," I retort, glancing over and giving him a bitter smile.

Not that I want to be rude, but this is for his own good. It's true, Everett will come at him if he hears Jax won't stop hitting on me. And this guy, he's new, I can have a new start.

I don't have to be a pushover.

But all he does is laugh. He actually laughs. Do I not sound threatening enough?

I am small, and clumsy, and seemingly innocent, and I don't do scary very well. But I was serious, and I said it in my serious tone.

"You're incredibly cute. You know, I was asking around about you. Oliver said you were shy and innocent, and were dating that skinny lacrosse player before. I didn't think you'd be this confident and bold."

"I'm just reading at the moment. And class is about to start, so I'd prefer to concentrate," I say with another bitter smile and focus back on my book.

"I'm guessing Oliver told you about the party this morning from the way you were looking over at me, checking me out—"

"I was not checking you out. I don't need to. I have a boyfriend for that."

Everett loves when I ogle him and drool like he's the most attractive man ever to have lived. I think he is.

"You coming to the party?"

"Like I told Oliver, no," I state firmly.

"No? You're turning down one of my parties? They can be pretty wild, but I thought a girl like you could handle it. I guess I was wrong."

"I guess you were."

He laughs again, shaking his head slightly in amusement. I have no clue what he finds so amusing. "Reverse psychology usually works."

"Well, that's when you're talking to people who have a low self-esteem and need to be validated by proving people wrong. I have a boyfriend, and a personal life, and I don't want or need to go to your party."

The words just flow out of my mouth—I can't stop them. I don't know what it is about this guy, but he infuriates me.

"Shit, I don't bite, but you definitely do. I was not warned you'd be so…resistant."

"Resistant? Because you get every girl that you want?"

"Yes," he replies quickly with his signature smirk. "I do. But it's clearly more difficult to get you. I like that, a challenge."

"Trust me, I'd stop trying. It's not difficult, it's impossible. If I told my boyfriend you're hassling me, which would be… maybe two or three more conversations away…

"He's incredibly protective and might do something I can't stop him from doing, that he'll probably regret later. But you will definitely be in a hospital."

All he does is laugh.

"Fuck, you're adorable. Those shoes, where'd you get them? I was thinking I'd buy some for my kid brother. What size are your feet?" he asks sarcastically.

He's comparing me to a child, like everyone does. But when Everett does it, it's…caring and protective and cute.

Before I can say anything else, the teacher strolls in, starting class, and it renders me silent as I attempt to listen. Of course, Jax attempts to catch my attention.

After class, Jax follows me out, making random comments, and I just ignore him. I empty my locker with Jax leaning next to it, continuously talking and flirting.

What the hell will it take to make him stop? I don't think he gets turned down too often, or ever, so me doing so is spurring him on, but what can I do?

We make it outside and I try to find Lucius's car.

"Who are you waiting for, babe? Boyfriend?"

"A friend. But it's none of your business," I remark, rolling my eyes at his interest. "And do you even know my name, or do you think it's Babe?"

"I know your name, Rory," Jax counters with a devilish smirk. "I'm Jax, if you didn't know."

"I know, I just don't care," I snark, which makes him chuckle.

His hand touches my shoulder and turns me to face him. I try to shrug him off, but he's certainly persistent. Before I can completely take it off, it's done for me, by someone I didn't expect to see.

"I see your hand on my girlfriend again and I'll cut it off and feed it to the hounds I know. You like your hand?" Everett growls darkly, squeezing the life out of Jax's hand.

It definitely threatens Jax. He literally looks like he's wet himself from shock and the tightness of Everett's hand around his.

And since the school day is done, the crowd is hurtling out, noticing the display, and deciding to watch the show.

"Yeah, I like my hand," he grumbles, struggling to escape Everett's grasp.

"Then keep it away from Aurora," Everett hisses before releasing Jax's hand, taking mine and dragging me to his car.

"Everett," I whine, stumbling over my own feet from the way he's dragging me—although I'm not sure whether that wouldn't happen if I was walking normally. "Everett!"

He twists around to face me and hauls me to the car,

pressing me against the side whilst he stands in front of me, looking down, dominating me.

"I thought it was an unspoken rule. I told you that you don't go near Eddie, but that was a generalization for all males.

"You don't even let one touch you if it's not me, or Lucius or Ace, whom I trust," he hisses lowly, his hands squeezing my hips.

"This isn't my fault. He wouldn't leave me alone. And if I was talking to him, it's not like I would do anything. I'm with you. But you don't trust me?"

"I smell other males on you. It's a wolf thing, if you didn't forget. And I'm an Alpha, so my senses are even more heightened. Tell me the truth now. You spoken to Eddie today?

"Because I can smell him," he seethes, grabbing the back of my neck, his lips hovering over mine. "Tell me the fucking truth, Aurora."

"I talked with him at lunch. I wanted to explain to him the breakup and the text. I thought he deserved that," I explain.

"He deserves shit if it means coming nowhere near you. You're my little mate."

"I didn't forget, Everett," I scoff, pushing him away from me slightly. But he barely moves, and when he does, it's only because he wants to—not because I'm strong enough to move the wall.

"I may be your mate, but you don't own me. You don't control me. I like you. Really like you. I have feelings for you, past the mate bond.

"And I like the protectiveness and the Alpha qualities and the sense of responsibility you hold. But I'm allowed to fight back against it when you're out of line."

"Out of line, am I?" he whispers, his lips hovering over mine again.

Why do I just want to kiss him right now? I'm mad, but I just want to kiss him. So I give in to the powerful urge and smash my lips onto his, which he meets halfway, already acting on that same urge.

Before we fall deeper into our make-out session, he opens the passenger door beside me, lifts me in and runs around to the other side.

We drive a good few blocks before he shuts down the engine and drags me onto his lap so that I'm straddling him.

And then we're kissing again, passionately. And fiercely. His hands grip my sweater and my hair, yanking my hair kinkily, and he starts to suck on my neck.

I can feel his bulge pressing against me through his jeans, and it turns me on so much. But I can't. I'm not ready. And he's not ready.

I know that having sex for the first time, for him it would be when he's ready to mark me, ready for me to become Luna. Neither he nor I are ready for that.

But he kisses me like he never will again. And his kisses make me moan into his mouth. I'm frustrated with him, and I'm kissing him and I want to kiss him.

I didn't want to kiss Jax when I was frustrated. But with Everett I felt so…heated, and there was tension between us, and it just exploded into making out.

I think I'm falling in love with him. All of him.

Chapter 31

Domesticity

EVERETT

"Where the fuck have you been? It's been hours since you left to get her. Did you fucking kill her?" Lucius questions, looking at the sleeping little girl in my arms.

"I took her to get some food, and she fell asleep in the car. We're going to bed now," I declare, heading up the Aurora-proofed stairs.

Everything is cushioned now. I wish I could just tape cushions all around her so if she does fall, it doesn't hurt. And cushioning her is easier than cushioning everything around her.

"Alpha," Lucius calls out. "I found out what pack she belongs to. Ace fucking knew. Red Moon. Alpha Nick and Luna Victoria. They're apparently the ones who tried to kill her."

"Apparently?" I growl a little. He doesn't believe my mate? She was covered in her own blood when I found her. Her beautiful exhausted clumsy self.

It's been a couple of weeks since I blew up at her for Eddie and that kid who put his fucking hand on her. And she yelled at me like the strong Luna she is.

I plan to mark her. I plan to be with her for the rest of our lives. But she needs to be ready, and I want her to love me.

Because I love her. I know I do. But I don't want to scare her by saying it just yet.

"Night," Lucius concludes, rolling his eyes at my protectiveness of her and closing his door.

I open my door and roll back the covers for my little mate. But she nuzzles her face into my chest and makes cute little mutterings, wriggling around adorably.

And all I can do is stare. She's so beautiful—goddess-like beauty. And she's so petite; I can hold her in one arm. And she wants me.

"She's the most beautiful mate ever," Chaos hums, sighing in contentment with our mate in our arms.

I place her gently into bed, lifting her over the cushioned barricades on either side of it, and roll in next to her, careful not to wake her. But her eyes flicker open and almost blind me with their luminescent color.

"Hello," she mutters with a dazed smile.

How could someone ever hurt my little mate? They tried to kill her. I'm going to kill whoever tried. She's going to have to see those fuckers again eventually, once she becomes Luna of the pack.

Especially if I get roped into this conference. Alpha Nickolas has always been a dick, coming with his father most years and supporting the *hate on humans* campaign.

I'll have to protect Aurora for the entirety of it, the whole week, never leaving her alone. She can't defend herself, especially against titled wolves, even if they aren't as powerful as wolves in this pack.

"Hello, little one." I kiss her sweet soft lips, deepening it as I grab the back of her neck and roll her into me.

These past two weeks, I can't seem to keep my hands off

her. I had no idea putting her back in school would have such a great effect on our relationship.

I just know she loves school and work and learning, and she's always made sure to keep up with it. And I needed to work for her forgiveness, but she just gave it to me, falsely even though she didn't know it.

Two weeks ago, when we fought, it showed that we have a connection, a relationship—a passionate one. She's not afraid to speak up to me anymore, and nowadays, she's probably the only one.

The only time Lucius says anything against me, it's to insult my mate, and any time Ace says anything against me, it's to insult me for my treatment of my mate.

"Is it night? I didn't think it was that late," she comments, resting her head on my chest.

Stroking her silky hair, I chuckle lightly as she feels my arm muscles. "You're very strong," she whispers dozily. She barely knows what she's saying when she's just woken up or we've just made out.

"Thank you, little one. I'm glad you think so."

"I do think so. I think so a lot," she says, looking up and pecking my lips, her eyes about to close once again.

After I settle her in, I decide to look into her old pack more. They have to pay for what they did, don't they? Even if she wasn't my mate, they tried to kill a human—not just a human, but a human who grew up in the pack.

She was a pack member, even if she wasn't a wolf, and they tried to kill her for no reason. But there are no laws against it.

The council barely gets involved in interpack matters. It's the Alpha's job to create order in their pack, and what they say goes. But she's my mate, so I have justification to bring them to justice. Although, that's not council law.

"Alpha, what are you doing out so late?" Lily asks, fluttering her lashes at me for some reason.

As far as the hating on Aurora goes, the females are more frustrated that I'm not their mate than by the fact that Aurora is human and they think she won't make a good Luna.

"Just doing some research and decided to get some fresh air. How are you, Lily?" I ask politely.

"I'm amazing now that I'm talking to you, Alpha. I haven't seen you about a lot."

"Well, I have work, and a mate now," I declare, making sure to emphasize the point that I have a mate.

"Oh, right," she mutters, tucking her hair behind her ear as she walks with me. She moves to touch my arm but I back off, avoiding her touch.

Aurora can't touch males or let males touch her; I'm not going to be a hypocrite about my own rule. And I don't want anyone touching me other than Aurora anyway.

"Sorry, Alpha. Where are you heading now?"

"Back to the pack house, back to bed with Aurora," I tell her.

I give her a polite smile before walking off back to the pack house. When I slide back into bed with Aurora as I left her, she snuggles up against me, still in a deep sleep, and I just hug her back.

Why does cuddling with her feel so good? I've never been a sensitive guy—protective but never sensitive. I don't generally like cuddling or, fuck, I don't even know.

I guess no one else is my mate. There's been no one else I would want to do it with. She's…everything.

I wake up to Aurora knocking against the cushion and then rolling back onto me from the bounce. I've tried to think of everything to Aurora-proof the place.

When I don't go to bed, I want to know that she won't wake

up falling out of it and injuring herself. A few more bumps to her head and she could have a concussion.

She's lucky that she's actually perfectly healthy, the doctor said, which surprised me a lot. Nothing broken, no serious injuries, nothing. Just a few bruises that fade and then get renewed at the next fall that I can't control.

"You okay?"

"It's actually fun to hit a cushion in the morning. It's refreshing," she says with a giggle, jumping up in the bed and crawling to the end to get off.

She's small, so it's a long way from top to the bottom, and she can't get off if it's not from the end—which, I'm realizing, might be a disaster in itself, so I grab her by the waist before she can get down, and I lift her off.

The fact that she can be like an excitable little kid does nothing to help her avoid the effects of her critical clumsiness.

"Sleep well, little one?" I ask, kissing her cheek from behind her.

"Yeah." She looks back at me and narrows her eyes. "What do you want to tell me?"

I sigh and reply, "You're getting good at reading me. Ace is taking you to school—and picking you up, maybe, if I don't get back. It's better than Lucius, isn't it?"

"Why can't you take me?"

"I have some errands to run."

I'm visiting her old pack, with Lucius as my backup. I want to see if they feel guilty for what they did without telling them we have her and she's my mate.

I want to see who tried to kill my beautiful mate. I've met Alpha Nickolas only in passing—his father was much more talkative when he was Alpha, with Nickolas following behind.

We set out early, the drive only an hour away. Aurora made it pretty far on foot in rogue territory and toward mine.

I thank the goddess that we decided to go out hunting that day and got caught farther out than we'd intended, perhaps destined to find Aurora.

By the time we get there, Lucius has thoroughly complained to me about the broken kitchen appliances I actually allow Aurora around, and about the many loud sounds that Aurora causes by accidentally bumping into things.

I'm glad to finally get out of the car and be led to the Alpha.

"Alpha Everett, what a pleasant surprise."

Chapter 32

Doubt

RORY

"Have a wonderful day, Aurora," Ace declares, attempting to mock Everett with his deep tone and the way he calls me *Aurora*.

"That's not what he says."

"What does he say then?"

"Try not to hurt yourself," I say in a mocking voice of Everett, too, rolling my eyes after.

"Aw, what an adorable farewell," Ace jokes before getting out and popping my car door open before I can.

"I can open my door, Ace. Now everyone is watching."

"You're my Luna, that's like being the fucking queen. Queens get their doors opened for them. Plus, Everett told me it's better to be close to you when you leave a car just in case you fall.

"It's apparently the prime chance for you to tumble, and I don't want my head to be literally bitten off."

He grabs my bag out of the back and places it in my hands with a bright smile. "Try not to hurt yourself, Aurora." Then he just scurries off.

"Where's Everett this morning?" Bethany asks, eyeing up Ace as he drives off—after sending me a bright smile and a bow of his head like I'm a queen.

He's taken to calling me the Luna already, even though Everett hasn't marked me.

"He's running errands," I reply, ignoring the stare of Jax, who's standing beside Oliver and Freya.

He actually hangs around with Oliver now, attempting to get closer to me, I think. Or maybe he's moved on to his next target by now.

After Everett threatened him, he backed off a little, taken by surprise. But he was soon back at it, flirting with me in class, despite my numerous warnings.

Maybe he does want to lose a hand. Everett did not look like he was joking when he said it.

"If he told you that, it's not a good sign," Oliver taunts as we enter the school. "Errands are vague. Vague is what you use when you're lying but you don't want to lie to that person. He's probably married or something."

"She would know if he was married," Skye states, rolling her eyes.

"My mom dated this married guy for six months before she found out he had a whole other family who just thought he went on business trips," Jax explains.

"That sucks for your mom," I mumble.

They don't know anything about Everett, and why is it any of their business? Well, why is it Oliver's business?

I understand Jax: he wants to discredit the guy and get with me. I understand my friends, who want to be supportive, and who get to know about my life. But Oliver is in a relationship and isn't my friend.

Why is he trying to mess with my relationship? Out of loyalty to Jax? And for all their trying, it will never work because I live with Everett, I sleep in his bed, everyone in the pack knows I'm his soulmate.

If he is keeping secrets, anything that doesn't involve me is probably none of my business at this time—especially since I'm hiding something massive about myself.

But I just don't understand it myself. I wouldn't know what to tell him, and I don't want to freak him out. I love him.

"Have you actually been to his house? Or does he always go to yours and take you out?

"If he doesn't involve you with his life and job and family, and tells you he's doing errands, he's definitely hiding things," Jax states with a smug smile.

"I got dropped off by his friend this morning," I reply with an expression that says, *What the hell are you talking about?*

"Friends don't count. They're normally in on it."

"In on what? Anyway, I know his aunt; I'm friends with her. And I've been to his place. And he doesn't have any other family."

I trip over a book on the floor and almost fall face-first, but am saved by my shoes keeping some of my waning balance. The faint chuckles of Jax and Oliver can be heard behind me.

"She's cute but she's clumsy as shit. You don't really want that, do you?" Oliver whispers, I'm guessing to Jax behind me. I turn around and give him a glare.

"You know I can hear you, right?"

"Why would an older guy want to date you? You're like a little child, falling over everything, including yourself. He must really like playing daddy," Oliver comments, leaning against the lockers and getting a light jab in the ribs by Bethany.

"Well, he calls it Aurora-proofing. Like my shoes and the stairs and the bed and shower. He makes it so I don't hurt myself. But our relationship is none of your business," I sass, which makes Oliver raise his eyebrows in amusement.

"See, she's hot," Jax comments, and I furrow my brows.

He turns to me and reaches out to touch me, but I flinch

backward. What's he doing touching me anyway? Everett made it a rule, aside from Ace and Lucius. And honestly, I can live without other guys touching me.

"He's really brainwashed you. Just because he tells you no one can touch you, you obey it?"

"Stay away from me, okay? He trains twice a day, fighting and running and lifting weights. He can follow through with his threats," I warn him before backing away from all of them and heading off to class.

I would have thought that would get Jax to leave me alone for a few hours, but here he is again.

"What does that mean?"

"What does what mean?" I question.

"Does he hurt you?" he whisper-asks, looking at me intensely. "It's hard to tell whether he's hurting you or you're just clumsy."

"He's not hurting me," I exclaim, although I can see how he could have thought that. I was just warning him to stay away. "I just want you to leave me alone. I have enough to deal with without adding you to it."

"I'm a problem to you?" he asks with a sly smirk. "I'd only be a problem if I was affecting you."

"You are. You're distracting me from school with your constant flirting and whining and staring. Will you knock it off?

"Everett's my soulmate. There's no way I'm ever leaving him. So you can try and get some other poor unsuspecting girl."

"Soulmate?"

"Is that all you got from that? It's like when I speak, the only things you hear are the words you want to hear," I complain.

"Soulmate. He really has you brainwashed, huh?"

"No one has brainwashed me."

"Errands," he says with a small chuckle. "Oliver's right. Guys never say they have errands. Shit, who uses the word *errand*? He's lying to you. It's probably something like he's cheating on you."

He's not cheating on me. But he's right, errands are pretty vague.

"Why don't you text him?"

"I don't own a phone."

"You don't own a phone?" he asks, actually shocked. "No wonder you wouldn't give me your number. Your parents didn't give you one?"

"I don't have a dad, and my mom's strapped. So, no, she hasn't given me one. And I live in a tight-knit community. I don't need a phone."

"You are the only teenager I've ever heard say that, ever," Jax remarks. "Everyone needs a phone."

"What would I do with it? My free time is spent reading or at an orphanage I help out at or with Everett, and anyone I want to talk to is either at school or lives around me, within walking distance."

"So it's easy for him to control your life? He or his friends take you to school, so if he doesn't, you're not going. He lives near you, so he can go to your house whenever he wants.

"He's bigger and stronger than you, so he can do whatever he wants. That's insane," he states, leaning back in his chair and looking at me.

It's not insane. He saved me when I had nowhere else to go. He takes care of me, looks out for me, cooks for me, Rory-proofs for me. I love him.

By the end of the day, I'm stressing like crazy about this *errand* thing. They got into my head. If it's work, Everett just says that, and it usually happens in his office or around the pack.

I get outside, with Jax hanging around me again, along with Bethany, Oliver, and Skye.

In my opinion, Bethany seems to be hanging around me more since I've come back—maybe because I'm dating an older guy and she thinks I'm cooler and boy crazy like she is.

Plus, she loves to gossip, and me dating a mysterious older guy is good gossip.

When I see Everett's car pull up, I stroll over as he gets out, deciding whether to ask him or what I'm going to ask him.

"Hey, little one, get hurt today?" Everett asks, raising my arms and checking me for any visible bruises or scratches.

"Where did you go today?"

He glances up at me, furrowing his brows at my tone. "I had errands, Aurora. I told you this morning."

"What errands?" I question.

"I'm confused. What is this?" he questions, grabbing my waist and pulling me toward him so we can speak more privately. "Aurora, why am I on trial?"

Chapter 33

Betrayal

EVERETT

A FEW HOURS EARLIER

"Alpha Everett, what a pleasant surprise," Alpha Nickolas greets us, leading us into the pack house where his Luna, Beta, and Gamma are waiting—informed, probably, just as we arrived.

"I'm wondering about the purpose of your visit though." He offers us a seat graciously and formally in his pack meeting hall, which almost makes this feel like an interrogation.

They're lined up on one side like I'm sitting for a fucking interview, clearly curious and wary as to why I'm here. They know their pack power is inferior to mine, which makes them all the more on guard.

"Your pack is the closest pack to my territory. There's the annual conference coming up, and I feel that I need to gauge some of the views of my neighboring packs.

"I rarely attend those meetings because my views are heard but not implemented. Instead of going there completely outnumbered, I'd like to share ideas with other packs one on one."

This gets him talking, sharing with me his own laws he's implemented within his pack since he took over, and the ideas and issues he's planning to bring up.

And of course, I play out this excuse, maneuvering into the human issues he has.

"What are your views on humans?" Alpha Nickolas asks, narrowing his eyes. "I know your pack has been about coexistence with humans and all that shit. I wonder if you've changed your mind."

"No, I haven't. I follow my parents' teachings whilst adapting to the modern era," I reply nonchalantly.

"But coexistence doesn't necessarily mean integrating them with our communities?" Luna Victoria questions, her arm wrapped around Alpha Nick and confidence oozing off her.

"These two tried to kill our mate," Chaos screams, his growls rumbling throughout me.

"Stay calm," I respond silently. "Aurora doesn't even want us here, so we can't make anything obvious. They can't know she's alive, not just yet. She wouldn't like that."

"Technically, no. I don't believe in integration. As long as we're living different lives, we should get along. You feel differently?"

"No," Alpha Nick declares with an agreeing smile. "Exactly. Humans shouldn't be part of a pack."

"You have a human in your pack?" I ask.

Alpha Nick and Luna Victoria look between each other before sighing.

"We did," Luna Victoria answers.

"You did?" Lucius questions with a fake confused look. "What happened?"

"We tossed the little bitch out," she replies, grimacing at the thought of my mate.

"Our pack raised her and she was fucking useless. I don't know why she was even allowed to stay. Humans shouldn't be in a pack, they don't belong in one."

"If she grew up here, doesn't that make her a pack member? She was integrated. Did she have any family? Why was she even here?" I question.

"An Omega brought her back after finding her in rogue territory. She was a weak little clumsy shit."

I had to keep my anger from exploding all over her for talking about my mate like dirt on her shoe.

I guess that's what she thinks happened to my mate: she became dirt, savaged by rogues and decomposed into the mud.

That Omega, Aurora's mom, I know Aurora misses her. She sometimes whimpers about her in her sleep, and about her old pack, the trauma they put her through.

They did that. Alpha Nickolas and Luna Victoria. They tried to kill my mate. They created her nightmares.

"Although that fucking Omega left. Went missing, just like that. She was on an errand in rogue territory and she didn't officially break ties, either. But that bitch probably went to find her daughter, not that she will."

"Why not?" I question, although I already know the answer.

"She's out in the human world. Probably making a buck on a street corner or something."

That's my fucking mate, you asshole.

I take my leave, knowing I won't even be able to meet Aurora's mom and deciding to pick up my little mate instead.

NOW

Maybe that was a fucking mistake, because now, my mate seems incredibly suspicious and paranoid.

"Aurora, why am I on trial?"

She doesn't trust me. But why? I did visit her old pack

without her knowing, but I've given her no reason not to trust me, have I?

"I want to know where you went. You don't want to tell me?" she questions, backing away from me. Why is she being like this?

"No, I don't, not right out here," I declare, scoffing and stepping closer to her.

But she takes another step back from me. I reach out to grab her and someone gets between us, a scent I've smelled before. I could fucking kill him right now.

"Don't grab her, you abusive asshole," fucking Eddie threatens, and the rest of her friends march over, protecting her like she needs protection from me.

She needs my protection. Abusive? What the fuck? Has she been telling them something?

"Aurora," I call out in a dangerous, low voice—my Alpha voice—to make her understand my frustration.

What the fuck is happening? Her friends are glaring at me like I'm the fucking devil, and she's gone all paranoid. Perhaps rightly so.

Through her friends, I watch her: those pleading green eyes that are asking me.

"I went to talk to Nick and Victoria," I blurt out, making her completely freeze altogether.

"You didn't...," she whispers, barely audible to the regular human ears around her, but caught by mine. "Did Ace tell you?"

"Ace shouldn't have had to. You should have trusted me enough to tell me," I lecture.

She barges through her friends, who are now confused. "Trusted you? You didn't even tell me you were going there. Did you tell them? Do they know?"

"No, they don't fucking know. But it wouldn't matter." I

reach out and grab her waist, wrapping my arms around her to feel the contact and soothe myself. "You don't need to be scared, little one. I'm here for you."

"You went behind my back. You told me you were running errands," she persists, her eyes watering.

They're telling me that she's really hurt. Really fucking hurt. And I did that. That's why I didn't want to tell her.

"I'm sorry, little one. I just… I needed to know."

"Know what? You didn't trust me? You didn't believe me?" she questions loudly.

"Of course I fucking believe you. I wanted to know how anyone could fucking hurt you."

"Really, you do it all the time," she blurts out.

And all I can do is stare at her in stunned silence. Did she really just say that?

"We've fucked up. Really bad," Chaos mutters.

"I think you should leave," Jax declares like an asshole. "I'll take her home. She clearly doesn't want to be around you."

"You should mind your fucking business!" I growl out, my entire body filling with an uncontrollable rage. And Aurora notices.

"No! I'm driving her home so you can go," he argues, although previously taken aback by my tone. "Let go of her!"

"She's our fucking mate," Chaos growls.

I'm about to go full-on wolf rage with this guy, but Aurora places her hand on my cheek, snapping my attention back to her.

"I'm sorry, little one. I am. I didn't mean to…"

"You did mean to. You think about every decision you make, right? You overthink most of the time. And I liked that about you. But you can't make the 'I wasn't thinking' excuse."

"Can't we just go home? Aurora…we'll talk about it at home?"

"No, I don't want to. I don't want… I need space. I'll walk."

"You'll walk? It's an hour and a half walk. I'm not letting you walk, you fucking know that, little one."

Fuck. She'll pass through rogue territory if she walks. And there is no fucking way I'm allowing her to.

"She can do whatever she wants," Eddie declares, touching her shoulder.

What is with this Jax and Eddie? They want my mate. My fucking mate.

"You've brainwashed her enough," Jax exclaims. "She doesn't need you. Take your hands off of her."

"I'm fine," she says, glancing over her shoulder to her friends—Jax, Eddie, Freya, Bethany, Skye, and Oliver.

I'm trying. I'm really trying. Because I care. I care about her life, and everything about her. I just wanted to know her. I love her.

"No, you're not. He's convinced you that you're meant to be together, that he loves you, all so he can get into your pants," Jax counters. "Don't go with him. I'll drive you to your house."

"It's a bit difficult since she lives with me," I sneer, holding her tighter to me.

His eyes widen and I just squeeze tighter, never wanting to let her go. I know I hurt her. I just wanted… I don't even know. I have to tell her about her mom. But at home. Not here.

"Please…come home with me. I can't force you, I won't. I've done enough shit. But there's something I need to tell you."

"What?"

"I should tell you at home."

"Is that just some way to get me home? I don't—"

"Please. It's important."

"Just tell me now," she demands, looking pained.

"Fine," I give in. "I... Fuck, I'm sorry, little one. Your mom, she's...missing."

"What does that mean?" she questions, now panicked.

"I'm sure she's fine. She left, but she wasn't forced to go. She went out into the woods, and she never came back. She'll be fine."

"You don't even know her."

"She raised you," I say, cupping her cheeks in my hands. "I'm sorry. Please let me take you home."

Chapter 34

Trust

——◆❖◆——

RORY

Mama's missing? In rogue territory? What if something happened to her? She would never leave; she has too strong a bond.

What if... What if it was this "she"? What if "she" has my mama?

I let this happen. I put her in danger. Anyone associated with me is in danger.

What about my friends? What if I'm putting them in danger? No one is safe around me. What about Everett? What if something happens to him? I couldn't live with myself.

"Aurora," Everett calls to me. "Let's go home?"

I can't believe he went behind my back and visited my old pack. The pack that killed me. If they knew I was alive, if Everett let that slip, it would create a lot of suspicion and curiosity.

And I don't know anything about this, any of this. I can't explain dying a number of times and then just coming back to life like nothing happened.

I feel angry—and betrayed. He knew I didn't want him to go there, and he went there anyway. That's why I didn't tell him which pack I was from.

But I knew that when I told Ace, it would come back to Everett. I just… I didn't think he'd go and pretend he didn't.

What if he let something slip? What if they already know and he doesn't know they know? He must have been asking questions about me to find out anything. Though, he's not stupid.

Everett has never been stupid. Although this entire thing may have been. He didn't need to go there. They couldn't tell him anything I couldn't.

He didn't trust me? Because if he did, why would he need to go? I don't understand.

"I can't go with you," I tell him. "You betrayed me."

I want to go with him. I so want to go with him. But…I can't… I don't know what to do.

He hurt me. Now I'm just supposed to go home with him? What do other couples do in my situation? Sleep on the couch for the night? Sleep over at a friend's?

I can't do that. I can't go with a friend, and sleeping on the couch, I wouldn't be able to.

"Do you tell me everything about yourself? You know that I can tell when you're lying." He has a point. I don't tell him everything.

I didn't tell him that I've died numerous times. And he can't expect me to. But this is different. This is about me. He went to my pack, to my killers.

"And I let you keep your secrets because I know you. And you know me. I would never try to hurt you.

"Trust isn't about knowing every little detail about each other, it's about putting trust in each other despite everything, knowing that we'll do what's best for each other," he explains.

"And going there is what's best for me? Is it? I'm certain that it's not," I counter, wrapping my hands around his wrists and prying his hands off my face, even though it kills me.

I crave his touch; I crave everything about him. I love him. But he did this. Am I supposed to believe he was doing this for me?

"Nothing happened. I didn't say anything. You're safe. You will always be safe."

"Were you even going to tell me?" I question.

"Yes, of course I was. At home."

"How do I know that's not a lie?"

"Because… Is that what's wrong? You don't trust me." There's pain in his eyes.

I know I've hurt him. But he's hurt me too. That doesn't mean he deserves it, but… I want him to know he's hurt me. I think he knows though.

The truth is, I do trust him. I'm just scared. I know he thinks he can protect me, and he can from Nick and Victoria. He's stronger and smarter and he cares about me a lot.

But against this higher being, whoever is after me, I don't even know my supposed enemy's name.

"I trust you. I do. But… you don't know what they did. It was horrible. I grew up there, my mom was there and they kicked me out, left me in the woods.

"Why would you go there when you know that? They wanted me dead. What did you even go there to do? What if you lost your shit with them? How would you explain that?" I question.

"I didn't. I try not losing my shit. It's difficult when I care about you so much. But I didn't. For you.

"I wanted to talk to your mom and to talk with Nick and

Victoria. That's all. I'm sorry. Tell me what you want me to do and I'll do it."

He cups my cheeks again, yanking me closer to him. I just want him.

I want him to hold me, to keep me safe from the monsters that seem to be looming. There are monsters at every corner, and I want Everett to protect me from them.

"Please, let's go home. We'll talk there, huh? Please," he begs, and I give in finally.

It's not like I'm walking home. I can't. Rogue territory is where I'm unprotected. Plus, Everett would never allow that. He would force me into the car. He just prefers to beg me first, which I respect.

I slide into the passenger side, catching a glimpse of my friends, who all stand bewildered and confused, before Everett drives off.

We drive in silence. Utter silence. I rest my head against the door and stare out the windshield. Out of the corner of my eye, I watch Everett glancing over at me every few seconds, just checking up on me.

As we reach the pack house, the silence continues into the house and into the kitchen. Until he turns to me, his eyes connecting with mine. And our lips connect too in a frenzy.

He slams me up against the wall, lifting my legs on either side of him so that they cling around his waist.

I feel his hard-on against my sex, and all I can think about is him, and being closer to him, and feeling him on me.

I don't even notice that he's walking up the stairs with me until my back is against the bed with him on top of me. His lips suck on my skin, my neck and collarbone and shoulder. I'm so angry at him, I just…

I push him away a little, but he doesn't move. He just

stops and looks at me, his legs and arms on either side of me, pinning me down.

"I'm sorry, little mate. I really am. I didn't mean to hurt you. I never did."

"I know. But…you went there. I didn't tell you for a reason. And I know you knew that. I thought you would start something, and you could have.

"And I would be caught up in everything again. I'm a weak little human, thrown into the deep end with wolves."

"You're not weak, and yes, you are small, but you're fierce. And they would never dare touch you, ever again. Never. I love you, Aurora," he admits.

I search his face for the truth—to see if he really loves me. And I think he's telling me the truth.

"I love you too," I confess, and he kisses me again.

I fall into the bed, relaxing, giving in to the safety he provides me with and the love he shows me.

"I'm scared."

I can't lose him; I don't want to lose him, ever. He's everything to me—everything and so much more. I feel whole when I'm with him, in a way that only people who have mates can understand.

There's no such thing as human soulmates. But wolves, wolves get them. And sometimes wolves get human mates. And I'm lucky enough to have him, an Alpha, someone who loves me, and someone I love back.

"I can protect you."

"I don't know if you can against this," I mumble as he sucks on my neck again, right where I want him to mark me.

"I'll protect you against anything and everything."

That's what I'm afraid of. He can't risk his life for me. Goddess knows I've had so many lives already, yet I'm only eighteen. I've died and revived and died again. I can't have him dying for me.

"You know I trust you, don't you?" I ask firmly. "Because I do. I trust you. I want you to know that."

"Yes, I do," he replies. "Do you trust me enough to let me make you Luna?"

Chapter 35

Virgin

RORY

His teeth graze my neck, my heart racing a thousand beats a minute and my breath hard and shallow.

He waits, asking for permission.

I can't even get any words out, so I bare my neck further for him, wanting him to do it, to get it over with. It'll hurt, I know it will. But I need him. I need him to complete me, to make us whole.

All I've ever wanted is to belong, to fit in somewhere, to have a real home. And as much as Mama tried, I just didn't belong there. I thought I wouldn't belong here either. But I was wrong. This is my home.

He's my home.

His teeth dig into my neck, making me let out a pained screech before sinking into delirious bliss. He moans, and the sound fills me with ecstasy. I feel like I'm floating.

"Are you okay?" he asks, stroking my cheek and breathing in my scent.

"I'm amazing," I tell him, reaching for the buttons of his shirt and peeling it off his muscled chest.

He helps me, tossing it across the room, over the Rory-proofing cushions.

I'm a virgin. It's pretty obvious to everyone, somehow. But I am.

And by tomorrow morning, I won't be.

But I won't lose it to just my first love. I'll lose my virginity to my first, my last, and my only love. He's my mate. Plus, I don't know how long I'll live with this impending doom.

I thought I would lose it to Eddie, after maybe a lot more months of dating, and then I would go to college and have normal human college experiences.

I still want to go to college. Although, I guess being Luna, that's not possible anymore.

"You have no idea how much I love you," he growls, sliding my top over my head and then throwing it across the room too.

He's seen me without my shirt on a couple of times. But he's never touched me. He wasn't sure if he wanted to mark me, and he didn't want to use me and then leave me. But he wants me now. He loves me.

"Tell me to stop, and I'll stop."

"I don't want you to stop. I want you. All of you," I tell him, giving him my permission to go all the way.

I reach around to unsnap my bra, which makes his breath hitch. He snatches it from me and just stares at my body.

"Fuck, you're so fucking beautiful," he mutters.

He undresses my bottom half, sliding off my panties slowly and intensely. And he removes his pants too, along with his briefs.

Being a virgin, and a real pure virgin who hasn't done anything other than kiss someone, I've never seen a…penis. What do I even do? Is that meant to go inside of me?

I didn't think it would be so big. And long. And…I don't know. I almost want to laugh, but I stifle it into a smile, which confuses him and makes him feel awkward. I can feel what he feels, with his mark on me.

"I'm sorry. I just… I've never seen one before," I say innocently.

"Oh, and it's funny, huh?" he replies with a smirk, taking my hand and placing it on his penis.

It feels… strange. But good strange. And he certainly likes it because his low groans fill my ears as I wrap my hand around it.

"Oh, fuck. Keep doing that and I'm gonna cum right now." He grabs my hands and plasters them to my side.

Then he presses my legs open, his breath on my private parts. "I love you, little one. You're amusing and adorable. You've never had someone touch you, have you?"

I shake my head, then bite my lip when his tongue touches me.

"Don't do that. Moan. And loudly. I want you screaming," he says, reaching up and removing my bottom lip from my teeth. "And you'll call me Alpha when we're doing this, hmm?"

"Yes, Alpha," I hum as his tongue moves back down between my folds, quickening in pace and building me up.

It's such a strange feeling. I like it. It's… different, and good. And I want more. His tongue swirls around and licks and sucks.

My whole body sparks, as though a match is being lit in every part of my body. My legs spasm, but he holds them down, pressed to the mattress.

That's when he slips a finger inside of me. And I gasp. And he chuckles. And I think I'm losing my mind here. I can barely think anymore. It's just him and me, and what we have together.

The finger starts to move, pumping in and out of me slowly, curling inside, whilst he continues to lick me. And I do just as he says, moaning loudly, not even in obedience but because I can't help it.

I'm at the edge. And I feel safe to fall off with Everett. Then he enters another finger, shocking my entire system and bringing me to the brink.

His fingers stretch my hole out, creating an uncomfortable feeling, but he makes up for it.

But then he just removes them. And I whine loudly at him. He chuckles, bringing his head up from between my legs to my face and pressing his lips to mine.

His penis pushes against my thigh, making liquid leak from me.

"This is gonna hurt, little one. You can tell me to stop and I won't be mad," he tells me sincerely, stroking my cheek with his hand.

"I don't want you to stop, Alpha," I reply.

"I'll be as gentle as I can, Aurora."

With that, he positions his penis before pushing his tip in slightly, easing it in as I whimper.

I try to silently squeak because I know he hates seeing me in pain, but he can feel it anyway, with the mark connecting us. I just hold on to his arms and squeeze to relieve a bit of the pain.

"I don't have to keep doing this, Aurora. I don't like hurting you."

"Don't stop. Please," I tell him, breathing through the pain.

He pushes in further, watching my face, wincing every so often as he does, but also growling in pleasure. Soon enough, I am too, moaning from the feeling of him inside of me.

"Ah… Alpha…" I start panting as he moves faster, sliding with the help of the liquid pouring out of me.

"You feel so good, Aurora… fuck… I fucking love you," he groans, his hands pushing up my legs and hugging them to his sides as he thrusts.

I can't even explain this feeling. It dulls any pain I once felt.

It connects me to him, like we belong together forever, like the only place I should be is with him, as close to him as I can get.

It's just me and him. Our sweat, our bare skin, our bodies becoming one.

Is mating like marriage? I never paid attention when people told me about mates growing up. I thought I would never have one. And now I do. And I'm not sure what all of this means.

But I do know that he loves me, and I love him, and this is both of us accepting each other into our lives forever. That should seem daunting, but it's not. It's... perfect.

I'm almost at the edge, at a climax higher than before, and I know he is too. I can feel it. And his growls get louder and lower and fiercer.

Tingles ripple throughout my body, a feeling between numbness and transcendence. My eyes widen and my lips form an *o* shape as I ride the feeling out, staring up at Everett and knowing all of this will change everything.

And I feel warm liquid squirt inside of me. I make a face at him, although it instills a warmth in me.

He chuckles a little, relief washing over him. A lazy grin takes hold of his face as he collapses beside me. Pulling me on top of him and tugging the sheets to cover us, he kisses the top of my head.

"What does this mean?" I ask in a small, tired voice, stroking his bare chest with my fingers just to feel its strength and power.

"Us mating? Me marking you? It means that you're my mate and my Luna. And you'll feel the strong emotions that I will feel, and I'll feel the strong emotions you will.

"We're connected now, fully, not just by the mate bond. We'll always be together and I'll always protect you, no matter what, I promise."

"Don't make that promise," I mutter. "I don't want you to get hurt protecting me."

"You don't have to worry about Alpha Nickolas and Luna Victoria. You're protected with me. They wouldn't dare go against me, and wouldn't win if they did.

"You're my Luna now. It's not just my desire or need, but my duty to protect you. I love you."

"I love you too."

It's not Nick and Victoria I'm worried about. It's "she." And I have this gnawing feeling inside that she's more powerful than even Everett can take on.

Chapter 36

Confrontation

RORY

"Morning, Alpha, morning...Luna," Ace greets us with a wide grin as Everett and I enter the kitchen, me in his arms because he thinks I've lost the use of my legs.

Cue eye roll, although it may be true—not just due to my clumsiness, but to the soreness between my legs.

Everett sets me down on the counter as usual, but with a smile adorning his face. He bends down to nuzzle my mark, and it surprisingly makes me moan. It's become a sweet spot.

"Please keep the PDA to a minimum. I had to hear it all last night," Lucius grumbles, strolling into the kitchen and glancing our way. "Morning, Alpha, Luna."

Even he is calling me Luna. Luna Rory. Well, Aurora. Everett calls me Aurora. I thought it was quite a Disney princess name. But it's Latin originally, before a children's princess took it.

I thought Rory suited me more, too—it's small, like me, casual, unisex. I just took to it.

But Aurora, Luna Aurora, it sounds...regal.

"Are you sure you want to go to school today?" Everett asks huskily, kissing my mark and tugging me closer to him. "I can think of other things I want to do."

I push him back playfully and make a face at him.

"Fine. We'll leave after you eat something." He taps my chin up before getting some cereal.

"Why are you still going to school? I mean, you're the Luna now, you don't need something to fall back on," Lucius says, leaning back in his seat at the table with a questioning expression.

"She wasn't going because she needed something to fall back on. She likes school, and if she likes it, she's going," Everett declares, flashing me a gorgeous smile.

I smile back. He's still letting me go to school, even though he's made me Luna, because he knows that I want to learn. He's perfect. And I know he can feel my joy at his words.

Once we arrive at school, I know the others will stick their noses into my private life again, although we did air some of our dirty laundry to them yesterday.

But since coming back to school, I've gotten nonstop questions about my relationship with Everett—from a lot of people. And more guys are hitting on me than before, but I just ignore them.

At lunch, because Bethany is more interested in me, she sits with me, Freya, and Skye, thus, so do Oliver and his friends. And now Jax too.

I guess it's because I'm not a boring Goody Two-shoes anymore, being with a grown man like Everett.

But I was never boring. I couldn't say anything about my life, and it's not like anyone really cared to pry. They accepted my excuse of having a strict mom. That was all I had to say.

I kiss Everett goodbye before clambering out of the car carefully, minding my step, and I watch him drive off. My friends, and well, Oliver and his friends, just watch, and expect some sort of explanation.

So, I decide to ignore them all and head inside by myself.

I don't want to be bombarded this early in the morning, particularly as I had such a good night and a good morning. I don't want them breaking my high and tearing me down.

I'm in love with Everett, and we connected our hearts, minds, and souls last night. They have no idea how that feels, and they can't understand. And I'm not explaining it.

They'll just tell me I'm brainwashed again.

In all honesty, if Freya was dating this guy and describing a feeling like I have now, I would believe she was brainwashed and tell her to stay away from him.

Everett and I are the equivalent of married, and we haven't known each other for too long—just a few months.

Like Everett, I lose all reasonable thought when I'm with my mate, when generally I'm quite reasonable.

Common sense doesn't bewilder me, and I know why Freya and Skye, and Eddie, are concerned, but he's my mate, and I know him. And they will never understand that.

Bethany just acts amazed at how I got him, and always pries about what's going on between us.

Instead, I steer our conversations toward her relationship with Oliver, which always just seems to be the same. I think she's getting bored with him.

I make it through the whole morning—luckily with no classes with any of them—without a single confrontation.

I know our fight yesterday may have seemed pretty dramatic, especially since they had no idea what we were even fighting about.

But it was dramatic. He went back to my old home. And Mama is missing. And Nick and Victoria are acting like they didn't kill me.

They believed they killed me—not let me be mauled by

rogues like I told Everett—but fully killed me, slit my throat. If, no, *when* they see me again, with not even a scar, they'll know something isn't right.

But it was unavoidable, right?

Perhaps I should have rejected Everett at the beginning. But at the beginning, I just thought the threat was Nick and Victoria.

Everett can protect me from them, so I thought staying with him would be the safest place to be. Then I started falling for him, and it was a steep fall.

I had no idea about Achlys or "she." And now he could be in danger, the pack could be in danger, because I'm there.

I don't want to get Everett hurt, and now I can't turn back. It was too late to reject him, or to make him reject me. How do I even tell him? Will he hate me for keeping it from him?

He knows I have secrets, he told me that. But he says he trusts me. I'm not sure he should. I'm not safe. I'm dangerous.

I always have been, with this clumsiness curse. Maybe it really is a curse. The ironic curse: the girl who can't die is the most likely to die.

As I sit down for lunch, it's unavoidable when the whole table fills up with questioning faces. Even Oliver looks deadly curious. And even Eddie now sits back at the table, his curiosity outweighing his pain and pride.

"What the hell happened yesterday?"

"You're staying with him?"

"Did you make up with him?"

"Are you okay?"

I'm bombarded with a million questions, and then Bethany exclaims, "Is that a hickey?"

I had completely forgotten about the mark and how it would look to everyone here.

Aurora's Secret

Back in the pack, it shows that Everett and I have accepted each other and that I'm their new Luna, even though they can all feel it. I'm a part of their pack, an actual member.

When Everett mated with me, he gave me ties to the pack, real ties, and a feeling of belonging. I'm the Luna.

"Did you have sex with him?" Bethany questions, her face shocked and excited at the same time.

The same can't be said for Freya, Skye, and Eddie, who look horrified. And Jax just looks pissed.

"Shit, you're glowing. Was he good?"

I just remain silent. She knows I'm not going to answer a question like that.

"I can't believe you actually slept with him," Skye hisses next to me.

I understand her reaction, but I had hoped she could support my choices.

"Did he force you?" Jax asks, leaning back in his chair and scowling.

"No, he didn't force me," I reply definitively.

"Why are you living with him?" Eddie asks. "What about your mom? What does she have to say about all of this?"

I decide it's time to come clean, as close to the truth as is affordable, just to make this all easier.

None of them have ever really known anything about me, and when Everett came along, it piqued their interest.

They decided that my life may actually be interesting after all. I have to give them something to get them off my back.

"My mom is missing," I admit, sighing. "That's what the fight was about yesterday. I was bullied back in the neighborhood I was living in and they were awful to me. They tried to hurt me so I ran away.

"I was hurt and tired, and Everett and his friends found

me, took me to a hospital. I had nowhere to go and Everett was there for me. And we started dating and I live with him.

"Yesterday, Everett went back to my old neighborhood to talk to my mom, tell her that I'm safe. He also met the people who hurt me. But my mom wasn't there. She's gone missing in the woods; no one has seen her."

They all just remain silent, some feeling awkward because they barely know or talk to me, and others feeling awkward because they think they're supposed to know me.

"I call bullshit," Jax declares with an accusing tone, a sour look on his face still.

I guess he doesn't like the fact that I slept with Everett, especially after the fight he tried to provoke. And he did provoke it. Although Everett was lying.

"About what?" I ask, raising my eyebrows at him.

"All of it. Why would you run away? What about your mom? Why would you just leave her? Wouldn't you just move, both of you?" he questions.

"She's lived there her whole life. She has friends, even though some people have treated her badly. I'm adopted, so I don't feel the same ties, and I couldn't ask her to leave with me," I explain.

"You're adopted?" Freya asks, and Eddie and Skye look like they want to know the answer to that too.

I really did tell them nothing. I didn't even know they didn't know I was adopted.

Technically, I wasn't adopted, just found in the woods. But Mama took me in as her own and raised me. I'd call that adopting.

"Yeah, when I was three. I guess that's why they bullied me," I answer.

"What does 'hurt' mean? You said they hurt you. Did

they just say some mean things and you decided to run away?" Oliver questions skeptically.

"They...had a knife, chasing me through the woods. They're psycho."

"They tried to kill you?" Eddie exclaims.

Chapter 37

Answers

---•❖•---

RORY

"How do you piss someone off that much that they want to kill you?" Oliver questions, again skeptically.

"I don't know if killing me was the goal." Yes, I do. They did kill me. And I apparently did piss them off that much.

"Why didn't you say anything then?" Jax asks.

"I mean, you don't act like a girl who ran away from people who tried to hurt you. You're just…normal. You do your work, you eat lunch, and you get picked up and dropped off every day."

"How am I supposed to act then?" I ask in an irked tone.

"Terrified. Scared other people would hurt you. Upset that you had to leave home," Eddie lists in response to Jax's question. "Why didn't you tell any of us what was happening at home? We could have helped."

"By doing what? My personal life has stayed personal up till now for a reason. I came to school because I have friends and a place to get away from all of it. I didn't want to share it. And I am scared.

"But I have a boyfriend who protects me. He's given me a home. I'd appreciate it if all of you could stop casting your judgment like you know either of us. You didn't even know I was adopted until two minutes ago.

"And Everett isn't married, nor does he have a secret family. I live with him.

"Every day, I sleep in his room on his bed which he calls Aurora-proofed because he put a barrier of cushions on either side so I wouldn't fall off.

"You can all stop prying and giving advice on what's best because none of you know," I rant, huffing at the end, getting out of my seat and marching outside for some air.

Everything feels different now. I feel stronger—a bonus of mating with a powerful Alpha. I think he's sharing some of that power with me, the strength and will to say what's necessary. He can probably feel my distress.

I can feel him working, decisions weighing on him. I feel his burdens, his responsibilities, how much it affects him. I knew he took them seriously, but this extensively, I had no idea.

And I'm another responsibility, another burden, although he wouldn't call me that. But I am. I am a burden. And he doesn't even know how big a burden I really am, and might be in the near future.

"I'm sorry," a voice from behind me mutters. Freya settles beside me against the gates.

"Freya, I don't need an apology. It's not necessary. I just want you to understand that when I say Everett is good for me, I mean it, and I know that he is."

"I just... I can't believe you lost your virginity," she says with a giggle, nudging me playfully. I giggle with her and bite my lip. "How was it?"

"Amazing," I reply. "Everett was gentle. And I've never seen him so playful and happy. It made me happy."

"You're in love with him?" she asks.

"Yes. Maybe too much, if that's possible. I don't know, he just seems to understand me. He can read me really well. Like whenever I hurt myself, I just brush it off and say it's fine even if it's painful.

"But he can always tell, and then he carries me or bandages me up and calls me clumsy whilst incredibly concerned at the tiniest injury. I've never had a protector like that before," I explain.

"He just sounds so perfect for you, I was surprised you could find someone like that."

"What about you? A guy you have a crush on? Still Jax?" I question.

She told me a few weeks ago about him, but was vague. I had no idea who he was. But I think it's faded seeing the interest Jax has in me.

He's only interested, like the other guys, because I'm someone they can't have, and I'm the girlfriend of a guy like Everett.

Everett's sexy, somewhat rich, dominant, proud, and respected—not to mention, older than everyone here.

He's a grown man, and the testosterone in guys makes them believe it's about beating the strongest guy around.

Which means hitting on me. It's not that they actually like me. Though maybe they've convinced themselves they do.

"No. Not anymore. There's one guy, but it's a small thing and I don't want to tell you yet unless it becomes bigger. Sometimes you have small things for many people and then you crush hard on someone.

"I haven't even had a boyfriend at eighteen, and you sound like you're ready to get married," she says with a chuckle.

She's not far off though. I practically am married. Freya's a great person—fun, sweet, generous—but she's shy and sometimes quiet. That's the result of years of bullying wrecking her self-confidence.

"Rory!" Eddie calls out, stalking over to me with Oliver, Bethany, Jax, and Skye following.

Aurora's Secret

I stand up, dusting myself off, and step back to create distance between Eddie and me as he comes closer.

"I can't touch you now?"

"No," I mutter, taking another step back.

"Living with him, it's brainwashed you. You're detached and you spend all your free time with him. He doesn't let you go out or do anything," Eddie exclaims, stepping closer.

"He doesn't even want me touching you. That's insane."

"I agree. What's the shit with the touching?" Jax says, inching closer to me and Eddie and shaking his head.

I take another step back, onto the sidewalk outside the school to create more distance.

"It's just his thing. He's protective and I like protective."

"That's not protective. That's just mental. But he's not even here and you're still backing away," Jax states.

I back out again and it all happens so suddenly. But it's just my luck, I guess.

And now I'm back in limbo.

It's the clumsiness, really. I took another step back and fell off the sidewalk into the road right when a car was zooming past. And it barreled into me at top speed.

It really, really hurt. I mean, it killed me after all. Broke a lot of bones. I heard most of them cracking.

It was... so strange. It came right at me, sending a shudder throughout my body from the impact, and toppling me. The wheels crushed me—my arms and legs.

How do I explain surviving this? That's *if* I survive. After all, I'm in limbo now, where "she" can get to me.

"You shouldn't be back here," the voice of Achlys utters hauntingly.

Her voice is a sad one, empty, hollow. It sounds like it would through a microphone, only in a big hall. It projects, yet it's melancholy, like the voice of a ghost.

"I got run over by a car."

"I know. With the curse she put on you, I'm surprised I don't see you here more often," she states. "The curse of clumsiness as a human."

So I am cursed. That actually makes me feel better, knowing there's a reason behind it.

"Who is 'she'?"

"Her name is Nemesis. She took you from your family and tried to kill you when you were a child, in rogue territory. The first time you died and came to me. You don't remember it, of course, you were only young."

"Why do you bring me back to life?"

"It's not by choice. Your presence here is not correct. You cannot be here, so I have to give you a push back into your body, back where you should be.

"But, she can get you in here, which is why she cursed you, knowing she'd get quite a few chances."

"Why does she want to kill me?"

"Your parents wronged her. And she requires vengeance."

"My parents? Do you know who they are?"

Just as she's about to answer, a gust of… something like icy wind… flies around us.

"She's here again. You have to go, Aurora. Try to be careful. I hope to not see you here. Inside packs and human lands are safe.

"Your mate, he's safe, he's an Alpha after all. He'll protect you as best as he can. Goodbye, Aurora."

Before I can question anything she has said, I'm pushed, *hard*, back through that green door of life, back into my body.

Which appears to be in a hospital.

"She's de—" My eyes flicker open and I hear faint gasps.

I'm incredibly tired, and a wave of exhaustion washes over me, knocking me out. But I have questions swimming around my head.

She knew about Everett. What does that mean?

What did my parents do to this otherworldly being? Who are they, even?

Why is Nemesis coming after me? Thanks to her, I don't even know my parents. I can't be held responsible for anything they have done.

But Achlys said Everett will protect me, and I know that to be true.

Chapter 38

Blame

EVERETT

A SLICING PAIN RIPS THROUGH ME LIKE A DAGGER TO the heart, and soul, and mind. And a scorching heat rushes through my body, making me clench my fists in pain in front of my Beta and Gamma.

"Alpha, what's happening?"

"Mate. She's… She's hurt," Chaos cries, distressed and heartbroken.

"She's not just hurt. She's… She's dead."

My heart is shattering into a thousand pieces. I can barely move without pain shuddering through me with a vengeance.

I need to go to Aurora. She can't be dead, I won't allow it. She can't die. I promised I would protect her. I promised.

"Aurora," I breathe out, clutching my heart and my head as I writhe on the ground.

Our mate bond has only just been solidified. It's the most tender time for us to be apart, let alone for one of us to be hurt.

She's at school. How is she not safe? Is it my fault? Did Nickolas and Victoria do this? Did I tip them off? I promised to protect her. I would do so with my life.

And yet…she is dying, maybe dead already. I need to get to her.

"What about her?" Lucius questions, crouching down to yank me up into my seat.

"She's hurt. She's..." I tune in to my waning connection to her, locating where she is so I can go to her. As I thought, she is in an ambulance, heading to a human hospital.

They'll better treat her there at least. The doctors here might not know how to help her. Someone needs to help her. I can't lose her. I can't live without her. My Luna.

"Get me to the human hospital close to here. Hurry! She's dying."

They haul me out and into a car. I'm in agony in the back seat, aching for my mate. My beautiful mate. She's clumsy, perhaps she is merely hurt. I hope that is true.

But it's not. I can feel it. I can feel her, her life force drained from her body. She's just a shell. She's dead already. But I am not giving up. I will never give up.

It feels like the longest drive possible. The human hospital is farther than the school is from the pack, which makes every minute excruciating.

My mate is suffering, and it was my duty to prevent that. She is my duty, my heart, my life. My beautiful Aurora.

When we arrive at the hospital, the pain begins to dull. Perhaps it's because I'm close to her now. I hope it's not because she's already gone and it's too late.

I run, as fast as I can, and when I spot her friends, huddled around with horrified expressions, I hurry over to them.

"Where is she?!" I exclaim, startling them.

"She's in the ER; they can't find a pulse," a girl says, tears filling her eyes and rolling down her cheeks.

She can't be dead. She can't. She's my life.

"Fuck...," Lucius mutters.

But Ace, he stays silent. He doesn't seem upset or

concerned. He almost seems curious. Like he knows something, or is waiting to know something.

We wait.

And wait.

And wait.

It wouldn't be like this if she was in the pack hospital. I could be by her side; I could help her. I could at least quell her suffering. But all I can do is wait.

When the doctors come out, I rush inside, not knowing the outcome.

"She's de—"

Like life itself has been thrust back into me, every ache and pain leaves my body. My heart is fixed, and I feel the beating heart of my mate, Aurora.

She's alive. I couldn't feel her, and now I can.

How is that possible? How is any of this possible?

I catch sight of my mate with doctors and nurses gathered around her, shocked expressions etched across their faces. I push through them, not caring about the protests, and clasp the hand of my now-alive mate.

I'm not even sure she died. She can't have. Although some humans die for a minute before regaining life. Humans call them miracles, although us wolves have never experienced anything like that.

When wolves are dying, there's nothing that can be done except easing their pain. Their wolf-healing genes ensure that any injury can be healed, as long as it isn't too grave.

But Aurora isn't a wolf. And that's what scares me even more. She doesn't heal like I'm used to, and she's fragile.

I can't take losing her, not now that I'm so in love with her that any future I can imagine will always include her by my side, my Luna.

"Sir, we need you to leave," someone declares.

"I'm not leaving my girlfriend," I state, clutching her hand in mine to feel her touch.

"Is there someone we should call? Family?" the doctor questions.

"No, she lives with me. I'm her family."

She's my family. She's the Luna of the pack, my family. She's the equivalent to my queen and wife.

"What happened to her? How badly is she hurt?"

"She was hit by a car. Her heart stopped for fifteen minutes, and that's when we got her in here. A pulse couldn't be felt."

"But she's alive."

"Yes, she is. It's a miracle. She has sustained many severe injuries. The hit damaged her spine; she may not ever walk again.

"Both her legs are broken and an arm. A few ribs also. If she survives, she'll have to be cared for extensively. She has no family?"

"Her mother is missing. I'll look after her," I state firmly.

I stay with her for hours, waiting for her to awaken. I just want to know if she's suffering. What if she never walks again? I would always care for her, but losing the use of her legs, I can't imagine that.

But I will be here. Forever. She got hit by a car? Why? How? Even she is not that clumsy, is she? It's because of those "friends" of hers. I know it is.

"Everett," a small raspy voice calls out, a little squeeze of the hand in my own.

Her gorgeous green eyes flicker open, dazzling me again. She has small and large cuts over her face and neck, and most probably all of her body if I could see it.

The one person I vowed I would protect merely this

morning is the person lying here in front of me, paralyzed, pained, and panicked.

Her eyes dart around the room to figure out her surroundings, but they settle on me and she sighs. "You're here."

"Of course I'm here, little one. I'm so sorry."

"Why? Did you run me over?" she asks with a small pained giggle.

"I promised to protect you."

She sighs and shakes her head at me.

"You can't protect me from everything, Everett. You have to accept that. Some things are beyond your control."

"Are you in pain?"

"No."

"Liar," I reply with a chuckle. "Seriously, little mate. Are you in pain? I can help, a bit. My touch, it will ease it."

"Can you...lie in bed with me? I-I can't feel my legs; I can't move my bottom half. I'm scared," she says.

Her words break my heart, but I attempt to keep it together, for her. She's being so strong; I can't be the one to break down.

"Anything for you, little one." I get out of my seat from beside her and lift her to get in slightly under her. "How did it happen?"

"I fell into the road."

"You're leaving something out. Lying to me again?"

"I fell, Everett. That's all."

"You died briefly. It's not a 'that's all' thing. That's serious. I can't lose you. I can't ever lose you. Your 'friends,' what happened?"

"Nothing happened. Leave it, Everett. Just hold me. I'm tired," she whispers.

Once she falls asleep again, I leave her room to speak with Lucius and Ace, only to be stopped by her so-called friends.

Aurora's Secret

"How is she?" a girl, Freya, asks.

"Paralyzed. A lot of her bones are broken. She's tired. You should all go home," I tell them.

"So you can brainwash her some more. Where is her family?" Jax questions like the annoying asshole he is.

"I'm her family. And this doesn't concern you. So go home," I state firmly, almost growling. "Or maybe you want to tell me how she ended up in the middle of the road at lunch?"

"It's because of you. Because you brainwashed her. She backs away when anyone tries to touch her. Anyone but you. You did this," Jax argues.

They tried to touch her. Jax tried to touch her and she stepped back. I guess that is my fault. And she is my responsibility. I'm supposed to protect her.

"You all stay the fuck away from her," I growl lowly. "Stay away."

CHAPTER 39

Freedom

---•◆•---

RORY

"**A**RE YOU JUST GOING TO CARRY ME EVERYWHERE? They gave me a wheelchair for a reason," I complain, staring up at Everett as he settles me on the kitchen counter for breakfast.

I've been home one day. After the accident on Friday, Everett insisted on taking me home quite soon, and now, Sunday, he's still carrying me everywhere. I haven't even used my wheelchair yet.

I doubt he'll ever let me return to school. He's terrified he'll lose me. Thus, he plans to be by my side all the time, so he can prevent any danger from coming my way.

But against Nemesis, I'm not sure even he can protect me. Sure, I'm safe inside this pack, beside its powerful Alpha, but Nemesis isn't of this world, which means she's probably powerful.

Although, if she's so powerful, how am I not dead already? I'm not powerful, I'm not special, I'm just a human. Achlys said my presence was not right in limbo, or wherever people go when they're dead.

I'm not sure what that means. I'm not sure what any of it means.

And now, I'm supposed to act paralyzed, at least for a while. My legs are broken, as are my ribs and my arm, but I'm no longer paralyzed.

Recovery doesn't miraculously happen though—especially not to weak little humans like me. And over a shorter time than should be possible, my bones will fix also.

I predict that within the week, I'll be healthy once more. And that is impossible for a human, maybe even for a wolf.

"You're not using that death trap. You'll probably get hurt again if you use it," he scolds, pressing a kiss to my lips.

The pack has been a little restless since my accident, some claiming that I shouldn't be their Luna. I haven't even been named as his Luna officially yet, but there hasn't been time with everything that has happened.

I died. Again. Not the first time, or the second, and definitely not the last, although that may be approaching. Even the name *Nemesis* doesn't fill me with security.

She wants vengeance for something my birth parents did, whoever they are. Maybe I can find out before I meet her, and find out about her.

But, that's only if I can get away from Everett long enough or research discreetly. He allows me to visit the orphanage, but only if he accompanies me.

A few weeks later, with Everett on my last nerve with his hovering, I sit, bored, in his office, having read the same book in my hand five times.

Pretending to have two broken legs and a broken arm is incredibly difficult, and it makes me dependent. Although, Everett's happy to be depended on.

He's more than happy to help me shower and change. He tries to hide his grin, but I know it's there. It's the mate bond. Like I know he knows I'm bored and fed up.

"Everett, can we do something?" I plead, pouting at him in hopes of getting my way. "The kids wanted to go to the mall, and I need an outing. I'm trying to regain the use of my legs in these leg braces."

"Leaving the pack? I want you to be safe, and safe is in the pack," Everett states.

I pout even more, appealing to the side that wants to please me. But his protective nature as Alpha and my mate overwhelms everything else usually.

"Alpha, please." I flutter my eyelashes flirtatiously and unbutton my shirt.

He just stares at my hands on my shirt, taking in a breath. "Please."

I work my way down the shirt until it's completely open so that he can see my bra. I bite my lip and lean over toward him.

"Aurora…stop it," he warns, clenching his fists in an attempt to control his lust.

"Stop what?" I ask innocently.

I would walk over to him if I could. Well, I can, it just wouldn't be the smartest move.

I was given leg braces that I can actually walk with a few days ago, and a brace for my arm too. But it doesn't look sexy to hobble over to him.

"And I thought you were a good girl, little mate. Fine, we'll take the kids and go to the mall. But if I tell you to do something, like if I decide I should carry you, I'm carrying you and you have to deal with it. Yes?"

"Yes," I squeal, excited.

He rolls his eyes and stalks over to me, picking me up so my legs are on either side of him, and attacks my neck with his mouth.

"You should be in trouble for that, but I liked seeing my innocent little mate trying to get her way by seducing me."

He brushes my hair away from my face, so that it's behind my shoulder, and smiles sadly at me.

"I just want you to be safe. I don't mean to make you upset with me, little one. But if it means keeping you protected, I'll do it."

"I was hit by a car, Everett. You would never let that happen. I'll be safe with you at the mall with the kids," I tell him, pecking his lips and easing his worry.

All the kids clamber into the SUV that Nellie uses for driving them around. They start singing and jumping around as Everett drives off, almost getting tangled in their seatbelts.

"Remember, this was your idea," Everett grumbles as the kids are chatting and giggling in the back.

"I know," I reply.

We reach the mall, constantly head-counting the eleven kids we have with us. At least Orion and Cassidy are older, so there's less to worry about with them.

The two little kids grab my hands, steadying me while also dragging me along with them while the other kids cluster around Everett, their Alpha after all.

They like how much time Everett has been spending with them, since he comes with me to visit. And the other kids at school, the bullies, have actually backed off, hearing that their Alpha is hanging out with the orphaned kids.

After all, both Everett and I are orphans ourselves—at least I think I am. If Nemesis is after me, that probably means my parents have already been dealt with, perhaps by her, perhaps not.

But my mama is missing, too, so I don't have any parents anymore. Everett and the pack are my family now.

As we watch the kids outside of a toy store at the mall, Everett buys some milkshakes for us. Before we can sit down, we're stopped by the sight of Oliver and Bethany, who are making their way over to us.

"Rory, hey, we haven't seen you in weeks," Bethany says, looking at me and my casts pitifully, as does Oliver.

"Well, I'm recovering from all the broken bones. They're healing quite quickly, though, so I hope to be back on my feet properly in no time," I explain with a bright smile to tell her I'm okay.

"When are you coming back to school?" Oliver asks.

I glance over at Everett, who holds a stern face, and I sigh. I do want to go back to school, but I understand Everett's fear.

"Um…I don't know," I reply vaguely.

"Rory!" Orion exclaims, rushing out of the shop and grabbing my hand, elated. "There's this toy that's so cool. It's got a controller and it flies. Please can I get it?"

I grin at his enthusiasm.

"You'll have to ask the boss man. He has the money," I whisper, looking back at Everett, who can clearly hear me.

"But you're his mate. Can you ask him?" he whispers back.

"I'll see what I can do."

Orion rushes back off over to the other kids.

I turn to Everett with a bright smile, which he scoffs at. But he nods anyway.

"Who are they?" Bethany asks, furrowing her brows as she looks in the direction that Orion ran off to.

"We help out at an orphanage and those are the kids. They're great, and Everett and I are both orphans, too, so we know what it feels like."

Bethany sends me a small smile.

"Rory," Cassidy calls out, taking the milkshake from my hands and sipping on it.

I give her a look, but she carries on drinking the stolen milkshake.

"Who are you?" she asks Bethany and Oliver.

"We're friends of Rory's from school," Bethany replies.

"Oh, right, the human school," Cassidy says, taking another sip before wandering off to Orion.

Human school? Did she really just say that?

Bethany and Oliver just look confused at her statement, but they decide to brush it off.

They hook arms as they watch my and Everett's positions next to each other. Everett's arm is wrapped around my waist tightly, slightly lifting me with his wolf strength to keep me off my perfectly healthy feet.

"We should be going. Bye," Everett declares without even waiting for a reply.

I can't take him anywhere. "That was rude," I scold.

"No, little one. That was necessary. You're not talking to them anymore. They got you hurt."

"No, they didn't. And I want to go back to school, Everett. I'll wait until I'm all better, which is going to be soon, but I've already missed a lot this year and these past few weeks."

He's about to protest, but I cut in.

"I'm not asking. You can't control me. We're partners, Alpha and Luna. I'm not someone you can just order about. But I want you to be okay with it."

He stares at me, assessing my serious expression and the look in my eyes.

"Okay, little one. But you'll stay away from Jax and Eddie. They were the ones who made you fall into the road, and they're too…in love with you. Please. That one condition."

"Okay."

Chapter 40

Love

RORY

"I haven't seen you in forever," Freya exclaims as she spots me in the halls, one brace still on my arm for show. "Are you okay?"

"Yeah, I'm better now. It just took some time to heal. Plus, Everett was hesitant to take me back to school considering I died for a few minutes in addition to all the injuries," I explain, walking beside her.

"I still can't believe you just live with him. So he decided whether you come to school or not?" she asks.

"Well, I told him I was going back to school whether he liked it or not, and eventually he just agreed to it. I can't get here without a car, so I did need him to like it," I tell her.

We begin to chat about gossip that's been around the school for the past few weeks. A lot of looks are being sent my way; everyone has either heard about my accident or seen me be taken off the road just outside the school.

Skye joins us, greeting me, then we break away from our classes.

"You're back," Jax comments. I forgot this was the lesson I have with him. "I can't believe the puppeteer let you out of his grip."

I decide to ignore that comment, waiting patiently for the teacher to enter.

"What do you see in him? Is it the money? Looks? Babe, I can give you anything. My dad is CFO of a massive tech company. If that's what you want, you don't need him."

I huff loudly to show him I'm not engaging in this conversation.

"Come on, Rory. You're not talking to me now?"

"Not if you're berating my relationship. We can talk about the book we're reading in this class if you want," I reply.

He chuckles at my response and leans back in his chair. "You know, Oliver and the other guys told me you were shy and sweet and innocent.

"When I asked about you because I had an interest in you, they laughed and told me you'd probably be easy, too, from the attention and my charm.

"But since I've known you, you've been anything but shy, sweet, and innocent.

"You're sassy, you can talk back, and you had sex with your adult manipulative boyfriend. You're nothing like they described; they don't even know what they described anymore.

"One guy changed you? And you don't even know it."

"It's not just him, although I'm grateful for him. Being sweet and shy and innocent has only ever gotten me hurt. Unfortunately the other thing that gets me hurt is my clumsiness, which I can't help.

"But I'd rather not almost die again with something I can change," I tell him seriously, and his eyebrows furrow at me.

He pauses, and I think I've stumped him. He just stares at me, and doesn't even stop when the teacher enters and begins the lesson. He keeps doing it throughout the lesson too.

"Does it hurt? I know you broke a lot of bones in the accident," he asks in a whisper.

"No, I'm better now. It's just my arm. I've been immobile for a while. I couldn't walk for three weeks and then I had to wear leg braces."

"How did you do anything then? I can't imagine not being able to walk," he comments.

"Everett helped. He stopped me from using the wheelchair where he could, just because he thought, with all that metal and the wheels, I'd probably hurt myself even more.

"And he's right. I've hurt myself just eating with a fork," I say.

He laughs quietly, shaking his head lightly.

"He doesn't even let me near most things in the kitchen. He sits me up on the counter and I just watch him cook.

"I slipped in the shower a couple of times, so he made the floor in there foam and fixed the settings to one place so I can't accidentally turn it up and burn myself."

He just stares again, completely fixated on me.

"Why would he do all of that? What does he get?" he questions.

"Because he loves me. But before, it was because I was his responsibility. He found me and helped me and decided that he was responsible for me because I had no one.

"The first thing that I respected about him was his sense of duty. He's not manipulative, or my puppeteer.

"He can be overprotective, most of the time, but I know it's for a reason and I know it's because he cares, and not anything malicious. I'm sorry that you like me and I don't like you back.

"I mean, I think you're a good guy. But I don't need someone trying to ruin my relationship so they can have one with me. You wouldn't like me anyway.

"I'm clumsy as shit, as most people tell me, I'm reading most of the time, I'm quite fragile and small and weak. And I've been through a lot. I'm…complicated."

"Yes, you are. You're very complicated. I don't even understand it. Any of it. Everything you said that happened back where you lived, that's insane.

"I'll back off though. You've found someone already, I'll respect that. But if he hurts you, or you don't like him anymore, you can come to me."

"Love," I correct. "I love him. And thanks. There's plenty of girls here though who have a crush on you. You can take your pick and have a new interest."

When lunch rolls around, Skye and Freya are arguing about whether the tater tots are healthy or not. Bethany, Oliver, and Jax decide to join us as usual.

Bethany and Oliver are disagreeing over some petty thing.

Their relationship appears solid, although Bethany was always complaining to me about Oliver before my little sabbatical, and she still does.

He's cheated on her a couple of times, just kissing people at the many parties he goes to. I would tell her she could do better, but now, I don't want to be a hypocrite.

I tell all of them that I can make my own decisions about my relationships, so I can no longer comment on other people's in such a way. But I still believe she could do better.

A tap comes at the window and I'm surprised to see Everett, dressed in a hot leather jacket with a white shirt underneath. He gestures for me to come out to him with his finger in that Alpha commanding way.

"Get your stuff. You're leaving school early today," he declares, muffled through the glass.

I nod and sling my bag over my back, heading out of the canteen to see what Everett wants. Before I reach his car, I hear

Eddie call out to me. I sigh, knowing this may be a big thing yet again.

Everett just watches, and even though Eddie believes we are far enough away for Everett not to hear anything we're saying, I know his wolf hearing is very superior to my own and he can easily hear us.

"Don't go with him," Eddie pleads, a pained expression on his face. "I know you're scared, but you don't have to be with him because you think you have no choice. I love you. I'm in love with you, Rory. Don't go with him."

What is he talking about? He loves me? This is crazy. I'm with Everett, in love with Everett. Why is Eddie saying this?

"I love Everett. We were only together for a month, Eddie. I don't know what you want me to say."

"How can you love a guy like that?" he questions, glancing over my shoulder at him. "He's possessive and violent and controlling. You love that?"

I look back at Everett, noticing that he's waiting for my answer, raising his eyebrows at me to Eddie's question.

"He's aggressive when he's protecting someone or something he cares about. He's incredibly protective and he hates seeing me hurt. He's an amazing guy and I love him. I have to go," I conclude, beginning to walk away.

But Eddie grabs my hand, which alarms me, especially with Everett as an onlooker. It's safe to say he'll be an onlooker no more.

I'm yanked away from Eddie by the waist and lifted into the air, my back hitting a broad muscled chest. My body becomes locked to this chest by tree-trunk-like arms caging me in.

"Lay a hand on what's mine again and I won't control my temper next time," Everett growls loud enough for Eddie to hear.

He breathes in my scent to soothe him, nuzzling his head

into my neck, which lifts me even farther off the ground. "Are you hurt, little one?"

He's acting as if Eddie's touch burned me, but I understand his Alpha and mate protectiveness. I'm Everett's and he's mine. It's an insanely strong connection between us, now that we're mated.

Being away from him physically pains me, creating this dull ache in my heart that gets stronger the farther I am from him.

But when we're together, right up against each other, everything feels perfect, and it's hard to be mad at him for such protectiveness, when I can understand it. I would do anything to keep Everett with me and safe as well.

"I'm fine, Everett," I mutter. "Where are we going?"

"Get in the car and I'll tell you on the way back home," he replies, setting me down on his other side, away from Eddie and closer to the car.

He nudges me toward his car as he takes my bag from me and follows after me, completely ignoring Eddie standing there.

Once we're strapped in and Everett pulls out of the lot, I ask the question again.

"We're going to the annual conference I told you about. Don't worry, little mate. I won't let anyone hurt you."

Chapter 41

Enemy

———•◆•———

RORY

I'm lost in a whirlwind of thought and worry. My anxiety is tenfold watching Everett pack some things to take with us for the week.

"Aurora, I can feel your panic. I told you, you have nothing to fear," Everett says once more, pecking my lips in an attempt to ease my nerves.

He picks me up and hugs me close to him, like I'm a monkey clinging onto a tree. I'm tired and scared and I don't want to go.

I hide my face in Everett's neck, comforted by his smell and his overall aura. It's the Alpha aura and mate aura that makes me feel so protected, and the love I can feel from him.

"I don't want to go," I whine, hugging him even tighter.

"Why? Nothing will happen. I'll be there, right next to you, all the time. Hmm?" He strokes my hair and tilts his head against mine for more skin contact.

"You're my Luna and my mate. Someone tries to hurt you, I'll kill them."

I'm going to have to wrap my neck so that it appears as though I'm just hiding the scar Nick and Victoria created when they slit my throat. In reality, I'm hiding the fact that I have no scar.

"I love you, Aurora."

"I love you too. I'm just scared. But it'll be fine. I have you." I reassure him that I'll be fine whilst he finishes packing.

"You're not mad about the thing with your ex-boyfriend, are you?" he asks, zipping our bags up and tugging me to my feet.

"No, I'm not. He was being weird," I comment, thinking back to all of it.

From the moment Everett put me back in school, things have been strange between me and Eddie—and then there's the whole thing with Jax too.

"Get your shoes on, little one," he orders, grabbing his car keys and discussing something with his Beta.

With this being a big wolf conference thing, many of the pack members are attending—many warrior wolves to protect their Alpha and Luna; the Beta and Gamma to join the discussions; and Ophelia is even coming, advising Everett.

There will be plenty of wolves to protect me.

After what is already a long drive, I find out we're only halfway there. Everett swaps driving with one of the warrior wolves in the car, and he sits with me in the back seat.

Dragging me onto his lap so I can have a comfortable sleep, he straps us in together and lulls me to sleep by stroking my back.

When we reach the place, it surprises me how tall the buildings are, and that they don't get any human visitors who accidentally wander through.

Everett tells me it's because they got a witch to cloak the place. I'm not sure how that even works, but it does.

They don't like humans, they just tolerate them, and that's for now. How will they react to me? Will it make Everett seem weaker because he has a weak human mate?

I don't want to harm his reputation among these wolves,

particularly because even I know that the Shadow Blood pack is one of the most powerful packs in the country—I knew that before I even met Everett.

And that means Everett is seen as one of the most powerful Alphas. But with a new human mate, he may look weaker.

Lunas are meant to strengthen the pack, sharing the load with the Alpha successfully. But I'm human.

I hold Everett's hand tightly as we enter a massive building joined to an even bigger one. Everett explains that this is where we are staying for the week, and the conjoining building is the wolf headquarters.

They make laws, set boundaries, handle external pack disputes. The council.

We have a good night's sleep, with me cuddled up soundly in Everett's big arms. He makes sure to strap me down with them since we no longer have the Aurora-proofed bed.

In the morning, we eat a quick breakfast before changing into our formal wear for the welcome party downstairs. This precedes the first meeting of the week, so that everyone can catch up.

Everyone will be there—most of the Alphas in the country will be there.

All that dominance in the room, I imagine, can raise some tensions, especially since one Alpha is my loving mate and another is my murderer.

I throw on a green turtleneck dress that, luckily, is quite suitable for the event as it covers up enough to make Everett happy, although hiding my mark. But it's also short enough to make it seem more formal.

Heading down the stairs with my hand attached to his bigger one, my heart is thumping in my chest so much, I'm certain every wolf around me can hear it.

Everett's thumb starts stroking my hand, trying to soothe me, which, in fact, does help.

Heads turn when we enter, eyeing me and the powerful Alpha holding my hand like I'm a little child who could get lost. And I probably can in here.

I squeeze his hand tighter as we continue to walk in, Lucius and Ace on either side of us.

I remind myself that I have nothing to be scared about with any of these people, besides Nick and Victoria, and I can't even see them yet, or any of their entourage.

"Breathe, Aurora. You have nothing to be worried about," he assures me, his hand moving from mine to my waist and tugging me to his side to make me feel safer. And I do. With him.

"Alpha Everett," a man, an Alpha, greets as we approach him.

Everett wears a polite smile, shaking this Alpha's hand and nodding over to a woman I assume is his Luna. This Alpha appears much older than Everett, perhaps close to retirement.

"Alpha Bruce, Luna Nancy, how are you?" Everett asks.

His tone conveys to me that he is genuinely friendly with these two and not faking the smile, like I assume he will do with many of the others.

He hates many of them for not supporting his justified and innovative ideas.

"We're great. I see you have found your mate at last," he replies, turning his gaze to me and sending me a warm smile.

"This is Aurora, my mate and Luna."

"And human," Alpha Bruce adds, studying me with narrowed eyes.

"It's a pleasure to meet you, Alpha Bruce, Luna Nancy," I say, deciding to step up and use my manners. Which seemingly surprises him as his smile widens.

"It's a pleasure to meet you, Luna Aurora," he replies, as does his Luna.

We move around, making the introductions, with some turning their noses up at me, a human Luna, as expected. I just feel comforted with Everett beside me, and nothing can ever feel so terrifying with him.

That's until I see them, and they see me. Their eyes widen. Victoria chokes a little on her wine. Nick narrows his eyes to make sure they're seeing correctly. Everett just nudges me along over to them.

"Alpha Nickolas, Luna Victoria," he greets. But they are utterly speechless, their eyes stuck on me. "I believe you already know my mate, Luna Aurora."

"Your mate? Curious why you didn't mention that when we met before," Nick states, immediately tense and wary of both of us. I've never seen him like this. I think he's scared of Everett, my mate.

"You know his Luna?" Alpha Bruce asks, cutting into the conversation.

"She's the usele—she's the human we exiled."

He was going to call me useless, but after glancing at Everett's cold and fierce look, he changed his mind. Victoria just stands there dumbfounded, utterly speechless.

"Exiled? You tried to kill me," I state, gaining my confidence from Everett. This shocks all but Everett as he moves to protect me even more.

"It's not a crime. You were on our territory; it's not against wolf laws," Nick replies.

"We'll see about that," Everett growls lowly, making Nick visibly shiver. He tugs me away and over to a corner of the room, attempting to control himself.

"I'm going to fucking kill him. I don't even care what the

laws are. What they did to you was fucked up. And more than that, you're my mate. They would have killed my mate."

They did kill me. But it made me stronger. It brought me to Everett and he makes me stronger. He gives me courage every single day.

"I would never have found you if they didn't force me out."

"I would have never found you if they actually managed to kill you, little one," he counters, tilting my chin up and pressing his lips to mine.

"If you knew we'd have to come here and see them anyway, why didn't you tell them I was alive before?" I ask.

"There's a reason. And you'll find out soon enough." He seems a little calmer now, taking deep breaths to prevent himself from exploding and taking Nick and Victoria out with him.

CHAPTER 42

Conference

EVERETT

"I bet they found it hilarious when they tried to kick out and kill our mate. They need to pay, Everett," Chaos seethes, wishing to come out.

But soon enough, we're led into the conference hall that's reserved for the council, Alphas, and Lunas.

No one else from the packs is allowed to attend, which makes it a more intimate affair, with a heavy layer of dominance filling the room.

I keep a hand on Aurora's thigh as we take our seats, needing her touch—all the tingles from our connection and love—to cool me down.

As the meeting starts—with sharp stares sent to Aurora, especially from Alpha Nickolas and Luna Victoria—I bring up the first issue, hoping to get the jump on them all.

"I think the law about humans should be changed. It should be illegal for wolves to hurt humans," I state, throwing the view I give them every year out there. Hopefully this time it will stick.

"It's not an important issue," a member of the council replies, like they do every year.

"It's an important issue to me. Wolves don't get another soulmate, and another Alpha almost killed mine," I argue with an underlying growl laced in my voice.

The council all look over at me, as does everyone else, and then they glance at my Luna, who looks perfect and innocent as usual.

"The laws state that I'm permitted revenge if another pack attacks a Luna, Beta, or Gamma. But Alpha Nickolas over here, does that mean I'm allowed to kill him for trying to kill my mate?"

"I didn't even know she was your mate," Alpha Nickolas comments.

"I know. So I would have lost my mate because there is no rule against it?"

The plan was to catch them all off guard with the arrival of my human Luna who was attacked because there was no law in place. Looks like Alpha Nickolas couldn't even think to formulate a plan against it.

"Perhaps we should consider new laws for crimes against humans then," one of the council members suggests, which makes the others agree.

I see a small smile on my mate's face and her hands clasp mine.

I couldn't imagine my life without my little mate now. She's the only person I want by my side. She's beautiful and smart and kind and strong.

And there should be a law against what others tried to do to her.

After much deliberation and many looks sent our way, a handful of laws are passed to prevent a possibly devastating crime that could have taken place. And I'm, for once, victorious.

My little Aurora must be my good-luck charm. I made the meeting my own personal platform for my grievances.

And dominating the first meeting is a great step toward gaining control at the conference—something I worked out a few years ago. But I never knew how to do that. So I barely attended, and I carried on leading the pack.

We head back up to our room and I collapse on the bed with Aurora crawling on top of me, smooth small legs on either side of me.

"That was amazing. I love you, Alpha," she purrs, filling me with lust and making Chaos excited to play with her.

I flip her onto her back, grinning and pinning her to the bed.

"I want to see Chaos again. I haven't seen him in wolf form since you met me."

She wants to see my wolf, and Chaos wants her to see us too. I get down from the bed and onto my hands and knees. As the bones click and snap, I hear tiny gasps from Aurora.

And Chaos takes full control, clambering back onto the bed and on top of Aurora. She's not scared, not in the slightest. Just dazzled. Chaos licks the mark on her neck, making her giggle and squirm underneath us.

"You're so beautiful."

He nudges her with his nose playfully in response and licks her face. She begins to rub our fur, stroking it, and I think I'm in heaven. She's a fucking angel.

I change back into my human form to immediately kiss her lips, making her gasp and melt into it. I rip her dress off, but before I can do anything else, a knock comes at the door.

I huff, pecking Aurora before throwing on some sweatpants from my bag to cover my naked body at the same time as getting a T-shirt for my little mate to cover her up.

I swing the door open, irritated that Aurora and I were interrupted by whoever is at this fucking door, to see Alpha Bruce, without his Luna, with a smirk on his face.

"You finally did it, huh?" he comments, chuckling a little.

"I just thought I'd warn you that even though the council

agreed to pass those laws and supported you, not all the Alphas do. Particularly Red Moon and Midnight Rock.

"They're attempting to lead the charge at the next meeting to reverse or pass something else that will create a loophole. Of course, I'm backing you, and seven others, but you're outnumbered."

"Not overpowered though. We're strong collectively. But I suppose we need to make a plan on how to start the next meeting." I turn back to Aurora, with Alpha Bruce greeting her once more.

"I need to speak with Alpha Bruce and some of the other Alphas. I'll have Ace and Lucius sent up here," I say.

"She can always stay with Nancy if you don't want her to be left alone," Alpha Bruce suggests.

Perhaps that's a good idea. Lucius, Ace, and some of the other warriors are out around the citadel, so it would take time for them to get back. But I can't have Aurora unprotected.

Of course, we already have a couple of warrior wolves guarding our room, so I send them off with Aurora to Luna Nancy and I mind-link Ophelia to go there as well.

"I would never have thought you would have a human Luna."

I narrow my eyes at him but he holds his hands up defensively.

"It doesn't matter if she's human or wolf," I say.

"She's strong. She'll make a good Luna. She's newly appointed to the job and the pack is already adjusting well. Of course, there was some resistance in the first week that just fizzled out."

"She seems sweet. You're lucky she was part of Red Moon before. Explaining wolves to an oblivious human is difficult, especially if that human is skeptical and believes we're just a myth.

"Your Luna grew up in a wolf environment."

"An environment that tried to kill her," I add with a slight growl.

"What happened there?"

"I found her in rogue territory covered in her own blood. Literally, her face was covered in blood. I think she slipped in it because there was so much." *And because she's clumsy.*

Alpha Bruce was a good friend and ally of my parents, and the alliance has carried through to me. I trust him. And his Luna. Which is the only reason Aurora is leaving my sight to go to Nancy.

"She was tired and cold and terrified. She spent the night out there."

"She spent the night?!" he exclaims, clearly shocked. "In rogue territory? She's human. She would get eaten alive."

"Apparently not. It's not the only time she's been mixed up with rogues and perfectly fine."

"That's strange. Maybe she's come across the rare rogues that are actually good," he suggests.

"Rogues aren't good. None of them are good." Perhaps I'm incredibly biased because rogues killed my parents, but rogues either choose to abandon their pack, or they're exiled for a crime.

Either way, they have no sense of loyalty. And being alone for a long time can change a person too—make them selfish and immoral.

"Maybe. But clearly there's some guardian angel watching over your Luna."

We formulate a plan for the next few meetings with the other Alphas, and the next meetings go the way we want them to go over the days. Although the other packs try to tear our strategy down.

Aurora's Secret

And even though Alpha Nickolas and Luna Victoria have been glaring at my mate in shock and confusion, they haven't managed to say anything about it, not that they can now.

When I leave Aurora with Nancy and Ophelia again, I deal with the Alphas I heard talking shit about my mate. I won't allow it.

She's stronger than any of their Lunas, and if they ever try to hurt her, I'll gut them.

Once I deal with them, threatening them, daring them to talk about my little mate again, my mind wanders to her.

My mate has always been a mystery to me—ever since I met her. Even now, she still is. Alpha Bruce is right. How is it possible that she's been completely fine all three times she's been around rogues?

In rogue territory when I found her, when she followed us out on a hunt and was with Ace, and when she was put in the rogue dungeons... She remained unharmed. And all her injuries, they heal so fast.

When she was hit by that car, the doctor said she was paralyzed and may never walk again. She proved him wrong within a matter of days.

He probably made a mistake, but all those broken bones, they healed fairly quickly.

A month is probably the least amount of time that it could take for a human.

My little mystery.

Chapter 43

Taken

RORY

"You're adorable," Nancy comments, chuckling as we play cards in her room. "Bruce can be a sore loser, all of the time. But you just congratulate me."

"She's what Everett needs really," Ophelia says, placing her card down.

"Yeah, I agree. I've known Alpha Everett for a long time, and he seems a lot less tense and…stiff with you around," Nancy tells me.

It's comforting to hear that I'm not bringing Everett down but helping him. I want to be useful. I want to help him.

He's done nothing but help me, doing everything he can to keep me safe. Even the little things like Aurora-proofing.

He's constantly thinking about what he can do to help me and protect me as well as having the responsibility of the pack.

And I do wonder what I do for him. I did save Ophelia, and Ace, but it wasn't something I really did; it just happened.

Just as Ophelia is about to say something, the door bursts open, revealing six large, I'm assuming warrior, wolves, all growling.

My eyes widen at the sight, and I back away with Ophelia and Nancy, over to the back corner of the room. So that tells me they're not in Nancy's pack either.

One of them charges at me, dragging me away, whilst the other wolves fend off Ophelia and Nancy, who fight and claw to try and get to me.

But I'm weak, and against these wolves—even one wolf—I would lose. That doesn't stop me from struggling, like before when the wolves from my own pack were hauling me into those dungeons.

"Where are you taking me? Who are you?" I demand once they begin shifting into their human forms.

But they continue to ignore my pleas, sliding me across the floor, out the back of the building we're staying in and into another building in the citadel.

When I'm thrown into a cold, dank room, I scramble to my feet, assessing my surroundings. Soon after, the faces I've dreaded appear in the room wearing sadistic expressions—along with the Beta and Gamma.

"Alpha Everett will kill you when he finds out," I state, backing away from them.

Even now, they have some sort of power over me that I can't explain. I hate it. He's not my Alpha anymore, not that he was ever any sort of Alpha to me.

But Victoria bullied me since I joined the pack, and even though Nick is older than us, he turned a blind eye or just joined in.

I was the token human of the pack, and therefore the punching bag, regardless of age. Even between Everett and me, age doesn't matter. Because we're mates. Like age doesn't matter with bullies.

"How are you still fucking alive? I don't fucking understand that," Victoria sneers, still wound up with confusion and shock.

Honestly, I am too. I still don't understand it either, so there is no point in asking me.

"You didn't kill me," I mutter, knowing it is a blatant lie.

I don't understand what they want with me. Everett is going to skin them alive when he finds out, and I don't know if I can control his temper.

Nick rips the scarf from my neck, only to find what he didn't expect: no scar—not even the faintest sign that I was ever hurt. Just my mark. The mark made by my Alpha mate.

I hate that I'm always relying on Everett to save me. He's done enough for me already. He's saved me so many times in so many ways.

He protects me in the smallest ways, too, with the Aurora-proofing just so I won't get hurt, even if it's only just a bruise. And I can't even defend myself now.

"I don't understand," Nick mutters, astounded, but quickly covers it. "It doesn't matter. You made us look like complete idiots, and all the Alphas think that the new laws passed are because of Red Moon.

"We won't make the same mistake. Let's go," he declares, grabbing my arm and trailing me along the floor.

The side of my body grazes the floor, making me squeal and flail like a bag on his arm in the wind.

Are they going to try and kill me again? What if they actually succeed this time? Because Nemesis might actually get me. And I won't get to say goodbye to my mate, or tell him everything.

I want to tell him the truth—about my entire life. It's strange to think that many months ago, I was just a normal human girl, and now I don't know what I am. Perhaps I'll find out this time.

I scream until I lose my voice and end up whimpering, which makes me sound even weaker. Everett can feel my distress, I know he can, through the mate connection that binds us. But I don't want him to get hurt.

I may be able to revive myself, maybe, but Everett can't. And if he gets hurt, he'll be hurt permanently if I can't save him. Perhaps it's better that he doesn't come for me, that I deal with this on my own.

I attempt to calm myself down so that Everett won't feel my panic anymore, but I fear it's too late.

Before I know it, I'm dragged out of the citadel and into a clearing in the woods, on the border of this wolf territory and rogue territory.

I guess this is a just place to die. This is almost identical to the first time they killed me.

"You're still pathetic, little Rory," Victoria taunts, kicking me in the gut as I collapse to the floor. I grimace but bite my lip, refusing to give them a reaction and let them win against me again.

I was so afraid before, terrified of what they were doing, and they showed me no mercy. They reveled in my pain and my panic.

This time, I'm not giving them that, because I'm stronger now, I'm stronger because of Everett and what he has taught me, and because I've died multiple times. They're not my biggest enemies anymore.

"You're pathetic, Victoria," I spit out, along with the blood rising from my gut. Victoria pulls back my hair forcefully and stares into my eyes.

"You think you're so strong now because you have an Alpha mate? He should have rejected you," she sneers, pushing me against a tree.

I stare at both of them, my cheeks wet with tears, my hair like a bird's nest on top of my head, my lip cut and bleeding out.

"You think he'll save you?"

"He can take your pack on no problem," I counter.

Laughter erupts from all of them, and I notice that other

Alphas from the meeting have joined us. Why are they all doing this?

"These laws that we've pushed aside for years have been passed," one of the Alphas states, "because of you. Alpha Everett used you as an example, and continues to do so. Lunas shouldn't be human.

"A human shouldn't lead a pack of wolves—not that a weak little girl like you could ever lead. With you gone, it'll weaken Shadow Blood, and we'll take over and put in the laws we want."

"The fuck you will," a familiar growl erupts from behind all of them, filling me with love and hope.

Everett is here to save me. But against all of these packs, I'm not sure if he'll win. And I don't want him hurt because of me.

"I'd let her go if I were you," Alpha Bruce yells, and I realize that he's not alone. He has other packs with him too.

"Your little human isn't worthy of being a Luna," an enemy Alpha says bitterly, standing beside Nick and Victoria.

Before anything else can happen, I feel a stabbing pain in my heart, slashing into my chest through the skin and twisting inside of me.

Through the crowds of wolves, my eyes meet Everett's crystal-blue ones, which entrance and comfort me in my overwhelming pain.

Victoria stabbed me. I should have known; she's always been impulsive. I squeak at the gut-wrenching pain, but there's not much I can do.

I can't be scared. This isn't it, not yet anyway.

Once I get to limbo, I know this time, Nemesis will catch up to me, and I have no idea how I'm going to fight her. I know that she's stronger than Nick and Victoria, and I couldn't do anything against them.

"Everett," I whisper, knowing he'll be able to hear me. "I'll be okay. I love you."

And I do. I really do. He came for me as fast as he could, bringing backup, too, to fight for me.

No one has ever fought like this for me before, sacrificing everything just to try and save me. I really love him. I just need him to know that.

Chapter 44

Dead

———•◆•———

RORY

NEMESIS COULD BE ANYONE, BUT I'M PRETTY CERTAIN she is a higher being.

While researching her, I learned about a goddess named Nemesis, the goddess of revenge and divine retribution. She delivers a righteous justice that she deems necessary, with no mercy.

What could my parents have done to enrage Nemesis to the point that she tried to kill me? I guess I'll find out.

"Aurora," Achlys calls out as I find myself surrounded by white mist once again, the chilling loneliness sending shivers up my spine.

As a child, I'd always wondered what death felt like. People would always ruminate any time a pack member would die or get killed. They would mourn and contemplate what would happen after death.

I thought it would be cold and lonely and dark. It's all of those things except for dark. No, it's light. Blindingly light. If this wasn't the afterlife, I would go blind, yet not everything works here like it works back on Earth.

It's different. Complex. It just feels…different.

"Aurora," another voice, yet a familiar one, whispers, snapping my head in that direction. And I see a woman.

Raven-black hair flows down her back to her hips. Her dress, a haunting white, wafts like Achlys's, yet there is still no wind, no air. A vicious smirk is set upon her face as she stares daggers into me.

And then I remember where I know her voice from: rogue territory. The voice that sent me astray, made me lose my way when following Everett. Just before Ace came. She was there.

And then when I died. It was her voice, one of the voices was hers. She's been stalking me for a long time—probably since she tried killing me when I was a child.

"I've been wanting to meet you for a while now, especially all grown up. Yet you always manage to evade me."

"What do you want with me?" I ask innocently.

"What do I want? I would think it obvious by now, from what that bitch told you. I want you dead," she states bitterly, edging closer to me.

"Stay away from her," Achlys warns, pushing her back with some invisible force. But it only maintains her distance, and ever so slightly she inches forward.

"Why do you want to kill me?" I ask.

Nemesis narrows her eyes at me before snarling at me.

"Your mother, that adulterous bitch. I was married, and she fucked my husband. She made him think that she wanted him, wanted to be with him. She made him fall in love with her. And I was pregnant.

"He didn't want to be tied to me anymore, and he thought a child would do that. So he killed my unborn child, poisoned me just enough to kill my baby, just for your mother.

"Of course, your mother, bitch that she was, didn't want him after all. She found your father, she wanted him. And I was left with an unfaithful, murderous husband and a dead baby.

"Now I'm going to kill her baby, her daughter, you. That's retribution."

"You took me from her. It's because of you that I don't even know my parents. How is it fair that I pay for their mistakes? I'm not their daughter; they barely parented me," I say, my hands trembling.

"Who were my parents then?"

"I suppose you should know who you are before you die. Your mother and father were divine beings—a god and a goddess, like me and Achlys. Which is how you are not just a regular human.

"I took you from your parents, took you to Earth where I thought you would be vulnerable. To go to Earth, gods and goddesses are no longer in their divine forms, but in human form.

"I thought I would be able to kill you. But I didn't realize the immense power you had, even on Earth."

A goddess? I'm a goddess? That's insane. I'm weak and human, and if I were a goddess, I think I would be able to at least stand up for myself.

"Immense power?" I ask almost inaudibly.

"Unfortunately, yes. You're not a strong human, by any means. And I cursed you to be clumsy to bring you here more often.

"But Achlys is always pushing you through that door you created before I can get to you and stop you from going through."

"The door I created?" There are so many questions I need her to answer, yet she is the enemy. I need to get away from her. But I need to know who I am, what I am, to understand it all.

"So clueless, aren't you, little girl? A goddess all this time, and to everyone else, you seemed like the weakest little human.

"Until you started to know better. Until you knew you

couldn't die. Then you thought you were better than everyone else, didn't you?"

"No," I squeak out.

"Little clumsy Rory. I've been watching you your entire life. Since your mother gave birth, I knew you would be my revenge.

"I killed my husband and your mother, of course, but not until you were born, just so I could see the look on her face when she knew I took her baby and she would never get her back, just like she did to me.

"But you, innocent, sweet Aurora, you're nothing like her. In fact, that's what made me misjudge your power. The door you created. The door between life and death.

"You can create a door that saves you; you can grant life to others with your own and then create the door to save yourself.

"And Achlys pushes you through it before I can get to you. Because your presence isn't right here. But it will be. When I kill you." She struggles against Achlys's force fiercely, trying to get to me.

"Run," Achlys commands.

It takes me a few moments to get out of my contemplative state and move my feet. And I dash off, running.

Luckily here I'm not so clumsy, perhaps because I'm no longer human in here, with my human body left behind on Earth.

Here, I'm not plagued with the curse, so I run. Run faster and smoother than I ever have done. And because I've never been able to run like this in my entire life, I feel like I'm flying.

But a hand wraps around my leg, dragging me across the mist, making me scream out. The hand feels like it's pure fire, burning me, scorching me.

I kick and I shout, pleading for a rescue like the weak girl I am, needing a savior every time. But I do. I need someone to save me.

"Aurora," Achlys calls out. "You're not some defenseless human anymore. In here, you're much more. You can fight. You may not be as strong as her, but you can still fight. Just fight."

So I fight, and fight and fight.

But it all seems impossible. I can't defeat her. I'm not strong enough. I can't even get her hand off my leg, and she's hauling me closer to her.

"Please," I whimper as another hand is placed onto my other leg, scalding me with a fierce heat.

"Little Aurora, so young and so pretty. Your beauty rivals your mother's—even triumphs it, I would say. She could always lure any man to her with that beauty and her trashy, seductive ways.

"But you, so innocent, so in love with your strong protective Alpha. Now, Selene protected you well there.

"She programmed every rogue to protect you if you needed protection in rogue territory, preventing me from getting you there so easily. And you mated with that Alpha; fate was mocking me.

"Luna of the most powerful pack in the country, with a handsome, respectful, smart mate. The moon goddess as you call her, as all you wolves worship her...she's like your aunt of sorts."

I can barely concentrate on what she is telling me, although she's disclosing to me everything I've wanted to know.

All too late, it appears.

"Please stop," I scream, still kicking, although I feel so worn down it's hard to do anything anymore.

"Stop? I haven't started. But I suppose I could make it quick. You are so innocent after all, so adorable," she almost coos before pulling me further toward her.

I want Everett. I want him with me. He may have felt our bond breaking, with me being dead. But I still feel it. I still feel

Aurora's Secret

him. Even though I can't feel it physically anymore. I can sense him. Far away, with my body.

I don't want to hurt him. And I can tell he's hurting. I don't want to die and leave him. I love him. I can't hurt him. I refuse to.

Out of everyone, I will not be the one to hurt him. And I don't want to lose him.

I push, harder than I ever have before. Harder than I ever thought was possible before. And I run, run faster than I have. Faster than I can even comprehend.

And I run to Everett. To my mate. My handsome, respectful, smart mate. My strong protective Alpha.

I don't stop until I see the door. A door I apparently made. Green like my eyes.

Green like the forest leaves and the woodland hills. Green like emeralds. And I push myself through. I didn't even know I could do that.

But I go. Back to Everett. Back to my love.

Chapter 45

Mourning

EVERETT

"Everett," she whispers as my heart cracks.

I can't breathe. The mate bond is waning like it did before, and my heart is going with it.

"I'll be okay. I love you."

I love you, too, little one. And I'll save you. I promised I would protect you and I will. It's not over. I can still protect you. Please.

When I see the blankness wash over her eyes and feel our bond smash to pieces once again, my rage takes over—over everything, my sense of duty, of faith, of composure.

This uncontrollable rage that makes me shift faster than ever before.

I thrash through enemy wolves, not caring who it is as long as they played a part in killing my beautiful innocent Luna. My Aurora.

I can't lose her. I can't. I love her so much that everything hurts now that she's not here. I can't live without her.

Wolf after wolf after wolf. I can't stop myself. Slashing and clawing and biting and tearing their fur and their necks. All in justice for my mate. My dead mate. My little Aurora.

My warrior wolves and allied packs join in, tearing at enemy wolves left and right.

"Alpha!" Ace yells, but I completely ignore him, blinded by

my anger and need for vengeance. "Alpha, I don't think Rory's dead!" he shouts across to me.

And my rage eases slightly at the mention of my mate and the fact he thinks she's not dead. But the bond has broken. That's how I know she's dead. When she died before, it broke like this; it shattered.

I growl at Ace for even giving me the slightest hope, and then I continue, trying to get to my mate's executioner, Luna Victoria. And of course, Alpha Nickolas.

I promised Aurora I would protect her from them, I would keep her safe. I told her she would be by my side, safe—that they wouldn't dare hurt her with me.

But they did. And they didn't just hurt her, they killed her. My Aurora.

I pounce on Alpha Nickolas, and am about to tear his throat out when Ace yells once again.

"Alpha! Stop! She's—" Before he can even finish, a tiny, almost inaudible gasp arises from the once lifeless body of my mate. And a connection is reestablished, again.

I feel her. I feel her soul again, interlocking with mine. I hear her little heartbeat. And then a scream. A piercing scream before she passes out.

Everyone else heard it too. And they stop. They're stunned into shock, as am I. I drop Alpha Nickolas on the ground and rush to her.

Her chest is rising and falling now. Little breaths are escaping her; her pulse is healthy and regular. And I can't find a wound. I can't find the stab wound.

I saw Luna Victoria do it. We all did. She stabbed her. So where is the wound? How can my little mate be alive? How did Ace know? How is any of this possible?

I lift her into my arms, hugging her petite body to me, and

storm off, needing to protect her properly this time. I get in my car and drive. Back to the pack, back where we're safe. Or safer.

The pack members in the clearing all mind-link me, informing me that they're coming back too, along with the Alphas and pack members of our seven ally packs.

Constantly, throughout the entire drive, my eyes flicker to her, still trying to make sure she's real and that she's really alive.

Once we get home, I ignore all the staring and horrified faces of the pack. Ace or Lucius most likely told them what happened, but they probably also felt their ties to their Luna break.

I just focus on my exhausted mate in my arms. I dash up to our room and lay her down on the bed, feeling her temperature and pulse and listening out for her breathing. But she seems fine. Completely fine, after dying.

I don't understand any of this. But why did Ace know? He knew at the hospital when she was hit by that car. He knew something. He knew that she would live. How did he know? What does he actually know?

At that, Ace and Lucius come barreling into the room with concerned and shocked expressions plastered over their faces. I march over to Ace, grabbing his neck and shoving him back against the wall.

"What the fuck do you know that I don't?" I growl, searching his face for answers.

"Alpha, I didn't know anything. It was just a feeling," he struggles to say, trying to breathe.

I drop him so he can speak, and he just sighs, taking a seat in the armchair in the corner.

"Alpha…she… Something happened that time we were

out in rogue territory. And it was strange. She... She's not a very good liar. In fact, for a girl who has told many lies since she's been here, she's quite awful at it."

"Stop insulting my mate and tell me what you know," I grunt, restraining myself from just torturing it out of him. He may be my Gamma, but he knows something about my Luna that he's kept from me.

"When we were out there, I don't really know what happened. I rationalized it as falling asleep and dreaming it up, and Rory lied and supported that.

"I thought it couldn't possibly be real because I was shot, by a hunter, with a wolfsbane bullet, which is why I thought it was a dream."

"You'd be dead if that happened," I say.

"Yes, I would. But I think my dream actually happened. When I got shot, Rory helped me get away and we went further into rogue territory. Then we ran into a group of rogues.

"I thought she and I needed protection, but something happened. She...took control. They didn't want to hurt her, and she knew that too. She knew they wouldn't hurt her, even though they wanted to tear me apart.

"And they told her the direction back to the pack. And she helped me to try and get there. And we were talking.

"But I was dying and I couldn't go on much further and I think I almost died. But she somehow saved me.

"She might be a witch or something. I don't have a wound and I should have died. But I didn't.

"Then I woke up and saw Rory passed out, and I thought maybe we had just taken a break, although I thought that would be incredibly thoughtless of me, to sleep out in rogue territory. But Rory agreed."

"But then she repeated something I said in the

dream—something I remembered telling her—and I knew something was strange. I don't know what she is, but she's been lying to you.

"I don't think she really knows either. But that's why I was following her before: not because I had a crush on her, but because she's a mystery. Your human, perhaps, clumsy, maybe fake, mate."

"Why didn't you tell me if this is true?"

"Because I didn't know whether it was true. But she got run over and the doctor said she would be paralyzed. But, a few days later her legs were just broken. I still didn't know."

"Aurora isn't faking being clumsy; it's not even possible to fake being that clumsy," I state.

"Exactly. How can anyone be that clumsy?" he questions skeptically.

"She's bad at lying. She's not a fake."

"Maybe she's faking being bad at lying," Lucius pitches in.

I walk back over to my innocent little mate and stroke her cheek. When they find their mates, they'll know why Aurora can't be a fake. I just know. I know her. We're bonded.

"She's my mate and your Luna and she is not a fake," I state adamantly.

"Even if I didn't know that to be true, it's incredibly hard to fake being that level of innocent and sweet. And she doesn't force anything."

"You're right. I was watching her and she was as pure as anyone could be. She could easily slip up when she thought no one was watching. And yet, she was still clumsy and cute. But I'm not sure what she is."

"She's not a what," I growl. "And whoever she is, she's still the Luna of this pack and you all will protect her."

I knew she was keeping something from me. I just didn't

know it was this big. But I love her, despite anything that happens or has happened. And I know her. I know what's in her heart.

She's strong and brave and innocent and benevolent. She's an amazing Luna, even if she is human and not as physically strong as everyone else in the pack.

But dying and coming back to life? That's definitely not a weak trait. I'm not sure what any of this means, but I know that I will always love her.

CHAPTER 46

Truth

RORY

I STIR AWAKE, GASPING FOR BREATH AS I REALIZE I'M ALIVE.
I'm alive.
I'm alive!

My eyes flutter open, landing on three anxious-looking wolves, the powerful Alpha more so than the others.

When his eyes connect with mine, everything melts away. He dashes to my side and searches my face for something—signs of ill health?

"You're here, you're alive," he mutters frantically, smashing his lips against mine before pulling back to give me some air.

But I love the tingling feeling of his lips on mine—and the sparks that fly between us and dance like a never-ending party.

"What is going on? Tell me what's happening, Aurora."

"I..."

It's time to come clean. I do know most of it now, at least the basis of it all, of everything that has happened. I know what I am now.

"I... It's hard to explain. I... The first time we met, when I was kicked out of Red Moon, Nick and Victoria didn't just try to kill me, they did.

"T-they killed me. T-they slit my th-throat," I stammer,

finding it hard to recall the memories with what happened to me and all the pain surrounding it.

"And I-I went into this place, a-and there… It was like limbo, or that's what I call it. And there was this door and I-I was pushed through it. A-and then I was alive again.

"I didn't understand. It was like a dream, but filled with so much pain. I couldn't breathe."

Tears start pouring down my face. I'm so tired, and I'm also tired of keeping all of this in, not sharing it with Everett. I just thought it was safer and easier for him, for us.

"And I-I woke up and I g-got up and I-I was in a pool of my own b-blood. It must've l-leaked out everywhere. And I-I didn't have anywhere to go.

"A r-rogue protected m-me that n-night. I-I was so exhausted, I-I just collapsed."

My eyes feel so heavy still. Having my life drained from me and given back again really takes it out of me—not to mention the fact that Nemesis almost killed me.

I feel myself start to drift off to sleep, but Lucius snaps me awake with his next question.

"What else?" he growls.

"Then you all found me," I say dozily. "I was in the hospital, with Ophelia, when it happened again. But I didn't actually die.

"Well, I did, but I cured her and then died for it, I think, like I did when Ace was shot in rogue territory. And then the car hit me and I died again. And I healed quickly when I woke up. I just faked my legs being broken."

I watch Lucius's eyes narrow at me, but Everett's still listening. He doesn't seem angry that I kept this from him, yet.

"My mom gave me a letter before I was exiled. It said that I had died and come back twice before. The first time was when she found me.

"She said that I was left out in rogue territory, killed. I found out who killed me. It… It was a goddess."

As I'm saying it, I know it sounds unbelievable. It was unbelievable to me when I heard it. But I just have to get it out there, because it's the truth.

"The third time I died, when Ace was dying, there was this woman. Her name is Achlys. She's a goddess too. And she told me someone was after me because of my birth parents. This time, when I died, I saw her.

"Her name's Nemesis, the goddess of revenge. She told me that her husband fell for my mom and that he killed Nemesis's unborn child for my mom.

"So to get her revenge, she stole me and put me on Earth so she could kill me. But it wasn't very easy."

Lucius is just shaking his head at this point, quietly scoffing at anything I say whilst Ace looks at me skeptically. But Everett just listens, not forming any conclusions just yet.

"She told me Selene, the moon goddess, made the rogues subconsciously protect me anytime I'm in rogue territory because that's unprotected grounds, apparently.

"Nemesis can get me there—and in limbo. And Selene paired me with an Alpha, too, because we're soulmates and because it's safest for me with an Alpha. Apparently, Selene is like my aunt.

"Which makes me a goddess too. And Nemesis cursed me, with clumsiness, so that I would die easier and she could get more chances to get to me in limbo.

"But Achlys gets in the way. But she was close this time. She got to me." I still feel the burns she gave me through my body, and I swiftly peel back the cover to see handprints scalded onto my ankles.

"What the fuck is that?" Everett growls at the sign of me hurt.

"I think the damage she can do is permanent," I mumble, gazing at the burn marks. "She grabbed my ankles. Her hands were like fire. They hurt so much."

"That's real, and new," Lucius mutters, looking at my legs in shock. "But none of what you just said can be true. It's stupid. You're cursed with clumsiness?"

I just shrug and lie back in the bed.

"Leave us," Everett demands in his Alpha tone, forcing Lucius and Ace to leave obediently.

He crawls into bed beside me and makes me face him so that I'm staring directly into his unreadable eyes.

"Why didn't you tell me?" he asks in a soft voice.

"Until a few hours ago, I didn't know most of that. I'm sorry. I shouldn't have kept it from you. But I didn't know if you'd keep me at first, and I was scared about what happened.

"And I still didn't understand anything myself; I still don't," I explain.

We're so close I can feel his breath on my face, and he can feel mine.

"That's why you were so scared to see Alpha Nickolas and Luna Victoria again? Because they actually killed you and you don't even have a scar?"

I nod slowly and he just stares at me. I yawn and my head falls closer to his.

"You're sleepy, little one. I just want to hold you."

"I want you to hold me. I was so scared to lose you."

I roll into Everett's arms and let his scent and his body engulf me. I rest my head on his chest, and the rest of my body lies sprawled out on his.

"I was scared I'd lost you. I promised to protect you, little one. You're my mate and my Luna and my love. I fucking love you. Nothing can ever change that," he whispers, stroking my arm. "Do your ankles hurt?"

"Not so much now. It just feels seared. They're fine though. You don't have to worry, Everett."

"I do worry, Aurora. I'm even more worried. There's some goddess bitch after you. I always knew you were a goddess; you definitely look like one," he says playfully, making me giggle.

"So fucking beautiful. I love your little giggles. I want to hear more, but there's always someone or something messing with our happiness.

"I just want to be with you. I don't care if you're clumsy, or as it turns out, cursed clumsy. You're perfect to me."

"Then you need your eyes checked," I joke, laughing lightly and making him growl playfully too.

"You are perfect, little one. Absolutely perfect. You need to understand that," he states firmly, sliding the sheets over me more to keep me warm.

When he notices me shivering, he grabs another blanket from the side of the bed and pulls it over us too.

"It's cold in limbo," I mutter.

"I want you to tell me more about all of it. You know that. I want to know everything, every detail. But you need to sleep right now, so we'll just cuddle and you'll nap and I'll watch you and protect you.

"I can't ever let you out of my sight again. I can't lose you. Which is why I need to know everything."

"I know. I'll tell you everything, Everett," I whisper in my daze before slipping off into unconsciousness in the arms of the man I love.

Before, he was very protective of me; now he'll be even more so, keeping me in his sights at all times. But I don't mind anymore. I want to be with him all the time. I can't live without him.

He's my light, my protector, my savior. He saved me from Nemesis. Just the thought of losing him, leaving him, hurting him, got me out of there and back to him.

And I know that with him by my side, we'll get our happily ever after.

Chapter 47

Plans

RORY

In the morning, Everett listens to me for hours in his office, asking question after question to try to understand everything, then he spends hours researching it all.

Now it's time to face the music. Everyone in the pack knows that something happened—that I somehow died and came back to life. Lucius still doesn't believe my story, whereas Ace is actually entranced by it.

I think it's because of what happened in rogue territory. It makes sense to him. Although how? I have no clue. It doesn't even make sense to me.

Everett gathers the pack and the other ally packs together down in the meeting hall, and hand in hand we walk in, my body trembling nervously and still in a dull ache after being stabbed yesterday.

It's packed in there, with a thick layer of dominance and confusion in the room. The Alphas all eye me with puzzled and shocked expressions.

Having waited for answers all day, and with tonight being a harvest moon, all the wolves are anxious and wary.

"My Luna Aurora and I need the help of all of you. Along with being targeted by the Alpha of her old pack and his allied packs, Luna Aurora is also being targeted by a vengeful goddess named Nemesis," Everett declares.

This doesn't clear up any confusion whatsoever; if anything, it increases it.

Before Everett can say anything else, a couple of guard wolves barrel into the room frantically, and all attention turns to them.

"Alpha, there's something outside that you need to see," one of them states, leading all of us out like the world is about to end.

But then we all understand when we see her. Who is she now? I've already met enough unearthly creatures—including myself—to last me a lifetime.

Dealing with the fact that my parents are divine beings is incredibly difficult, especially when I've thought of myself as a weak, clumsy human for all of my life.

"Who are you?" Everett asks for all of us.

When her eyes meet mine, she smiles gently and her eyes then flicker to my and Everett's intertwined hands.

"I'm Selene," she announces.

"The moon goddess," I mutter in amazement, stepping closer as I feel a sense of familiarity with her. She is my kin, I suppose.

"That's right, Aurora. I heard what happened with Nemesis. She hurt you—almost killed you—although I have tried hard to prevent that. But she is incredibly relentless.

"The only way to make her stop is to defeat her," she explains, drifting toward me and Everett.

But Everett pushes me behind him protectively, narrowing his eyes at her.

"It's okay, Alpha Everett. I mean your Luna no harm. On the contrary, I wish to help."

"Why?" I ask in a small voice. "Why have you helped me?

With the rogues and everything? Nemesis said you were like my aunt. I don't know what that means."

"I'm a distant aunt. I'm very old, Aurora. I've been around for billions of years, but we are related. I helped your mother give birth to you. Do you know what Aurora means?"

I shake my head.

"It means 'dawn.' When your mother looked at you, she knew you were a light-bringer, a life-bringer. Which also fits your abilities, to give life.

"When you were taken, your mother wept constantly for days, until Nemesis came for her too. So I vowed I would look for you and keep you safe—for her, and for you.

"When I located you, I realized Nemesis put you on Earth so she could kill you with her powers from above. But she can't kill you unless she does it physically herself.

"I knew that she could only get you in rogue territory or if you died," she reveals.

"Listen to me, Aurora, because I can't stay here long for the same reason that she doesn't want to kill you here. For a goddess to walk on Earth, she has a human form.

"It decreases her powers and also it makes her mortal. So I made the rogues subconsciously protect you because Nemesis doesn't want to get killed before she gets to you.

"But if she gets you alone, she may come to Earth. And then she's mortal."

What she's saying is that if I'm used as bait to lure her to Earth, we can trap and kill her.

That sounds like a plan—a dangerous one that I'm not sure Everett would go for, but it's a good one, and the only way we'll be safe.

"I have to go, Aurora. But I'll see you soon." She turns to Everett and gives him a hard look.

"I mated you two together because you were born for each other. A powerful, protective Alpha and a young cursed goddess in need of protection. So protect her," she states firmly before completely vanishing into thin air.

"What the hell just happened?" Alpha Bruce murmurs, staring at where Selene once was.

The moon goddess was here, on Earth, to give us advice. She knew my mother. My birth mother.

I always thought my parents gave me up, just left me in the woods, but I know better, and I can no longer blame them for having never known them. It was Nemesis's fault.

Like it's her fault that I will never get to meet my mother now. She's dead. It doesn't matter though. I have Everett and my mama is still missing.

So I need to go through with this plan to make sure that Everett doesn't get hurt, that none of the pack will get hurt protecting me and keeping me alive.

"I know what you're thinking, Aurora, and the answer is no," Everett states, turning around to face me with a strict expression on his face.

"It's the only way, Everett," I reply. "And Selene told us that's what should be done."

"There are plenty of ways. And the ones I like are the ones that involve you staying completely out of harm's way."

"If I'm out of harm's way, she's not going to come. And if I die again, I won't be able to get away this time."

"I can't risk you getting hurt, little one," he whispers, pressing his lips to mine.

"I'm confused right now," Alpha Bruce says, snapping us out of our trances. "Luna Aurora is a goddess?"

"Yes, our Luna is a goddess," Ace replies, joining my side.

"And we just met the moon goddess, the goddess we pray to all the time."

"Wow," Alpha Bruce mutters, laughing a little in shock. "I shouldn't be surprised with what I saw yesterday. Coming back from the dead."

"We need to know if we have all of your support," Everett announces to the many onlooking wolves.

And specifically to the seven Alphas, whose support we may need to defeat Nemesis, and to definitely get rid of Nick and Victoria.

They killed me. Again. There weren't even going to be any consequences for them before they killed me for the second time. I don't know why they did.

Perhaps it was the pressure from the other Alphas, since I was used as an example to make laws against killing humans.

"My Luna and I have found ourselves with enemies everywhere now, some not even of this world.

"We need your help, but what just happened now, it gives you insight into what we're up against, and if you're not prepared to fight, that's fine."

"My pack will fight with Shadow Blood. Our alliance doesn't just extend to convenience. We are allies and friends and we'll help," Alpha Bruce declares, shaking Everett's hand and nodding to me in respect.

"So will we," Alpha Connor states in agreement, shaking Everett's hand and nodding to me in the same way.

Then the other Alphas follow suit, still a little shocked by the recent display, but all agreeing that we should fight together.

Most of the wolves go for a run around the territory in the full moon tonight, knowing that tomorrow, we'll begin making plans.

Everett doesn't want to go along with Selene's, so I'll let

them rack their brains for another plan. When they don't find another option, the only one left will be Selene's.

Everett walks with me back to our room, and we get into bed, me resting on him with his arms caging me in, our legs tangled together.

"I'll keep you safe, little one. I promise," he whispers.

"Please don't promise that. I don't want to see you hurt because of me," I reply.

"You can't stop me, Aurora. I can't let anything happen to you, I just can't. And I'll get hurt a thousand times just so you can be safe."

I know. That's what I'm scared of. If it comes down to me or him, he will sacrifice himself for me.

When a furious knock comes at the door, it breaks us out of our alone time and Everett growls at the interruption. Nevertheless, he goes to answer it and is met by two guard wolves dragging three bodies across the floor.

"Alpha, these humans were lurking in our territory," one of the wolves declares.

"Oh, fuck me," Everett grumbles.

I peek over his shoulders and have the exact same reaction.

Eddie, Jax, and Oliver.

What the hell?

Chapter 48

United

RORY

"WHAT THE FUCK DO WE DO NOW?" Everett hisses as he pulls me to the side.

"Maybe you shouldn't have been so hasty making those human laws," I joke, although upon seeing Everett's expression, I quickly realize it's not the best time.

I have no clue what we're going to do. Who knows what they've seen, what they know. They're passed out right now in our room.

Although, Everett cracks a little smile that disintegrates just as fast as it came.

"I'm being serious, Aurora. This is fucking crazy. We don't just get humans walking onto our territory; it just doesn't happen. And on top of that, they're people we both know."

"What do you normally do in this situation?"

"This doesn't happen. Wolf packs have evolved from living in the woods, making their homes out of wood and branches and anything they found. Soon, these packs were integrated and we built homes.

"Humans don't just happen upon our territories. I don't know how these three found this place; they must have followed us home on Friday. How long have they been here?"

"This is my fault. I'm sorry. I wanted to go back to school, and they wouldn't be here if it weren't—"

"Stop, Aurora," Everett commands, grabbing my cheeks in his large, warm hands and comforting me. "I led them here, this is all me. But it doesn't matter right now. What matters is what we're going to do now."

"We just have to find out what they know and work from there," I suggest, and he nods.

The three do look pretty beat-up at the moment, dried blood staining their faces. It must be due to the guard wolves' violent ways. I'm sure they'll survive though.

Why would they do this? Why would they follow us? I thought Jax was done with me, and what the hell is Oliver doing here? He doesn't even like me.

The only reason he even says anything to me is because I'm friends with Bethany. That's it. And he was my former bully also. Why is he here?

We leave them in our room for the night, locking them in whilst we sleep in a spare room next door. But the night feels dreadfully long as we stir, attempting to shake the anxiety from our minds.

"I've been sleeping a lot over the past few days anyway," I mutter as Everett tries to lull me to sleep. I just crawl up him so that our faces are aligned, with me on top, and I peck his lips.

Before I can pull away, his hand drags my neck down and his lips attack mine with uncontrollable passion. He rolls on top of me now, pinning me to the bed.

"Everything is fucking chaos right now, but I'm so fucking glad you're here with me to weather this storm."

"It's because of me that there is a storm," I say as his hands roam my body.

"I needed to find you, and once we get past this and you're

safe, we can finally have peace, together. I just want to be with you, Alpha and Luna of Shadow Blood. My little Aurora."

"I'm always called *little*," I mutter.

"It's because you are. You don't like it? I like that I can easily pick you up; it makes the keeping-you-from-being-clumsy thing easier. And you're mine, my little goddess Luna.

"How does it feel to be a goddess quite literally? I always thought you were heavenly, but to be an actual goddess?"

"I don't know. I don't suddenly have powers, like lightning shooting out of my arms or the strength to lift a truck. It just… explains a few things.

"And makes me think more about my birth parents. What would my parents be like if they actually had a chance to parent me?"

"They would love you, Aurora. It's hard not to. That's probably why those three are in that room right now. You're amazing and sweet, and it was very difficult for me to resist you.

"You're just so pure that it draws people in. And I want to protect that, that innocence. It's beautiful, you're beautiful."

I feel my cheeks heat up furiously as he dazzles me with his compliments and kisses.

He lies down next to me, pulling me onto him once again, and we just rest there, just breathing—just taking a break from all the chaos in our lives.

Morning rolls around, and we're woken up by loud banging from the room next door, along with the yells of my human "friends."

I used to think I was human, that I belonged around them rather than the wolves. But now, being of a different kind, I wholly believe that I belong with my mate and the pack. They're my family.

But I do have a human form, a mortal form. I possess the characteristics of the humans. The only thing different is the fact that I can die and come back, even though it may not be for much longer.

"Let's go deal with this, little one. Ace and Lucius are helping too," Everett declares, picking me up out of bed and sliding his T-shirt over my cold body.

We prepare ourselves before entering our own bedroom, with Ace and Lucius following behind. All three faces drop as they stare at us in disbelief.

"What are you doing here?" Everett questions, leading the charge whilst holding my hand to ease the irritation he fears he'll get.

"W-what the fuck is going on here?" Eddie queries, standing his ground, but the fear is evident in his tone and his eyes.

Jax and Oliver just stare at all of us, confusion and fear laced through their expressions. But what do they fear? The guard wolves did give them a beating, but maybe they know about wolves.

"Rory? Tell me what's going on. We saw grown men turn into wolves."

So they do know something. Everett and I glance at each other, and I squeeze his hand nervously.

"Then you're hallucinating as well as trespassing," Everett states with confidence and authority, attempting to make it seem like they're just losing their minds.

To be honest, if I didn't know about wolves and I saw what they saw, losing my mind would be more believable to me.

But I doubt myself a lot. Jax and Oliver and possibly even Eddie all appear sure of themselves usually.

"Trespassing? What? You own this place?" Jax questions, believing he doesn't.

"Yes, I do. I own all these lands, and you three are trespassing. So, I'll ask again, what the fuck are you doing here?" Everett demands more forcefully like the Alpha he is, which clearly intimidates all three, though Jax attempts to hide it.

"We're here to save Rory—from you," Eddie declares.

Everett scoffs and glances at me. "Do you need saving from me, little one?"

I need saving from everyone but him.

"No, I don't," I state firmly. "What are you actually doing here? I don't need saving."

"Yeah because he's making you say that. We came here to help you and we got beat up, because of him," Oliver states, pointing at my mate. "That's the sort of man he is."

"We weren't even here for the past four days. We just got back, and we've basically just stayed here," I say. "He didn't tell those guys to do what they did, but you all *were* trespassing."

"Are you serious, Rory?" Oliver questions.

"Why the fuck are you even here?" Everett grumbles to Oliver, clearly fed up already.

I think he's getting sick of my human friends all believing that he's some perverted manipulative guy who just wants to use me, especially when everyone here treats him with the respect he deserves and has earned.

"You don't even fucking like my ma—girl." He almost slipped up and called me his mate, but it probably wouldn't mean anything to these three.

"I do like you, Rory. I don't know why you think I don't. I'm just as concerned as these two are. I mean, look at this fucking place.

"Your boyfriend acts like he's the king here and you're his little toy he can mess around with," Oliver exclaims.

"You're fucking insane," Everett mutters.

"I'm insane? You don't even let her touch anyone else. How fucked up is that? Rory's your little toy you can control, and because she's young and innocent, you think you can get away with it.

"You make her think she's in love with you, and she'll do what you want her to," Jax says. "And you get all your friends here to make sure she stays under your control. The king and his fucking knights."

"I am like the king here, and Aurora is not my toy, she's my queen. She's mine," he states, his hand leaving mine to move his arm around my waist.

"Alpha!" a voice yells from down the hall, drawing our attention away.

What's going on now?

"For fuck's sake," Everett growls, twisting me around. "Nickolas is here and not alone. I want you to stay here with Ace, Aurora.

"I'll get Ophelia over here and a couple of others to protect you, but as long as you stay here, you'll be safe. Don't leave here, little one. I'll be back."

"Be safe," I whisper, kissing him.

He kisses my forehead before hurrying out along with Lucius. I stare after him, praying to the goddess that she will protect him.

But I know Everett is strong—much stronger than Nick. Nick was never the enemy I was truly worried about.

It was always Nemesis.

CHAPTER 49

Fight

―――― • ❖ • ――――

RORY

"What's going on?" I ask Ace, knowing that he's keeping up with what's happening through the mind-link.

"Everett's talking to Nick right now. Don't worry, Rory. He'll be fine. You didn't see him before at the citadel," Ace reassures me.

Everett did tell me he ripped tens of wolves to shreds along with the rest of the pack to avenge me, even though I wasn't truly dead. But, I could have been.

If I wasn't a goddess, I would have been. I wouldn't even have met Everett if I was human. But perhaps then I wouldn't have been mated to him.

"You'll tell me if he gets hurt, right?" I ask.

"Rory, you're worrying over nothing. After what they all saw back at the citadel, they're more confused than strong. They want to know what happened, whereas we all know. We're in the better position."

"What the fuck is going on?" Oliver questions loudly, gaining all of our attention.

"Nothing you need to worry your small brain about," Ace snarks, then opens the door for Ophelia.

She hugs me tightly and fusses over me like a mother would.

I haven't had a chance to talk to her since I was taken by Nick and Victoria.

"Thank God you're okay. Everett left me to take care of you, and I let Nick get to you. I'm so sorry," she apologizes, but I just shake my head.

"You don't have to be sorry. There was nothing that could have been done. Plus, I brought them all here. I just hope everyone will be okay. I just want peace."

"Who are they?" Ophelia asks, pointing over at the three puzzled humans on the other side of the room.

"My so-called friends from school: Eddie, Jax, and Oliver."

"Eddie? Your ex?" Ophelia questions.

"Who are you?" Eddie asks her accusingly.

"I'm Everett's aunt. I believe you've met him," she says bitterly, responding to his tone.

She respects manners and will treat others with the manners she receives.

"Rory, what's going on with the whole Nemesis situation?" she whispers.

"I don't know. I wanted to lure Nemesis out into the woods. She would think I was alone and, in fact, everyone would be there.

"She would be mortal, in human form, so we could defeat her. But Everett thinks it's too dangerous for me."

"Using you as bait is very dangerous for you." She's agreeing with Everett.

"I agree," Ace chimes in, making me huff.

"What? Because I'm a weak little girl? This is the only way, and I need people to advocate that to Everett. It's going to be a lot harder on my own, and by then, it might be too late. There's no other plan," I rant.

"There's no other plan right now because those fucking

three are here with no fucking reason. Once we sort out each issue, we'll figure out a way," Ace declares.

I roll my eyes at him. I'm his Luna and yet they all still side with the Alpha.

I understand their loyalty to him, but I'd have hoped these two could be logical and see that this is the way to keep us all safe, to defeat her.

She's a goddess. It's already quite impossible to defeat her as it is, but trying to keep everyone safe in the process is just not possible.

"I knew you would side with him."

"I want to keep you safe like he does. You may not be mine, but we all love you here, Rory."

"You have to keep me safe, but Everett can just go out there without a care?" I question.

"Everett is not…"

"Not what? Not defenseless. Out of all of you against her, I'm the closest match. I know more about her than any of you."

"That doesn't make you safe, and Everett would kill everyone if you got hurt again. Fuck, he'd kill himself if you died."

I grimace at that, even though I fear it's true.

"Shit, Nick and the others are gone. But they'll come back."

"But they're gone? They've left the grounds?" I question.

He nods in response, and I rush out of the room to see my mate. They all follow me, including the humans, who are under watch by Ace and the guard wolves outside our room.

When I spot Everett a little bloodied, I jump into his arms and hug him tightly. Even though I knew he'd be okay, I'm still relieved to see him unharmed. Just his knuckles scraped.

"I told you to stay in the room, little one," he whispers with a relieved sigh when he takes in my scent.

"Ace told me it was over."

"You still should have stayed there until I got you," he says sincerely, not in an angry way. "He only wanted to know what happened really.

"But they'll come back. I'm not so worried about them—not as much as I am about the evil bitch goddess targeting my Luna. I heard your conversation with Ace. I can't put you in danger."

"I'm already in danger, Everett. I've put you in danger. What's happening with Nick and Nemesis, that's all on me. They're my battles, and it's fine if you want to fight them with me, but they want me."

"Exactly, which is why you have to be as far as you can get from them."

"It's not ever going to be far enough with Nemesis. None of this is over until I face her. Last time, I was clueless about everything, and I wanted answers. Now, I go into this knowing her motives."

"That's not enough. I can't guarantee your safety."

"What if we had every rogue in the area on our side? I'd be protected from all sides."

"No. No, no, no, no, no. No."

"I know you hate rogues, but it's a smart move," I say.

He pauses, staring deep into my eyes with this glossy look, as if he's reliving a memory.

I didn't mean to make him reminisce about painful experiences with his parents and the rogues. I just wanted him to consider this.

"Fine. I'm telling you now, I don't like this plan and I'll do everything in my power to protect you from harm, little one, so you need to be careful."

I embrace him again, squeezing him tightly while on my tiptoes and nuzzling my nose into his neck as he does the same.

"I love you, Aurora."

"I love you, too, Everett. I want us to be safe, to keep the pack safe. I want us all to live happily ever after."

"They should go. Should we just let them leave?" He asks for my agreement on this decision as a partner in leading this pack.

I haven't really gotten a chance to yet, what with getting run over by that car and going to the citadel to die again.

"Yeah. They don't know anything anyway. They're just…a little lost on everything, which doesn't matter, I guess," I reply, and he nods in response.

Guard wolves are ordered to escort the humans out to their car and to watch them leave, which the boys reluctantly do, although still curious.

Having this…subconscious protection from the rogues, it forms an alliance with them.

Rogues will never attack this pack again with me as Luna, and thinking to the future, that's incredibly useful. We have every rogue on our side, good or bad, unconditionally.

I pretend like I'm sneaking out of the territory, because of everything that has been going on. I'm not sure whether it will work, but I have to try.

All the wolves hide out in rogue territory, with the pack continuing as normal so as not to raise suspicion. It's late at night, so everyone should be asleep anyway.

I take a step over the border, fear creeping in and making me shiver. Anytime I notice movement, anxiety hits me, but then I realize it's just the rustling of the trees or a small animal.

Attempting to trap and fight a goddess is a nerve-racking situation—even more so when it's at night and I can barely see.

Aurora's Secret

You would think that as a goddess, I would get some more abilities, like heightened senses. But no such luck.

As I travel farther into the unknown, seemingly alone, I feel Everett close, keeping me safe. I just hope I can keep him safe.

This is my fight, and I'm overjoyed that all these wolves are joining me and helping me. But, it's still my fight, my responsibility this time.

"Innocent little Aurora is trying to trap me, huh?" a voice says behind me, making me whip around.

My eyes widen at the sight of Nemesis, who is not alone. She has a whole group of monstrous creatures behind her. But what terrifies me right to my core is what I see in her arms—who I see.

My mama. Trapped and with tears streaming down her face.

CHAPTER 50

Nemesis

———•◆•———

RORY

THE WOLVES BEGIN TO CREEP OUT FROM THE WOODS, knowing they've been made by the powerful goddess. And Everett is quick to join my side.

Our hands interlock, reassuring each other that everything will be fine, even though this goddess has my mama in her clutches.

I had hoped that my mama had just gotten away from Red Moon—a very toxic pack, particularly to her. She was treated like dirt on their shoes, a slave, cleaning and cooking for the pack.

I just wanted her to be free and happy, what she deserves.

My mama's eyes connect with mine and I watch her visibly relax, eyeing the protective Alpha beside me with his mark imprinted on me.

How did Nemesis know this would be a trap? How did she know? This would have been a good plan if only she hadn't known.

"Wolves are hard to control. They're impulsive, they have two identities that can take control: their wolves or their human forms. It makes them less suggestible than humans.

"And of course, I can't cross into pack territories, especially with all those wolf guards. But humans, well, they are incredibly suggestible.

"Put one idea in their heads and it will take the second time. Their minds are less complex, their motives simple. And especially when one of them already cared for you."

What is she talking about?

"Eddie's sweet. It didn't take much to brainwash him into trying to ruin your relationship. Jax was harder, as was Oliver. Then when I realized that they were getting nowhere, I had to raise the stakes.

"That whole touching thing that got you run over, I just had to get there fast enough, but Achlys always tries to one-up me.

"Then Eddie declared his undying love in a last attempt to break you away from your protective Alpha mate. I had to settle for them sneaking into your pack and hearing your plan."

Oh no. This is on me. All of it. It's actually incredibly ironic, since they continuously said *I* was brainwashed. I don't know what was them and what wasn't.

I've only known Jax since I went back to school, so was all of it fake? I consider him a friend, but maybe he would want nothing to do with me without Nemesis's influence.

I knew something was up with Oliver though—and with Eddie when he declared his love to me. And that's probably how all three of them found the pack.

"The Omega wolf you love so much is with me. How much do you care about her? Your life for hers," she declares.

"And even if you don't take that deal, all these titans behind me are going to hurt your pack, the wolves you're supposed to protect."

I start to move toward her, accepting my fate. We can't beat her without wolves getting hurt, and she's right. I'm their Luna. To sacrifice my life for all of theirs is my duty and my purpose.

And she doesn't even need to threaten me. Just having my mama ends the entire game.

She is the woman who saved me, who brought me up among wolves against all protests, who tried to protect me. I have to give up my life for hers. I owe her everything and I love her.

But Everett halts me, grabbing my arm and pulling me back roughly.

"You want a fight, you have one," he yells to her, which makes me give him a sharp look.

"No, she has my mama. I have to go, Everett," I tell him and everyone else. "If me giving in keeps you all safe, that's what I must do. I can't hurt my mama."

"I'm not letting you just go. You're fucking insane if you think I'll let you sacrifice yourself," he growls, tugging me back.

"If she wants to go, she wants to go," Nemesis says with a devilish smirk.

"What if I make this fair? The little girl, and she alone, can fight me. She has a chance to win. I'm giving you a chance, Aurora. I suggest you take it. Goddess against goddess."

"Fine. You and me," I accept, shaking off Everett's grip.

I hear him growl and try to take me back, but I step up to Nemesis. She tosses my mama to the side and some wolves help her.

"No!" Everett growls louder than he ever has before.

Which is the exact moment everything goes into chaos. Everett tries to get to me, but is rushed by a couple of titans from Nemesis's army.

And an attack on their Alpha sends the rest of the pack, ally packs, and rogues that have emerged from the woods into a full-out war.

But Nemesis continues toward me, with everything around

us in uproar. Her hand shoots out to grab my neck, her power of burning me carried over into her human form.

Searing my neck, her other hand grabs a knife from my pocket; she is about to use it when Ace, in wolf form, jumps onto her.

I want to clutch my neck to ease my suffering, but that would probably make the pain all too real. Ace protects me, standing in front and growling loudly at Nemesis.

"You want him to get killed for you, Aurora? You did save him in rogue territory once. If you wanted him dead, why save him?" she sneers, squeezing the knife in her hand.

A titan pounces onto Ace's back, busying Ace and leaving me open once again to her attack.

"Maybe your pack won't be unharmed now, but at least your mama is safe. Give yourself up and you can prevent more harm from coming to these wolves," she states.

I don't even notice the knife that plunges into my gut and twists, producing a throbbing sharp pain that courses through my whole body.

Along with my burns that are screeching at me like a teenage girl yelling at her parents, the excruciating pain becomes unbearable.

My knees give way and I just give in to her, watching her pull the knife back and waiting for the plunge that will end me.

I'm already weak and I barely have any life left. But it's not enough to kill me.

It's enough to hurt and weaken me, but I need the final blow to end it all. I just want Everett to know I love him, and I want to protect him and the pack.

I wait for death to come, finally. I don't know what it will be like. Will I go back to limbo and see Achlys? Will I stay there forever, or is there somewhere else, somewhere worse?

Is death peaceful or full of suffering? Even though I've died several times, I don't know anything about it.

But it doesn't come. Instead, something much worse happens.

Everett dives in front of the knife, letting it plunge right into his heart and render him powerless.

No! No! Please, he can't... Why did he do this? Please. I can't let him die for me. I can't live without him.

Nemesis appears to be taken aback, dropping the knife in shock and eyeing my dying mate.

My mate who sacrificed himself for me. A mate who is the best, most dutiful Alpha and is needed by his pack, by me. I need him. I really need him.

All the fighting halts as the wolves in the pack feel their Alpha slowly slipping away. Tears flow down my face, dripping onto Everett's body as I press my hands against his wound and try to save him.

But I'm too weak. I know it. I just don't want to believe it. The aching in my gut is draining me as blood oozes out of the gash. And I can't save him. He's the only one I need to save and I can't do it.

What's the point of being a goddess with the ability to save people from death when I can't even save my own mate?

"Please don't leave me," I whisper to him, my voice breaking along with my heart and soul.

And our mate bond wanes, I feel it. It's horrifying.

Losing the connection slowly feels worse than any physical pain I have ever felt. This must have been what he felt, twice, when I got run over and outside the citadel.

I can't lose him. I really can't lose him. I can't do any of this without him. I can't lead the pack.

Who will be the Alpha? Will I even stay in the pack? I won't ever be happy without him. He's my light, my life.

Out of the corner of my eye, I notice Nemesis picking up the knife again and coming for me. I grab Everett tightly, gather all my strength to avenge him, and grasp her hand with the knife in it.

Although it burns, I welcome the pain of it all, having already gone past my pain threshold. I hold tight to Nemesis, not letting her go.

I want her dead. I want to destroy her. She is the reason I never met my birth parents. She's the reason why I can never meet my mom. She's the one who kidnapped my mama.

She's the one who brainwashed my friends and tried to take me away from Everett. And she's the one who has stabbed Everett with a deadly blow.

When she starts to grab her neck, gasping for air, I just watch, unsure of what's happening. As is everyone. They all just watch. My tears blur my sight, but I still watch the scene play out.

She falls to her knees like she can no longer stand, and she attempts to remove her hand from mine weakly. But I keep my hold, squeezing her scalding hand even harder.

"What are you doing to me?" she breathes out, collapsing to the ground.

Chapter 51

Future

RORY

AND THEN HER EYES CLOSE.

And the continuous burning sensation stops.

And she looks like a lifeless corpse.

And I suddenly feel no pain, and the mate connection is restored.

I turn my attention back to Everett and observe that his gash has closed completely. He's no longer hurt. What just happened? He's not dying anymore. He was, and now he's fine.

I wasn't strong enough to save him. I couldn't give him my life force because mine was waning itself. But I no longer have a stab wound either. What the hell?

"Aurora," an angelic voice says.

I look up to see Selene again with a dazzled expression.

"You defeated her. You were too weak to give Everett your life, so you took Nemesis's and healed yourself and Everett and all the wolves."

I glance around, expecting to see hurt and dying wolves along with titans. But the titans have disappeared.

And although there is blood, there are no signs of scratches or wounds or gashes. The wolves even search themselves in confusion, knowing that they were hit and suddenly they're not.

And I look back down at Everett, my Everett.

"You saved me, little one," he whispers, regaining his strength.

And I pass out on top of him from the exhaustion, a pleased expression on my face.

We're going to be okay. We're going to live. The pack is going to live. And Nemesis is gone.

―⁂―

"She must be worn out," a voice says as I fade in and out of consciousness.

"Everett?" I call out, a little panicked, needing to know whether he is alright.

I feel sheets on top of me, indicating that I'm in a bed.

"I'm right here, little one."

My eyes flicker open to see Everett's concerned face, and Ace and Lucius too.

"Is everyone okay?" I croak out, pouting a little in fatigue.

"Yes. Thanks to you, Aurora."

"Good," I reply with a small smile, extending my arms like a little child in need of a hug.

"Leave," he growls out to his Beta and Gamma before crawling into bed with me and taking me into his arms.

"How long have I been out?" I ask, pecking his lips and missing his taste.

"A week," he answers, making my eyes widen in alarm.

"A week?"

"I was really worried about you, but you were still alive and still breathing. I figured all of it took so much out of you that you just needed to pass out for a week. But you're awake now."

"What did I miss?"

"A lot, little one. I got Alpha Nick and Luna Victoria jailed for what they did, and because everyone else heard about what happened here, they're all backing down.

"They're scared of us, of you, of how strong and powerful you are. You can cure seven packs of wolves and rogues and save my life."

"Why did you jump in front of that knife?" I ask, although, of course, I know the reason why.

"You know why. I would protect you with my life."

"I can't live without you."

"You don't have to now. There's no more danger, little one. We did it. We defeated them. And everyone in the pack loves you now."

"Who knew it would take healing all their wounds to get them to like me?" I say with a little giggle.

"They always loved you—well, most of them. The warriors were hesitant, but they aren't now. They all call you Luna Aurora."

"What day is it?"

"Thursday."

"I want to go to school tomorrow," I reply.

"What? Why? After what those humans did? And you're not even human. You belong here, in the pack.

"I know you loved school because you felt like you belonged there, but the pack accepts you, and you belong with me."

"But I like my friends. Freya and Skye and Bethany and I have almost finished senior year and graduated. I'm closer to human than wolf."

"Are you? You can resurrect yourself and heal people. That doesn't sound very human to me."

"Doesn't sound very wolf either."

He chuckles and pulls me up further so we're face-to-face, with our noses touching.

"If you want to, I won't stop you. There's no more danger,

no more threat. I understand that you have friends there. I'll take you tomorrow. I have a lot of time, having caught up on work over the past week."

I press my lips to his, snuggling even closer. I don't know what I would have done without him. He means everything to me.

"What about Mama? Did she go back to Red Moon?" I question.

"No, I invited her to join the pack and she agreed. We've had many conversations, and she's been up here watching over you whilst I've been working."

I smile brightly at him and kiss his lips again.

"I don't know if she likes me. I've never had to worry about impressing a parent, and now I don't know how I've done."

"I'll talk you up," I tell him with another giggle.

"She'll love you. I love you. And even though I don't like the way you moved in front of that knife, I know you did it because you love me and you want to protect me. And I love you for that."

"I'm just lucky you're so special. I'll always protect you, little one."

I know.

The next day, after breakfast, we head out, and I have never had greetings like this in any pack. They wave, or smile, or say, "Good morning, Luna."

Everett walks beside me, pulling me into him by the waist, leading me to my mama.

When we arrive at the small house he set my mama up in, we enter to see my mama's grinning face. She runs and hugs me tightly, sighing with relief.

"Oh, Rory, thank the goddess you're awake and safe," she says, tears of happiness pooling in her eyes.

"I missed you, Mama," I whisper.

"I missed you, too, Rory," she replies. "I'm so glad that you found your way without me. Your mate seems to care for you a lot, and he's an Alpha."

She glances back at Everett with a genuine smile, showing me that she definitely approves of him.

"We should get going if you want to get to school, Aurora. We'll come back after," Everett informs me, and I nod in response.

I hug my mama goodbye and let Everett lead me out to his car.

"I don't know how that whole brainwashing thing worked, but I'd be wary of all three of them. Everything has probably worn off now that she's dead, but you never know," Everett warns me as we near the school.

"You're right. I'll just test the waters and stand back," I reply, easing his fear that I could still get hurt.

He kisses my lips and helps me out of the car. Unfortunately, even though Nemesis, the curse-maker, is dead, I'm still cursed. Curses stay for life.

So I'm always going to be clumsy, but I don't think anyone in the pack is judging me for that now. They seemed to practically kiss my feet this morning.

When I spot Freya and Skye, I skip over to them, minding my feet, and their eyes widen.

"Where have you been?!" Freya exclaims, hugging me.

I've only been away for a couple of weeks though.

"I've just been dealing with things at home. I found my

mom, and the people in my old neighborhood who hurt me got arrested," I tell them.

"Really? Wow," Skye says, smiling sadly, maybe at the fact that I got hurt in the first place.

Throughout the day, everything appears to be normal—not like the normal before I met Everett, but Oliver doesn't seem any more interested in me than as his girlfriend's friend.

Bethany, Skye, and Freya all seem to notice his disinterest, not even knowing why he's changed.

Eddie just returns to giving me a small smile and a few words in passing. And I see him chatting up other girls.

I don't think the guys even remember what they did when they were under Nemesis's control. They definitely don't remember what happened at the pack.

Jax does talk to me—flirts with me, rather—in our lessons together, but he flirts with other girls, too, returning to the player I originally thought he was. He certainly is less intense. But we're still friends.

I like that. I like him, as a friend. He's funny and entertaining. He sits with me and Freya and Skye at lunch, whilst Bethany and Oliver take seats at their normal popular table.

Everything appears to have settled down now. Nothing is out of the ordinary, and my days are a lot calmer and smoother.

Everett and I continue to run the pack together, and I even join in on warrior training sessions, with no one giving me sideglances like the previous time.

They just accept me and my clumsiness, knowing I can't help it and that they want me as their Luna. The pack wants me, and I feel like I belong.

I've struggled with belonging my entire life. But now, with Alpha Everett of the Shadow Blood pack, I finally belong.

Thank You

Thank you for reading the Alpha & Aurora series.
You can find all other books of the series and hundreds of other bestsellers on the Galatea app.

Scan this QR code to download Galatea and use the code **ALPHA20** to receive a 20% discount on the subscription.

Made in United States
Orlando, FL
10 June 2024